Look for these titles by *Lauren Dane*

Now Available:

Chase Brothers
Giving Chase
Taking Chase
Chased
Making Chase

Cascadia Wolves
Wolf Unbound
Standoff
Fated

Reading Between The Lines
To Do List
Always
Sweet Charity

Print Anthologies
Holiday Seduction

Praise for Lauren Dane's
Trinity

"I've been in love with the Cascadia Wolves since I read the first book in this paranormal series, so I was thrilled when I learned Ms. Dane was releasing Trinity. ...The sex, passion and desire is sizzling hot... I can't wait to see what happens with the next release in this keeper series."

~ *Literary Nymphs Reviews*

"Lauren Dane's wolves make me howl. I love everything about them..."

~ *Romance Novel Reviews*

"I would recommend Trinity to any paranormal romance fan who loves stories with bite, passion and heart. Ms. Dane has a history of writing stories that touch your emotions while making you sweat from the heat in the bedroom...or living room."

~ *Whipped Cream Erotic Romance*

"A fantastic story full of adventure and lots of super hot sex scenes... Ms. Dane has done an amazing job with this book and continuing this series. This book is definitely a keeper for me and one that I look forward to re-reading in the future numerous times."

~ *The Romance Studio*

"Set against a background so artfully drawn you can see it, Trinity is an emotional thrill ride that will draw you into the lives of Jack, Renee and Galen leaving you unwilling to have the story end."

~ *Veiled Secrets Reviews*

"TRINITY is a book I was anticipating and I was not disappointed. If anything Ms. Dane surpass my expectation and then some. The characters connect, the storyline flowed and the little issues that I had were just not issues enough to take away from how much this books rock..."

~ *Erotic Horizon*

Trinity

Lauren Dane

A SAMHAIN PUBLISHING, LTD. publication.

Samhain Publishing, Ltd.
577 Mulberry Street, Suite 1520
Macon, GA 31201
www.samhainpublishing.com

Trinity
Copyright © 2010 by Lauren Dane
Print ISBN: 978-1-60504-797-3
Digital ISBN: 978-1-60504-694-5

Cover by Natalie Winters

First Samhain Publishing, Ltd. electronic publication: October 2009
First Samhain Publishing, Ltd. print publication: September 2010

Dedication

This one is for all the Cascadia Wolves fans who've supported me and the series from day one. We're taking a right turn here and heading into National Pack territory now, hang onto your hats.

Ray, as always, thank you for being a fine example of hero material and for all that um, research.

Renee, Fatin and Mary—you're all so wonderful and supportive, I send a special cyber hug to each of you.

Last, to Angela James, who has been a fabulous editor and a friend. I wish you much success (though I have no doubt you'll achieve all you want to, you're just that amazing). Thank you for buying *Giving Chase*. Thank you for making me a better writer and thank you for being awesome.

Chapter One

Renee wiped the counter down, smiling as she swayed her ass to ABBA as they told the story of Fernando. The warmth pressing against the windows and outer walls of the building brought a languid fluidity to her muscles. She envied Sam, the fat feline sprawled in his high perch, furry belly flopped to the side. It would have been an excellent day to simply lie in the sun and nap the hours away.

Wisps of light from the high casement windows played through the air, swirling down over her little juice and coffee bar, catching the crystals and other such stuff her stepmother had hung up all over the place. Dust motes danced to the hum of energy in the shop. More despite Susan than because of her.

The shop was a metaphysical bookstore and magick shop. Owned by a woman who did not believe in magic. The irony of that wasn't lost on Renee, but since she *did* believe in magic, the shop seemed to be fine with the current state of affairs. Each day she entered the shop she felt embraced by it, which made those not so welcome feelings from her stepmother slightly easier to bear.

Renee had chosen the space in a sunny archway inside The Willow Broom when she'd signed the lease. At first she'd decided to set up shop there because it would keep her in her father's life somehow. She'd at least have a regular opportunity to see him. Their relationship hadn't been strained, but it wasn't close either and she craved that.

But from the moment she'd walked in, the space had called to her. That alcove fed her energy each day. It kept her warm in the winter and cool in the summer. The light through the stained glass created colorful dances across the walls and over the floors and shelves. The shop was located on a busy street near the T stop so there'd been a steady stream of customers all day. No one bothered her about what to serve and when. She kept her own hours, loved the space and her customers. Best of all, the bar enabled her to pay her half of the mortgage rent and it kept her in shoes so what did she have to frown over?

She didn't even need to glance toward a clock to know it was time to leave for the day. Time to head home to Galen. She smiled as she pictured him changing out of his suit and into jeans and a threadbare T-shirt. Mmmm. All that gorgeous, lean, hard muscle laying flat against his body. He moved like the predator he was, quiet and purposeful, big brown/black eyes never failing to take in everything around him. But wrapped in a most charming and stylish package. Sexy and totally focused on her. To be cherished and adored by a man like Galen was one of life's greatest gifts. She had no idea how she'd lucked out, but she planned to keep him forever.

"I'm out of here," she called out after she'd put away her cleaning supplies. The pale green scarf Galen had given Renee for her birthday was soft and cool against her neck as she wrapped it a few times before pulling her cardigan on. The air outside wasn't cold yet, but it had a bite and the sun would be going down soon.

She neared the front door and slowed, pausing to look around slowly. It wasn't time to leave yet. Just...wait. The decks of tarot cards on the nearby display beckoned and she fondled them. So pretty and colorful. The shop smelled of rosemary and sage, of amber and magic. Briefly she wished Susan could see just how special the shop was, but at that point, Renee knew it was a lost cause. Ah well, she could enjoy it just as easily.

Her phone rang and she smiled, relaxing as she picked up. "Hello there, handsome. I'm getting ready to leave now."

The sound of his voice was like caramel, thick and sweet. "Evening to you, babe. Just calling to check in. I brought some dinner home from the deli."

"Yum. I'm good, just leaving now. I'll be home in about ten minutes. I love you."

"See you in ten. I love you too."

She was still smiling as she got outside while she fumbled to tuck her phone back into her bag. She hadn't even noticed where she'd been going until she ran straight into someone a few steps up the street.

"I'm sorry." She bent to help him pick up the things he'd dropped, oranges, apples and fresh bread. "These look good. Mrs. Unger has the nicest produce." She finally looked up as they both stood and everything just sort of stopped as pale blue eyes met hers. And saw straight to her bones.

Her knees went a little weak at the energy between them. Wow. So not her usual type, it was as if a Southern California surfer boy simply appeared before her eyes. Olive-toned skin, golden-blond hair, just a tad too long, an open, assessing gaze and from what she could tell with the clothes he had on, an athlete's build too.

A breeze brought it, the scent of forest and loam. She breathed deep, turning the notes of the music the smells made over on her tongue, in her brain. Sometimes Renee experienced things differently than most people and right then, this blond man had flipped every switch in her brain and body. Just looking at him and smelling his skin threatened overload and still she could not get enough. The sharpness of it, the total unexpected edge of desire she felt in her gut alarmed her even as she tasted the rich and heady flavor and craved more.

But at the back of her mind she knew this was not okay. She pulled herself back from that edge and shook her head a bit.

He reached out and touched her arm, just quickly. And yet she felt the echo of it even after he'd moved his hand away.

"Are you all right?"

What a voice. Lazy, redolent with sex, deep.

Hopefully he didn't hear the slight breathy quality of her reply. "I'm fine. Your apples might be bruised."

A puzzled look skirted over his features briefly until he smiled. Big white teeth, pale blue eyes, that hair. Renee took a step back to try and break the connection forming between them, but he took a step forward.

"I'm Jack Meyers." He held out his hand and she took it. Instead of shaking it, he turned her wrist, bending to press a kiss just there, his lips against her pulse.

He straightened slowly and she practically yanked her hand from his grasp, even as his gaze held her still. Those golden threads of connection she'd felt just moments before were back.

"I really need to get home. I'm glad you're okay." Her smile was too bright, she knew. Too false and cheery. But he did something to her insides. Her insides belonged to someone else, thankyouverymuch.

"Wait." He took her hand again and she didn't want him to let go, which startled her into doing just that. This was not okay.

"I need to go. It was nice to meet you."

"Have dinner with me." She tugged and he let her hand go, but she saw his features, knew he didn't want to. "Candlelight, wine, and a few slow dances."

Something inside her liked that, responded to the idea and that scared her. She loved Galen. He was her man and she wasn't supposed to get all tingly and breathless about anyone else. She was being stupid and it was time to simply walk away right then. "Thanks for asking, Jack. I'm flattered, really. But I can't. I'm with someone. Really with someone. I don't have dinner with anyone but him."

That was the truth, or as simple as she could make it anyway.

She took one step, and then another, letting the threads of connection between them pull and snap, feeling her connection to Galen right where it should be. "Night." She raised a hand to wave and turned away from him, toward home where she belonged. Once she'd done that everything felt better and she relaxed.

"Hey!" he called out and she kept walking, but turned her head. "You never said what your name was."

"I guess I didn't. Night, Jack." She grinned and turned away again.

Jack stood rooted to the spot on the sidewalk as she walked away. As his mate walked away. The strain on his muscles burned as he held himself back, held his wolf from grabbing her and heading for the hills.

One moment he'd been caught by the glimmers of gold and burgundy in her short, curly hair and the next, as he kissed her wrist, he'd been breathing her in, filling himself with her scent until he nearly shook at the recognition of who she was. She was in him, rushing through his veins, becoming part of him.

Just beneath her scent, lay the scent of a cat.

A cat and sex. And as she'd been there, reacting to him, her body had warmed and the spice of her want of him had taken over everything within him. His skin tingled with awareness and need. The need to claim her and mark her as his until not even the memory of that cat remained in her mind. Tension washed away with the knowledge that he'd found her. The ever-familiar ache, wanting the one woman he couldn't ever have, he realized, was gone. He let his breath out slow.

For the first time since he'd become Grace Warden's anchor bond, *she* wasn't the woman dominating his thoughts.

He rolled back, balancing on the balls of his heels as he inhaled her scent on the breeze. His wolf wanted to howl with delight. Something else. More than a cat in her bed. His mate was something more than human. She smelled of magic, of amber and lavender sugar. He smiled at the memory of the sugar his foster mother made for tea in the winter. It boded well, this memory. This woman was meant to be on that sidewalk when he'd walked by.

Of course it couldn't be easy, no. He'd watched his friends find their mates and not a one of them had just bumped into another wolf at a dinner party and mated, end of story, happily ever after achieved. She'd said she was with someone and he scented a cat. From what he understood of cat shifters, they didn't idly live with others, especially in a romantic sense. They shared their space with their imprinted mates, their spouses under their law.

Still, he didn't need to jump to conclusions. If she was mated to another, she couldn't have rung his own mate bell. The mate bond wasn't so cruel to a wolf that he'd find his other half and have her totally unattainable.

This called for some thought. She needed to be courted, showered with attention. He was old enough to realize most modern, non-shifter women would not appreciate the wooing of the wolf sort straight from go. No scooping up and claiming against a wall with feverish urgency on the first date for her. He'd loved women long enough to have perfected the art of seduction and this would be the most important seduction of his life.

Smiling as he watched the last of her turn a corner a few

blocks away, he turned and headed into the shop she'd just exited.

A magick shop of sorts. But her stamp wasn't the one on the place overall, not that he could tell. There was some overkill, especially toward the registers. His little witch didn't seem to be the overkill type. Still, her magic hung about, intertwined with the magic of the place. It liked her.

"Excuse me." He sent his most boyishly charming smile at a woman nearby.

She looked to him, assessing his wallet most likely. The woman had crafty eyes. He'd studied people long enough to know which people to avoid. This one was bound to come with trouble. "Can I help you?"

"I'm looking for a woman who works here. God, I...her name escapes me just now. Small, probably about five feet or so. Dark, curly hair, big eyes."

"Renee?"

He nodded, relieved. Her name was Renee. Mentally, he rolled the sounds around, liking them immensely. What he didn't like was this woman he was speaking to. She of the shifty eyes and thin, sharp scent of lies. His mate was in contact with this woman every day? He shuddered inwardly but kept his smile in place.

"She went home for the day. She closes the coffee and juice bar down at three thirty every weekday. If you're looking for a coffee, there's a diner across the street."

"Thanks. I'll drop in to see her another time."

The woman he'd been speaking to crossed her arms over her chest. "You a friend of hers?"

"Yes. Have a nice night." He turned and waved as he headed out the door.

He had his work cut out. Of course he never doubted he'd be successful. She was his mate; their connection and attraction would be very strong. Strong enough that once she got to know him and trust him, she'd drop this cat and come to him. If she hadn't been his, he'd have felt guilty about trying to break up a relationship. But she was and he was meant to have her. He looked forward to spending every moment of the rest of his life making sure she was never sorry.

Starting the next day, he'd make himself a regular part of her life. He'd be there and get to know her, let her know him. It would be a challenge, but one he relished.

Satisfied, he headed toward his condo, opposite where she'd gone, and relished the next part of his life. The last years had been pretty quiet, peaceful, and he'd been dying inside each day as he watched Grace and Cade together, totally in love and united, their children underfoot and just as loveable as their parents.

He'd known being an anchor meant that male would feel bonded to the female much like her mate did. But no one told him what it would be like to love Grace and know he could never have her. On top of knowing how much Grace adored her husband, Cade and Jack had become close friends. They were his family and his love of them was double edged in a way Jack knew Cade understood very well until the moment he'd met Grace. Cade had loved his sister-in-law for a very long time as well.

He changed course, heading toward the building just a few doors down from his, where Cade and his family lived. He wanted to share this with them.

Chapter Two

"Jack!" Grace looked up from where she sat at the kitchen table, trying to guide a spoon into baby Henri's mouth. The boy ate like he was not quite convinced he'd come into contact with food again, guppy lips seeking the spoon and sending the food half into his mouth and the rest all over his face and Grace's arm.

Henri said Jack's name a few times until Jack leaned down and brushed a kiss on the top of his head. "Hey there, kid." He stepped back, moving to the fridge to get a soda. "Hey, short stuff, what's happening?" he asked Grace.

She smiled up at him, looking just as lovely as she always did, and while he appreciated it, loved it because it was part of her, he wasn't affected by it the way he was when he thought of those wine-hued curls.

"Something exciting must have happened. It's all over your face."

"Weren't you just here two hours ago?" Cade wandered into the kitchen, Annabelle on his hip, her fingers wrapped in the front of her dad's shirt to keep her balance.

"I was. I left. Flirted with the ladies at my local produce stand only to have a woman rush out a door and knock my apples to the pavement." He paused when Becca bounced into the room. Becca, Cade and Grace's oldest child, was the spitting image of her mother and while her mom and dad were first in her heart, Jack followed a close second. Jack had long since decided that was a good place to be.

"You're here!" Becca launched herself toward him and he caught her, hugging her tight.

"I am, dollface. Give me some sugar while I try to look hungry enough to get invited to dinner." Jack kissed her upturned face, reaching out to tweak Annabelle's toes when she swung her fat little foot into his reach. He wanted this. He wanted a family of his very own. His babies, his mate, his kitchen.

"Stay for dinner?" Grace wiped Henri's face and began to clear away the remnants of his meal. "Meatloaf, mashed potatoes, asparagus, salad, bread and macaroni and cheese."

"Awesome!" Becca looked up at Jack, as he put her down, her face expectant. "Will you stay?"

He knew without a doubt that he was welcome. He was family, as they were to him. "Sounds good. I'll even set the table."

"Typical. Show up after I do it." Cade rolled his eyes. "Grab an extra bottle of wine from the rack behind you."

"I'm off duty, boss man." Jack snorted and waited to see if Cade would rise to the bait.

Cade just raised one of his eyebrows. "Must be why you're here, mooching dinner."

"Pfft, I'm here to look at your women. All lovely ladies you don't deserve."

Becca giggled and patted his hand before reaching to take her dad's.

"Fine, fine. For meatloaf, I can get the wine." He looked down at Becca. "And some milk for these sprouts."

He and Cade spoke about nothing in particular as Cade put Annabelle into her toddler seat. Grace returned with Henri, who happily sat in his high chair now that he had been topped off.

18

Becca put some crackers on his tray and he grinned before shoving two of them into his mouth.

Dave, Cade's cousin and Grace's personal guard, strolled into the room and put the potatoes down on the table. "Yo. Akio says to check your voicemail. He had to make a shift change and wanted you to know about it in advance."

Jack laughed as he poured milk for the kids and wine for the adults. "Akio's been one of my top lieutenants for ten years; I'm sure whatever choices he made were appropriate. You people would have outsiders think I'm an ogre."

"You are. Other things I can't say in front of the children too." Dave sat across the large table from Jack. "He appreciates your respect. You do a good job with your people. Don't repeat that, I have a reputation to uphold and all."

"Secret's safe with me." It pleased him that people thought he was good at his job. He worked hard at it, had spent his entire adult life in the job, protecting the National Alpha pair and the pack itself. Protecting wolves nationwide because they were his too. He knew he was feared, but being respected had to go hand in glove with that or he'd have gone too far.

No one spoke for several minutes as food was dished up and people started eating. Slowly, people began to talk and laugh, Becca talked about school and Jack relaxed happily. This was his life and even before he met Renee, it was good. But now that the ache, the longing for Grace was dulled by his attraction to Renee, it felt even better. The *what ifs* were all things he could have instead of those things he never would.

He had a future. Filled with possibility. It washed over him, bringing a satisfied smile to his face.

Grace finally sent an amused look Jack's way. "Are you going to tell us or what? You've been a terrible tease to hold it back this long."

"As it happens, I do have something exciting. I met my

mate today."

Everyone began speaking at once and Jack continued eating until things calmed down.

Finally, true to his nature, Cade whistled and told everyone to quiet down. He turned to Jack, a grin on his face. "What's the story? Where is she? Why are you here without her instead of Claiming her?"

Of course Cade would ask these things. Because Renee was Jack's mate, she'd also be one of Cade's Pack, wolf or not. Cade took care of people, he had been born and bred to be an Alpha and Jack was his right hand. They'd been through a lot together, had forged a family of wolves there in Boston and all across the country with Cade at the helm. He was proud to be part of the new future they'd all forged when they'd taken Warren Pellini out five years prior.

"She doesn't know. About being my mate. It's complicated. No, don't get that look, it is." Jack shrugged. "She's human, well, more than human, she was dripping magic. I'm pretty sure she knew I wasn't human, though. She was attracted to me, we had amazing chemistry, but she's with someone." He sighed. "So I had to let her walk away. For today anyway. As for where she is, at her house, I'd wager. Hardest thing I've ever done, watching her turn a corner, knowing she was going to someone else. Yeah, that part." He sped ahead, cutting off the question he knew Grace would ask.

"It wasn't a man she smelled of. She had cat on her skin, in her hair. She lives with this dude, I can tell that much. I don't know why though, cats aren't one for casually living with partners."

"Well what did she say exactly?" Grace's frown was brief, but Jack caught it anyway. He wasn't sure if it was that he'd found someone or if she worried about him getting hurt or a combo of all those things.

"I asked her out, she told me she was with someone and

said no. But I know, my *nose* knows, she was interested." He didn't go into any more detail with kids at the table but her body had warmed to him; he scented her arousal, it wound around him, tying him to her, needing more of that scent. "She's mine, but I'm going to have to show some creativity with this woman. I have to approach the situation carefully and be strategic."

Grace exhaled, her impatience clear. Despite her size and how quiet she usually was, she was just as much an Alpha as Cade. Jack hid his smile behind his steepled fingers. "Can it be that she's *mated* to this cat? Well, no it can't. Of course it can't or he wouldn't have connected with her that way." She put more potatoes on Cade's plate and added some more meatloaf to Dave's. "Too bad for the cat then. No one else can have her. She's Jack's mate and that's that." She decreed it, so it must be true. He loved that about her.

"Of course she is, beautiful." Cade looked to his wife. "From what I understand about big cat shifters, they don't mate. At least not like wolves do. They imprint on their partner, a sort of chosen mating rather than the genetic mating we have. Maybe that's it in which case, well, let's not go there. It's probably that they're together, but not imprinted. Makes it easier, and yet harder for Jack, I'd wager." Cade tipped his chin in Jack's direction. "I'll call my grandmother to see what she thinks."

Lia Warden was an elder of the Cascadia Pack and had been the Alpha before Cade and then her other grandson, Lex, took over. After years of knowing the woman, Jack was convinced she also had some serious magic type mojo too. She knew a hell of a lot about shifters and their history so she'd most likely have some answers. Answers would be good, give him more tools to blow Renee's house down.

"Thanks, Cade."

"I'll call after dinner. With the time difference she should be home from her afternoon volunteer gig at Gabby's school by then." Gabby was one of the Warden nieces, the daughter of Cade's brother, Lex, and his mate, Nina. They also had two sons and a house that was chaos personified. Jack wasn't sure how Lex handled his bossy but undeniably sexy wife and all those high energy kids, but the Alpha of the Cascadia Pack seemed quite happy with his lot in life, and that was what Jack wanted. Needed.

Galen heard her key in the lock and put his book down, moving to meet her in the entry. He missed her, loved this time every day when they came together after work and relaxed.

His day had sucked. He'd been in and out of court, had a million phone calls and emails and an argument with his brother. Seeing Renee's smile as she came through their doorway eased it all away. Soothed his cat while comforting the human on the outside too.

The setting sun came through the bank of windows on the far wall, highlighting her hair, bathing her with warm light. She never looked away, even as she dropped her bag on the table near the door.

"Something smells good." She came into his arms where she belonged and nuzzled his neck. Gooseflesh broke over his skin and his cock strained against the zipper of his jeans. How perfectly she fit there, made for him. "Mmm. That's much better. Hi. You smell way better than anything else I've ever smelled. Why is that?"

He kissed the top of her head and tipped her chin. Every freckle, the sweep of her lashes, the curve of her cheeks, the dimple just to the left of her luscious mouth—all burned into his memory.

"Because I'm yours, right down to the bone." He inhaled

her, tasting her day. The sharp scent of wolf wafted from her ever so faintly. "Why do you smell like wolf?" He wrinkled his nose as his cat puffed up, affronted by the scent on its mate.

Her nose wrinkled for a moment as she thought. "Wolf? Um, I don't know. I wasn't near any animals but you today." She grinned.

"Funny. No, a shifter, not a full wolf. It's just a thread of scent. You probably brushed against something at the shop, not knowing. There's a Pack here in Boston, *the* Pack, if I remember correctly. I've met the Alpha male, Cade Warden."

"Werewolves? Awesome! I'm totally going to keep my eyes open from now on. What else is real? Mummies? Zombies? Vampires?"

He sent what he hoped was a quelling glance but given her smile, he doubted it. "You worry me sometimes. Vampires, yes. I don't think so with mummies and zombies. Though technically, I suppose mummies exist in that there are bodies preserved after death that way. None of that matters though, Renee. Whatever exists will be something to approach carefully or not at all. Stay out of trouble." For such a small and utterly competent person, she did manage to get caught up in stuff from time to time.

"I can't tell you what it does for my ego that you seem to think I'm one of the Scooby gang." She rolled her eyes. "I did totally plow into some dude as I left the shop today. Made him drop his groceries all over the place. That'll teach him to get in my way. And yet, I still got it. He asked me to dinner."

"Hmpf. You sure do." Galen kissed her cheeks, the tip of her nose and then settled in, his mouth against hers, kissing her slowly but deeply. He swallowed her sigh, relished the way she molded her body to his. She smelled of him. Of their home and their bed, of her shampoo and of magic. She tended to deny that last bit, but someday she'd have to finally admit what she possessed was more than knowing when the phone would ring.

She also held the scent of outside. Of the store, a bit of coffee, sometimes the green vibrancy of wheat grass or the bite of mango. He wanted to rub himself all over her body, knew she'd not only let him, but she'd love it.

"I know that smile." She tossed her scarf on the peg near the door and followed with her sweater. "That smile means I'm going without dinner." One of her eyebrows rose. "Not that I'm complaining."

He laughed and took her hand. "One more reason to love you. Much as I'd love to strip you naked and have my way with you for a few hours, you should eat. I know you probably went all day without taking a break." Knew too that many considered her flaky or flighty but she lived in her head a lot. Not because she wasn't capable, she was. Not because she wasn't intelligent, she was one of the smartest people he knew. But because Renee saw the world in ways most people never could. It made her more beautiful to him, but he knew she struggled to accept it in herself.

"Look at it this way, I'll just have more energy for the sex afterward if I eat." She pulled away to poke her head into the fridge, grabbing two cream sodas and some glasses with ice. "I had a smoothie and some yogurt for breakfast and heaven knows I'm not in any danger of wasting away." She indicated her body, the body he adored and knew every dip, every fall and curve, knew her scent, knew her taste.

"Your body, mmmm." He hugged her again before drawing her to the table. "You are rich and warm. You're cookies from the oven, brownies with nuts. You are succulent and delicious. If that's because you like to have two pieces of pizza instead of one, I'm just fine with that. I love your body so get eating."

They sat side by side at their kitchen table, spooning up pasta salad and sharing the sandwiches. They'd bought the loft three years before and had spent a lot of time making it their own. The pictures on the walls, the art, the couch so heavy and cumbersome to move he'd toss it out the fucking window before he'd move it again—these things were a tangible marker in their history.

He reached toward her, twirling a curl around his finger. "How was your day other than mowing down an unsuspecting dude?"

"Hey, he was way bigger. I totally took his apples to the pavement." She sniffed and took a sip of her soda. "The usual. Phoenix—" she paused to roll her eyes at the use of her stepmother's fake new name, "—was all agitated about some letter she got. Dad came in and took her shopping and to lunch or something because she was calmer when she returned. Calmer than her normal state of up my assery, anyway."

"Maybe he bent her over something. Always works to get you to relax."

Her nose scrunched up. "Ew. Galen! If you're still keeping sex on the menu for later, the comments about my dad and stepmom having sex need to stop."

"We all got here somehow, babe. We all got here somehow." He winked, knowing she'd get all ruffled up about it.

"Don't make me stick my fingers in my ears and start singing. How was your day? Did you kick ass?"

"I always kick ass. Work was work. Hit my hours target for the year so that's a load off."

"Kinda stupid to have a billable hours requirement when the damned firm is all family." She stole a pickle from his plate, but he'd put an extra out there specifically for that reason so he let it pass.

"Still have to pay bills. Even with family."

"Things improve with Max?"

He sighed and she put her head on his shoulder briefly. Galen was very close to his older brother. The two of them were a lot alike, which was the reason they fought all the time. Max also filled the spot of Renee's biggest fan within the jamboree; he defended her, sang her praises and generally adored her. In that, they were in total agreement. But they were still brothers and they acted that way. "After I punched him and broke his nose I know I felt better. Don't know about him though."

She tsked. "Galen. You two have to stop maiming each other. It's very hard to get blood out of your shirts for one thing. For another thing, you're not supposed to act that way with your own brother. He's single, it'll be harder for him to land himself a woman if he's bruised up and battered all the time. If I had a sibling I would not waste time by punching him or her in the face."

"You do know that when you get all judgy on me it only turns me on, right? All that moral indignation is hot. You're like a school teacher I want to rumple and seduce into doing naughty things."

She blushed, even as she laughed. "You know I'm right."

"Babe, I know anyone else in the jamboree will definitely think twice before challenging me, Max or my father because they know we will kick their asses if they try. They've seen me fight. They've seen Max and my dad fight. This is shifter stuff, you know human rules don't always apply to us." He shrugged. They were not humans, they didn't solve family issues the same way and he wasn't going to apologize for it.

"You guys really need to call yourselves something tougher than jamboree," she teased. "A gang. Oh! A cabal!"

He rolled his eyes at the familiar joke. "We don't need a tough name. I can rip someone's throat out before they can draw a breath. We could be sparkly unicorns and still eat your face off."

"I still say if you call yourselves the Hell's Jaguars or something you'd be even scarier. Better PR. As for eating? I like my face, Galen. But you can eat other parts of me." She blinked her eyes, smiling innocently. Part of her allure, the naughty girl down just a few layers.

"But you do taste so very good." He looked her up and down again. "Are you wearing a bra?" he asked, distracted by everything about her. She called to him, her magic, the way she sounded, the corkscrew curls she hated but wore better than any woman ever could. The combination was like catnip.

Her eyes darkened. Her eyes were the first thing he'd noticed about her back when he'd met her four years ago. Amber with flecks of gold and brown. In some light they looked hazel. Her combination of features, if they'd been separate on other people's faces, would have been odd. But on her it worked. There was no one like her in the world.

Faster than he could put his glass down and move to her, she was in his lap, straddling his body, and those delicious breasts were at eye level.

"Now you can see for yourself." She arched into him, her hands braced on either side of his shoulders.

"Like a present to be opened up." Taking his time, he slid his hands up her torso, over the curves he loved.

She was his. That knowledge filled him, gave him purpose and satisfied him down to the bone.

He licked over the upper curve of her right breast. A breast high and proud, and as he'd thought, totally unrestrained by a bra. Crossing her arms, she reached down and grabbed the hem of her shirt, pulling it up and over her head, tossing it to the side.

The way she moved on him, grinding herself against his cock over and over as her fingers wove through his hair, drove him crazy. Magic bled from her, washed over him, inciting his senses.

Without pause, he stood and began walking to their bedroom. While he wasn't opposed to fast and hard on the dining room table, he wanted to take his time that night. He wanted to lay her out and love her from head to toe and back again.

"I love you, Renee." He put her down and she finished pulling the rest of her clothes off, her eyes never leaving his body.

"I love you too." She held a hand out and he took it, following her body down to the mattress.

The shock of skin on skin, the rush of pleasure as they connected physically as well as emotionally, knocked him over. "You feel so good," he murmured as he licked down the side of her neck.

The energy between them swirled thick, her magic, his magic, bound together as they were. Each new time he had her, this was the case, more and more connection, a deeper bond. There was no doubt inside him, not with man or cat, that he had imprinted on her and she him.

In his world that was enough. They were married and mated and she was a member of the jamboree via her connection to him. She was family. She referred to herself as his wife and that's most certainly how he considered her too. He'd asked her to marry him all human style as well and she'd agreed. The problem was, she really wanted all his siblings to accept her and wanted to have a closer relationship with her father and stepmother so everyone would be at the ceremony. He was pretty sure that would never happen. Her father was disinterested and his wife too interested in herself. She didn't care about Renee's happiness and barely tolerated Galen. They'd consistently refused to meet his family or even speak of what he was out loud. Both the jaguar shifter part and the fact that he was biracial. They liked the lawyer part and he took care of her well, so her father never quite put into words what it was clear he thought.

None of that shit mattered. He'd taken to a new line of argument lately, that they needed to just do it because she'd never be close to her stepmother and father and he'd never get his sister to stop being a bitch and to accept Renee.

She wore his teeth on her skin, bore his mark proudly. She opened herself to him in a way he knew she never did with anyone else. They were united.

But there was something. He didn't know what. He only knew she felt it too. The air held expectation. Something was about to happen, something that would change them. There was no fear. He knew what he felt, knew it was genuine and he knew without a doubt Renee returned those feelings.

Still, as she was fond of saying with that smirk/smile she so often wore, you know what they say about cats and curiosity.

Her scent drew him in, made the other thoughts fall from his head. His lips knew her, his hands, fingers, cock. On his knees, he looked down at her, at those lush lips, at the sleepy, half-mast eyes banking a fire just for him, her curly hair in disarray around her face. Her body, petite but lush, was the most perfect thing he'd ever seen. Curves, dips, valleys, the puckered tips of her nipples, the scar on her hip, the birthmark on her left wrist.

She began to speak, hesitated and smiled instead. He knew. Knew how she felt because he felt it too.

Her palms slid down his back, urging him closer. She leaned up enough to kiss his thigh, licking closer and closer until that mouth, hot and wet, reached his cock, just a wisp of her touch but enough to bring a moan to his lips.

Renee still couldn't quite believe the man in her bed was hers. That someone who looked like Galen would even take a second glance at her, much less treat her as if she were the most precious thing he'd ever seen.

Acres of taut, caramel skin beckoned as she slid her palms against him. Over the flat belly, across hard thighs and toned shoulders. He was so incredibly gorgeous she never quite knew

Lauren Dane

which part of him to look at first.

His muscles flexed against her touch. She knew they were bound, the brilliant strands of the ribbons of emotion held them, drew then together. Not stifling, but assuring. Being with Galen, thinking about him gave her comfort even as it titillated her with the need to taste, to touch, to pleasure and take pleasure from. Just as he'd imprinted on her, she had with him. Their magic so very different, had reacted, melded and they'd bound themselves together. She belonged to him, body and heart.

His cock, fully erect, lay in her line of sight and she leaned up a bit to lick the head, tasting the sweet/salt of his body. He groaned her name, the sound wrapping around her, pulling her closer.

The power in this, the way she knew with her hands and mouth, with body, she could bring him to his knees, bring him pleasure like no one else, filled her, heady and sticky-sweet.

Rolling to her knees, she locked her gaze with his, falling into those brown/black eyes. One hand on his chest, over his heart, over the spot where her name lay inked into his flesh, she pushed until he gave in and fell back to the bed.

Inky-dark hair, just a bit longer than it should be, spread around his face as she leaned down to kiss him. His lips, as always, brought a shiver to her. So very good, that mouth. Kissing mouth, body, pussy, it didn't matter what part of her he touched with his mouth, he did it always with an intensity of purpose. Now was no different as he kissed her with slow sensuality.

Galen knew her body, knew her heart like no one else ever had.

With some regret, she left his mouth and kissed down his neck, across his chest, down his very sensitive side, across his lower belly until the hands gently cradling her head tightened, urging ever so gently downward.

30

She looked up, into his face, met his eyes and smiled. "Did you have a request?"

"My cock does and I'm its spokesperson."

She laughed. "I suppose it wants to go to Target to get some socks."

Her laughter died when he caught his bottom lip between his teeth. "Um, no." He swore in three languages when she licked up the line of his cock.

Sexy bastard. "You taste very good. I think I'm addicted." Wrapping her hand around the base of his cock, she angled it to take him into her mouth.

"Good God," he mumbled as he arched into her.

Over and over she licked and swallowed, kissed and sucked. Over the years she'd come to learn what he liked and what he didn't but it didn't feel boring or repetitive. Each time she was with him this way she learned something new about him and herself as well.

She knew he was getting closer, he hardened impossibly more, the electricity of his climax charged his skin, arced between them, stealing her breath.

He moved his hands to her shoulder, squeezing gently. "Stop, stop. I want to be in you. I've been thinking about it all day."

She sighed, sad to part with his cock that way, but pleased to scramble atop him.

"Impatient!" He rolled her to her back. "Let's be sure you're ready."

"Ready? I'm ready, believe me. Put your cock inside me already!" She writhed as he licked over her nipples, left to right, over and over until she nearly panted.

"I'll be the judge of that," he said as he continued south.

Well. Okay, then.

He nudged her thighs wider and settled in before delivering a devastating lick from her gate to her clit. A secret benefit to having a man who was a cat shifter? The tongue. Whatever cat thing he had, which thankfully did not include a barbed penis—ouch—meant the broad, nubbed surface of his tongue was like a sex toy or something.

She laughed and he paused. "You thinking about my tongue again?"

"Yes, now get back to work!" He didn't just give marvelous oral sex, she'd never, ever had a man go down on her and bring her as much pleasure as Galen did. What was there to complain about? Oral by a man who wanted to eat her alive with a super sextoy tongue. Bonus.

He pushed her hard, his mouth insistent, demanding. He took her from aroused to arching, begging and gasping out in climax in what felt like seconds. Her muscles still trembled, spasmed as he reared up and the head of his cock nudged against her, pressing inside her body.

"More. Ohgod, more. Deeper." Digging her heels into the mattress, she pushed against him, taking him deeper inside.

Caught between amusement and desire, Galen stared down at her as he thrust deep and pulled nearly all the way out. "Greedy." And she was. She may have looked like a sweet little pixie but in truth, his woman liked it hard and fast. Not that he'd complain. She also liked it all the time, which made her a rather perfect match for him in that department.

"And you love me anyway."

"Yes. Yes I do." He sped up, enjoying the jaunty bounce of her breasts as he plunged deep, fast and hard.

Orgasm rode him, urged him on. White-hot pleasure spread through him, outward like a blast as he guided her hand to her clit and she gasped, her pussy contracting around his cock. It didn't take very long for her to start coming again, thank goodness, because at the first, hard squeeze she tipped him right over with her.

"It's always this way with you." He pressed a kiss to her temple as he collapsed next to her on the bed.

She stretched, more like a cat than she ever knew. "How's that?"

"I can't get enough. One touch is never enough. A thousand touches aren't enough."

"Is that a bad thing? Do you resent not knowing if what you feel is real or the result of the chemicals between us? Between me and your cat?"

He rolled to face her. "My cat is hotter for you than the human part is. My cat doesn't care about whatever human conventions demand. My cat just wants to love you and fuck you and keep you safe, what anyone else wants bedamned. My human agrees but realizes it's important you're along for the ride willingly. Don't doubt any part of me. I've never given you cause to, have I?"

She shook her head. "No. I don't doubt what we have. I just...I've just seen some of your family seem upset by it. By you and me together when you have females within the jamboree who they think you should be with."

Anger coursed through him. "What happened?" He saw her hesitation and it was his turn to shake his head at her. "Tell me. Please, babe."

"Beth. She came by the shop today, in the morning. She's pregnant."

He only barely resisted the urge to grab the phone and call his sister to kick her ass. The only thing preventing that was the knowledge of how much he'd hurt Renee that way. He'd deal with Beth later.

"I know. She told me earlier today." He paused. "You know what she's like. I'll talk to her. She knows better than to hassle you. Anyway, so what? You know she's damaged. You and I will have children when we're ready and she has nothing to do with us."

"Mentally damaged. She's a humanphobe, or whatever you want to call it. Your genes are too precious to waste on my weak human ovaries."

He was going to kill his sister.

"My mother dropped her on her head a lot when she was a baby. I told you long ago not to listen to her because she's an idiot. Did something happen today other than that?"

He smoothed his hands over her skin, needing the contact. She sighed and snuggled closer.

"No. Not really. I guess it's just...it feels like the air right before it rains. Something will happen. Soon. It's making me impatient I suppose."

"I feel it too, sweet witch. You and I though? Nothing wrong there. The only thing I'd love more is if you married me all human like." He nipped her shoulder playfully, but left a mark.

A mark she loved and would look at again and again. Renee couldn't really explain why to anyone but him, but that he'd mark her, make sure everyone knew she was his, it turned her on and made her feel safe.

"We already said we'd get married next year. As for everything else? Of all the things I know in the world, I know you and I are okay and will be. You are my cornerstone, my foundation. I just wish I knew what it was. This thing we're waiting on." She knew that to be true more than anything else she'd ever known. Galen was hers and she his. They would be together when they were old and gray. She'd have his children and yes, they would get married though she'd prefer to just go to city hall and do it quietly than have some big event. Susan didn't really care about Renee, but she'd want to take over and spend lots of money, Galen's money, on some swank affair with eleventy million guests she didn't even know. That wasn't who she was and it wasn't who Galen was either.

"Soon enough. Now, let's finish dinner. I'll make you a lemon drop and we can catch a few episodes of Buffy before bed? Oh and more sex later."

She rolled off the bed, padding toward the door without bothering to put clothes back on.

"Of course more sex. You think I'm with you just for how smart you are?" She winked at him, loving the rich sound of his laughter as he jumped up to follow her back out to the table.

Chapter Three

Jack looked around the shop as he entered. Wall to wall woo woo. He wondered if Renee was one of those new agey types, wondered if she would put crystals in the window sills and refused to make decisions if Mercury was in retrograde.

But none of that mattered. None of it mattered because he'd accept her quirks much the same way he knew she'd accept his. Excitement warmed him. He'd not been this interested in pursuing a woman ever.

Which was as it should be, of course. She was *the one* after all. Getting to know her would be fun.

He didn't even have to search to find her. He felt her before he laid eyes on her. Spice? What was that? Following his senses led him around an aisle of shelving and there she was, a huge smile on her face, cat-eye glasses perched on her nose, a tight T-shirt with some sort of sweater over it. She wore little or no makeup and her hair curled around her face in no real pattern. And yet she was the most breathtaking woman he'd ever seen. She was...unexpected.

The citrus and cinnamon of her scent mixed with the pungency of mango, the sweetness of strawberries. He shook his head, trying to free himself from the siren song of her existence but then let go, let himself fall into it because it was hers and that was how it was supposed to be.

"That looks really good. What would you recommend?" He

leaned one elbow on the counter and sent her his very best charming grin.

"Well, look here! It's Jack. Hello, Jack." Her smile in return caught him in its artlessness and lack of guile. Not that she was naïve or innocent, there was definite mischief there dancing in her eyes, but she wasn't trying to sell him anything, not trying to get him to have babies with her. Though, holy shit, did he want to have babies with her.

That rocked him. He liked kids, other people's kids though. Cade hadn't been kidding about the impact of a mate bond. He wanted to bury himself inside her, wanted to take care of her, to build a whole lifetime. For a man like him, the depth of that need took him by surprise. What he'd had, had always seemed like it was enough, until he stood there looking into Renee's face and came home.

How did a male process all this stuff and keep his shit together? His estimation of Cade went up a few thousand percent knowing he'd dealt with this intensity of feeling and had managed to deal with a fermenting war at the same time.

Still, Jack realized that despite the challenges he faced, the biggest, most important thing was that he had met her. He knew this woman before him would be tucked next to him at night, every night for the rest of his life. How he'd work it all out wasn't clear just then, but he would. There was no reason for him to believe fate would put Renee into his path and not provide a way to work things out.

He took a deep breath and kept his composure. Barely. "You do have me at a disadvantage. You know my name and yet, here I am not knowing yours."

She laughed, not beautiful, lyrical laughter, but a full on, throaty laugh. He bit back a groan at the raw sensuality of the sound.

"Are we pretending you didn't come in here after I left last night to ask where I was?"

Busted. Here he was, an Enforcer, supposedly the biggest badass in the country and he'd been busted by a smidgen of a woman. Good thing he'd been best friends with a woman this size who could scare any smart man twice his size. Grace Warden would like Renee a lot. Once they got over their initial hatred of the other. The stories about the first meetings between Grace and Nina Warden after Grace and Cade had mated were legendary.

Getting ahead of himself. He needed to focus again. "It's my turn to blush."

"Blush?" She cocked her head and looked him up and down. "Why do I get the feeling blushing isn't something you do very often?"

"Given the right circumstances I totally blush." He bet she could get him to blush all the time.

"Like when you get caught checking up on a girl who tells you she's with someone?" Her smile faded into something else. She froze, blinking her eyes rapidly, cocking her head as she looked at him.

"Are you all right?" He didn't smell fear or anger, but clearly something was going on with her. His wolf pressed against the human skin, alert, needing to protect and comfort.

"Well now, this is interesting. You're a wolf. The wolf Galen scented yesterday."

He looked around. Someone approached and she shifted her attention, smiling brightly at the newcomer. "Hey, Pete. The usual?"

"With a shot of wheat grass too, please." The guy leaned against the counter and sent moony eyes at Jack's woman.

Effortlessly, Renee put a bunch of stuff together and used the blender to mix it. Pungent and sweet scents married, carried along with her essential spice. She slid it to the other guy with a smile.

He thanked her, dropped some money on the counter and toddled off, oblivious to Jack's glare. And that's when he saw it, the bite on her shoulder. She'd been marked by this cat, which meant way more than a simple dating relationship.

"Now, for you?" Renee looked him up and down, her shirt falling back into place and hiding the bite mark once again. "Obviously you need something with protein in it." She turned and began to fiddle with stuff.

"How about a coffee? I'm not one for health food." He hoped he didn't sound grumpy, but he felt it anyway. And then he let it go. She was his and this cat, whoever he was, wasn't going to keep him away.

Renee wanted to roll her eyes at his tone, but stopped herself. He was a freaking werewolf and he wasn't one for health food? Something inside her bolted. No, he was going to take care of himself.

"You'll have a smoothie." She assembled an orange mango power smoothie. The protein powder would help keep his energy up. She made them for Galen twice a day, shifters needed extra protein and calories. Coffee would not do.

"You're very bossy." One of his eyebrows rose, but the smile on his face made her nervously giddy.

"I am. You're a werewolf." She shrugged. The world was so magical, most people simply had no understanding of the dozens of layers the world had. This made her laugh and his expression made her laugh even harder. Susan/Phoenix looked up from her perch behind the counter but soon went back to chatting with her customer.

"How do you know?" Wonderment, not anger.

From a very early age, she'd known things. She'd known when the phone would ring or when something very good or bad was coming. And she saw. Most people looked around and kept from bumping into things, but Renee saw. At certain angles or in the right sort of light she saw within people, their true nature often revealed and they had no idea. Many times, Renee wished she didn't have any idea either. Some people's true selves were not so pretty and most of them were human and not supernatural beings.

She pushed the smoothie his way. "Drink it and I'll tell you."

She should not be playing with him this way. This one was so very clearly a predator, but she couldn't help it. It amused her to push him around. This was dangerous. The man was way more than the normal flirty customer. This man got to her. Part of her wanted to run, warring with the part of her who needed to follow this path with Jack Meyers to see where it ended up. It was more than flirtation. So that made her wary. She might like to look at a handsome man in a totally carnal way, but that didn't mean she'd actually *do* anything about it. Renee loved Galen de La Vega more than she could ever put into words.

"Is this like dingleberry nuts with some tree fruit hand harvested by tame monkeys in the Amazon?"

His silly tease brought her attention back to him, to that surfer's face with those big white teeth and eyes that held a teasing light.

"You're psychic. I'm the executive director of the tame monkey union."

He stilled a moment and sent her a smile she felt way down to her toes. And um, other places too. She'd seen that smile on many an alpha male's face. Male shifters were a handful and she wished good luck to the woman this one settled his attentions on. But she already *had* an alpha male shifter who wanted to "take care of her" and one was more than enough, even if this one was a whole bunch of hotness. She would never risk hurting Galen and she'd certainly never break the trust they had. But there was something here, something she felt like she had to let happen. That evening she'd discuss it with Galen to see what he thought of the situation.

He took a sip and one more. "Okay, you win. You and your monkeys. It's good. What is it?"

"Other than dingleberry nuts? Which by the way, you do know what a dingleberry is, right?"

He grinned again. Her whole system redlined for a moment and she had to start coring strawberries to tear her mind away from that face.

"Is there like a fourteen-year-old boy living inside you?"

"Sometimes. Anyway, banana, mango, strawberry, apple juice and protein powder. Oh and some frozen yogurt to make it like a milkshake. How many calories a day do you have to put away?"

"How about I answer all your questions over some lunch?"

"Jack, you're very handsome and I'm totally flattered. But I'm with someone. I told you that. I'm in love with him, we live together and we're married."

"Human married? Not mated?"

"In every way that counts, yes." She narrowed her eyes at him, but before she could say anything else, his phone rang. With an agitated sigh, he looked at the display and picked up.

"What?" he barked as he answered.

She tried not to listen. Well, that was a lie. She tried to listen without anyone knowing she was listening. But he did that male guttural thing. Grunting single word answers.

"You owe me so big." He hung up and when he turned his gaze back to her she felt it like a shove. "I'm sorry. Work." He put a five on the counter. "Keep the change. I'll see you tomorrow, Renee. We can talk about where to go to lunch then."

"I'm not going anywhere with you, Jack Meyers. I told you, I'm taken," she called out as he left.

"What do you think you're doing?" Susan/Phoenix approached once the shop emptied out a bit.

"What are you talking about?" Renee wiped down her counter and did her best to not be agitated by her stepmother's presence, or to let her make Renee feel guilty over something she hadn't done. It was a near thing. For pretty much most of Renee's life, the woman had sought to keep her under her thumb, to tear Renee down when she felt it was necessary. The woman was all about drama and emotional outbursts. She had been since the first time she'd gone out to dinner with Renee's father. Of course, she'd been Susan back then. The facets she'd seen in her stepmother hadn't always been so bright and full of love. But some things didn't bear obsessing over. The past couldn't be undone.

She didn't doubt Susan/Phoenix loved Renee's father, but the feelings between the two women were far more complicated. Obligation was there, but love? Renee didn't believe her stepmother had the capacity to love anyone but herself and Renee's father, and him only marginally. There was more jealousy than affection, which Renee used to regret, but she was too old to feel sorry about other people's choices. She made her own, good and bad, but she always tried to protect those she loved and cared about.

However, being accused of something when she'd never given any reason for anyone to doubt her really pissed Renee off.

"This guy. He's the one who came in here last night. Do you want to blow things with Galen by cheating so publically? Are you really so stupid that you'd risk yourself this way? Don't be dumb. He's a great catch even with the drawbacks."

Renee put the cloth down and turned her stare to the other woman. "Drawbacks? Cheating? What the hell are you talking about? Of *course* Galen's a great catch. That's why I'm married to him and live with him. That's why he and I are engaged to be married in my world too. That's why I *love* him. As for Jack, I made the guy a smoothie. A guy I've seen exactly twice in my life for maybe a total of fifteen minutes. I didn't have sex with him. I run a retail cart, interacting with customers happens every day. Men and women both flirt with me every day. He's a customer. He flirted, I told him I was engaged. He wasn't rude. What should I have done? Slapped his face for asking me to lunch?"

"You have bad judgment. Like your mother." Susan/Phoenix threw up her hands like she was just so fed up with the world. Fucking drama queen.

This had become a bigger issue over the years as her stepmother began to insult Renee's mother more and more often. Not much made her angrier. Renee's mother had died when Renee had been seven. Susan/Phoenix hadn't entered their lives until her father had moved them to Boston a year later. He'd been married to her for twenty years, but it didn't make Susan an expert on Cindy Parcell and it certainly didn't give her the right to ever make disparaging comments about a woman people said only good things about. Fact was, even if Cindy had been a three-dollar-handjob whore, it wasn't up to Susan to say one negative word.

Renee shut down rather than punch someone. "You have no right, Susan. Now leave me alone. You've said whatever you needed to say."

The day went on, annoyingly long, but it had been busy enough that Renee hadn't had any time to obsess or stew over her fight with Phoenix earlier. When she closed up, she walked past the front counter and said nothing.

The walk home did her some good. She kept a brisk pace, took in the sight of the leaves changing, the scent of dark coming, and let go of the anger the best she could.

The condo was empty when she got home. Galen's absence made the place a bit chillier, made her feel a bit more lonely.

Galen was her best friend, she wanted to share with him about the fight today, wanted to talk to him about Jack.

She'd lacked close friends growing up. When her mother had died, her father just sort of distanced himself from her. They'd never really gotten that closeness back. They'd moved to Boston a year later. Her life had been one thing, and then it was suddenly something else and she'd never really been allowed to look backward. Looking backward was difficult, cloudy. They'd avoided discussing it and Renee had never had the opportunity to talk about it with anyone else because her mother's family had refused all contact with her years ago. No one else knew her, knew her mother before. It felt like a dream sometimes.

Maybe a hot shower would help. And a glass of wine or two. By the time she was nice and relaxed, Galen would be home. She'd pounce on him and in the afterglow, tell him about her day. She knew she'd feel better once she got his input.

Galen looked up from the stack of papers before him. The clock had to be wrong. Eight? Already? Damn. He pulled his cell phone out and saw he'd received one text message from Renee some hours before. Not nagging, just a question about what his schedule would be that evening. And he'd been offline and in the middle of this damned case for hours without even realizing how late it had gotten. Working late wasn't that unusual for him and she didn't keep tabs, but they kept each other informed about their schedules.

He dialed home quickly. Her voice, when she answered, made him feel immediately better.

"I'm so sorry, babe. Time got away from me. I had the phone off during a conference call and I must have forgotten to turn the ringer back on."

"Okay. No big deal. I know what your job can be like sometimes. When are you coming home?"

He heard her rustling around and knew she'd perched herself on the big couch with blankets, a glass of wine and a movie. Holy shit did that sound good. Unfortunately, as he looked back at the screen and the pile on the desk, that wasn't going to be happening any time soon.

"I got a case dumped on me this afternoon. I need to file a motion tomorrow and get this brief done by Friday. I'm sorry to say I won't be home for another several hours."

"Oh. Okay. Well, I understand. Can I bring you dinner? Have you eaten?"

Had he? God it felt like forever ago that he'd eaten last. A big lunch after court and then another meal when he'd met with Max and had been given the case he was currently working on.

"I'm going to order something right now. I promise. You sound funny. Are you okay?"

She paused and the soft sound of her sigh tore at him. "I'm fine. Just tired. If you promise to eat, I'll probably just go to bed early."

He sat up at the emotion in her voice. Sad. Lonely. His system responded, needing to rub himself along her body to comfort, to give affection.

"I'm coming home now. I can work on this tomorrow. I'll just come in early."

"No you won't. You have a job to do. I can hear how stressed you sound. I'm going to order your food the minute we hang up. That way I know you're eating right."

This woman, God, how she got to him. Under his skin. Into his heart and soul. "I can hear how *you* sound. You think I'd just abandon you when you're so obviously having a bad day?"

"You're going to make me cry. Stop it. Really, I'm all right. Just a crappy day, that's all. Nothing earth-shattering. I got into a fight with Phoenix. She said stuff about my mom. There's this thing happening I wanted to run by you. None of this is urgent.

We have the weekend, we'll talk then."

"You need to move your cart. There are better locations for you and then you won't owe her anything. You won't have to deal with her every day. It's not good for you." Which was an understatement. Phoenix always had an agenda. He didn't trust her at all and that she made Renee so unhappy drove him insane. He'd been trying to convince her to move the cart for the last year, but she stayed, trying to have a relationship with her father. Phoenix was toxic to Renee.

She sighed again. "Cool. Not the Susan thing, but the fact that I was just able to order your dinner from Luke's via their website. You need to call downstairs to have the doorman let them up."

He laughed. "Thank you for taking care of me, babe. I'll try not to be later than one or so. What did you mean by *thing* happening?"

"The wolf you scented was this guy I ran into last night. The apple guy. I saw his inner self when he came into the shop today to get a smoothie. It feels odd. I wanted to bounce ideas off you, get your take."

Everything went still inside him, a cat with his woman in harm's way. "Does he scare you? Did he harm you or threaten you?"

"No! Not like that at all. He's very nice. Or not threatening anyway. Odd as in unusual. It's complicated and long and I wanted your opinion. I'll tell you about it tomorrow night. Really, I promise, I'm okay. I just miss you and I'm tired. If you have to stay super late, just sleep there. Coming all the way home at three to have to get back there by seven seems pretty silly when you have a place to sleep and spare clothes there. I hate you being out that late."

"I'm coming *home* when I finish. I want to sleep next to you tonight, like I do every night. Drink some tea, read a while and then go to bed. I love you."

"I love you too. Be safe and eat every single thing I ordered for you."

When he hung up, he made sure to deal with the delivery instructions for the doorman and then he dived back into his work so he could finish up and get home to her.

Chapter Four

Jack groaned as he shuffled from his bedroom into the kitchen. Too early. Too bright. Way too short a time between the moment he'd dropped into bed and that very second. And he itched to see Renee, to hear her voice and revel in her scent.

Since that couldn't happen any time very soon, he needed to get some coffee. That was thing one. Coffee, something quick for breakfast on the run, and back to Cade and Grace's. There'd been an incident at Grace's health clinic. A male whose mate had been injured severely in a car accident some months before had shown up angry and full of blame for Grace. Then there'd been vandalism and a fight between two neighboring packs down south and Jack had to get on a conference call and threaten to maim people if they didn't get their act together. Just another insane day as the National Pack Enforcer. Busy, agitating, but thrilling and satisfying too.

He gulped coffee as he nuked a breakfast burrito and thought of Renee. Wondered how the rest of her day had gone after he'd had to go so quickly the day before. He'd thought of her, even as he'd been so busy he'd been rushed off his feet the entire time.

The day outside his door was clear, the morning cool. He'd need to go on a run in the next few days. All the pent-up energy of the need he felt for Renee, his desire to Claim her and win her too, put him on edge. At the same time, he wasn't panicked.

It would happen. She was a human woman, most wolves had to court their human mates before they mated through the Claiming. His father had been human, his mother a wolf. They'd dated for seven months before having unprotected sex and performing the ritual that solidified their mate bond. As long as she let him in, he could move more slowly than he would have if she'd been a wolf.

He arrived just in time to walk Becca to kindergarten and drop Annabelle off at preschool as he pretended not to keep an eye on Grace. Grace brought Henri to the clinic with her a few days a week and the roly-poly sixteen-month-old grinned at passersby and talked nonstop to his mother as they went. She listened intently, laughing and speaking to the boy like he was making sense and contentment settled around Jack at the wonderful familiarity of the moment.

Dave, Grace's personal bodyguard, appreciated the backup and Jack never interfered with how he did his job so things were fine by the time he got back to the house and sat down with another cup of coffee and a plate heaped with a real breakfast.

"Appreciate you getting here early to go with them all this morning. Everything okay?" Cade asked as he read whatever was on his Blackberry screen. Shortly thereafter, he turned to his food and to face Jack.

Of course he'd shown up to escort them safely. It was his job and his pleasure.

"You know your wife. She's not gonna let something like this get to her. I interviewed the male last night, he's falling apart. Deep down he knows Grace isn't at fault. But he's watching his mate have to go through painful physical therapy because so much damage was done through the accident even being a wolf couldn't spare her entirely."

Cade nodded. He wouldn't punish the male too harshly because he understood what it meant to be afraid to lose one's ff0ff mate.

tpp G *Lauren Dane*

mate.

"Becca is at school. Annabelly is at preschool and Grace is at work along with your son and their bodyguard. No shots fired. No new graffiti. She's calm and relatively happy, even with an increased guard presence at the clinic today. I left them in good hands to come over here and listen to you yammer on all day about work crap. I need to head out in a little while to go see my woman."

Cade's smile softened for a moment as Jack spoke about the Alpha's family, but his sly amusement returned at Jack's last comment. "Did you tell *her* this yet? That she's your woman?"

Jack snorted. "Not yet. But, Cade, she looked at me yesterday and knew I was a wolf. I don't know how. I had no time to follow up because she told me she was married right after she said she knew I was a wolf. And then *you* called and I had to rush off."

"Sorry about that. I really am. Married married or shifter married?"

"That's what I said. She just said in all the ways that count. Which means not human married. What it does mean I don't know for sure. I just know I would not have met her if I wasn't meant to. I *know* it."

"I think so too. For us, fate is strong. You're meant to be with this woman. Until then, well I know what it's like not to have your mate. I know what it feels like to have such strong feelings about my anchor. I've noticed the difference in you. You're relaxed, satisfied. It's good to see."

"It's good to *be*. I know it's partly the mate connection, but she's exceptional. I've never met anyone like her."

"I remember the moment Grace walked into the room when I saw her the first time. Before I got close enough to scent her, I wanted her. I was fascinated by her. I still am. The truth is,

50

Jack, no one else is like her. No one can be. And while she's not the only female on the planet you'd have a potential mate connection with, she's the one you met first. You're *meant* for each other and she is unlike anyone else you've met or ever will."

He totally got it. Jack had heard the mated males talk about this stuff and it seemed natural enough, but he couldn't have understood. Couldn't have known the immensity of what it meant to man and wolf to find home in another person. Until Renee. Now he did.

"Yeah."

Cade put his cup of coffee down and looked to Jack with a raised brow. Jack sat back and waited for it. "My grandmother called a few minutes ago while you were out."

He only barely resisted the urge to lean forward. "Look at you with that casual taunt."

"All those years living in the same house as Nina honed my skills." He grinned and Jack didn't doubt it. Nina Warden, Cade's sister-in-law and anchor bond, was a sharp- tongued woman, no doubt. And gorgeous. Lex Warden was a brave and lucky man.

"Okay, consider yourself successful. I'm curious, what did she say?"

"She said you should call her at one our time since she was going to an early yoga class and then to breakfast with my mom. Now I have the image of my grandmother in Lycra in my head, so you should know how much I'm doing for you to facilitate this. She did tell me to relate to you that it was possible for you to mate with Renee, even if she was already imprinted by this cat. She said some other stuff but it was like five in the morning there so she'll fill you in more when you talk to her."

Jack breathed a sigh of relief. It was possible. The next

hurdle would be whether it was probable. It was no small thing if she'd imprinted with this other male.

So he'd wait to talk with Lia and then he'd go see Renee.

Galen woke up, his arms around Renee, the need for her, as always, thrumming through his veins. Her scent, sleepwarm, sexy and his, rose to his nose and he buried his face in the softness of her curls.

She stirred, and he didn't push, just waited for her to wake up on her own. While Renee was one of the sweetest women he'd ever met, giving and compassionate, she was *not* a morning person. He'd learned that the hard way. She was a sexual being, but if he pushed her to wake up too fast, she'd pop him one. Something he admired, something that made her an awful lot like the female shifters he knew.

Though he didn't share that fact with her. He knew there were problems with some of the females in his jamboree. His sister, Beth, was one of the females who reacted most strongly. Luckily his mother adored Renee, as did many others. But there was jealousy and no matter how kind Renee had been, they just didn't want to be won over.

He'd warned them all off and it reminded him he needed to talk with his parents about Beth and what she'd done earlier in the week to Renee.

"You're all bunchy," she mumbled, not moving her face from where she'd buried it in the pillow.

"Bunchy?" He smiled. "Here?" He rolled his hips, grinding his cock into her thigh.

"Mmmpf. Not." She rolled to face him, slowly opening her eyes. God she was beautiful, even when she frowned and looked slightly dangerous. "Look at you. It's ridiculous for anyone to look as good as you do in the morning. Makes me grumpy."

He risked life and limb to steal a quick kiss and laughed at her expression. "Babe, you're gorgeous. Every morning I want to eat you up."

"Hmmm. Don't move." She got up and headed into their bathroom. He heard the water run and the sound of teeth being brushed.

The sun was beginning to pinken the sky as she came back to him, sliding under the blankets and into his arms.

"Better?"

"As better as it can be at this hour. You never told me what was making you bunchy." Very perceptive eyes took him in.

"You never defined bunchy for me, babe. When you use Renee-speak, I need a dictionary sometimes."

"You're tense. Not so much now that you think you're getting some morning sex, but earlier. Your muscles were bunched up."

"Am I?"

"Bunched up?"

Leaning in, he drew a deep breath, his lips just touching her throat. His system went into overdrive. "Getting morning sex."

"You're going to get your junk punched if you don't tell me what had you all stressed out."

"God you're sexy when you're like this."

She pinched his side, not to hurt, but to get his attention. He tried to not laugh, he really did, but she was a tiny scrap of a woman who wouldn't even let him kill a bug in the house if he found one. Fierce, yes, but did he worry about her ever harming him on purpose? Not so much.

"Let's fuck. That's much nicer. I was just thinking about family and work. Nothing earth-shattering."

"Why do men think they can do that and get away with it?" She threw the blankets back and got out of bed again. Damn, this was not the way he planned to spend his morning.

But before he could say anything else, she spun and glared his way. The beast within sighted its mate, a female that despite being physically small, was not small in her ferocity or her ability to bring the pain should she need to.

The moment stretched and the anger left her stance. "How do you do this to me?" she murmured, moving back to him, taking his hand and letting him draw her into bed once again.

"Because I'm awesome?"

She rolled her eyes, but didn't make any move to leave again.

"Because you know I adore you and your strength? Because I know you and I love every part of you?"

"Yeah, that might be it." She leaned forward and laid a kiss over his heart. "Beating for me?"

"Since the first moment I laid eyes on you."

"How much time do we have before you have to rush back to work?"

"You do realize," he began as he looked at the clock on her side of the bed, "how difficult it is for me to not give my sexy smile of triumph."

"No limit to your classiness."

He didn't feel classy when her hand found his cock, squeezing just the way he liked. He rolled, pinning her with his body, and she wrapped her legs around his waist.

Hot and wet. He closed his eyes against the rush of pleasure as his cock brushed against her pussy. So damned good. A groan rumbled through his body, echoing through his bones.

"I love when you make that sound," she whispered, a sly smile on her mouth. "Your cat knows me."

He laughed, a sound swallowed in another groan of delight

as he sank into her body, surrounded. "My cat does. You're mine, babe. Cat and man, just one heart and you own it."

"God you're good at the words." Rolling her hips, she took him deeper. "And this too. I don't deserve you, Galen."

He kissed her to silence the doubts he knew she bore about him. More from the place of seeing her involvement with him as keeping him away from what he was supposed to be doing. As if anyone in his jamboree, anyone but her, could see him the way she did.

The soft spaces of her body, the cadence of her breathing, the silky stroke of a stray curl as it brushed against his skin while he moved over and within, all wove together, told a story he yearned to hear over and over.

Their early morning coupling wasn't about sensuality. It wasn't a slow seduction. It was hard and fast, bodies meeting, sliding in a slick of sweat, the ache of desire, the spice of their attraction hanging around them. Her nails dug into his sides as she came, her body clasping his with such heated ferocity he had no choice but to give in and climax.

When he walked out from their shared bathroom, she was ready to go, holding a travel mug of coffee and a breakfast burrito. "You don't eat enough calories when you're in court all day. I'll know if you don't eat it all so don't try it."

He took them from her after slinging his messenger bag over a shoulder. "I'm eating this before I get anywhere near the courthouse or I'd have to fight off those assholes I share parents with." The coffee was dark and sweet, no milk. Just how he liked it. It was the perfect complement to the breakfast burrito with extra eggs and a bit of jalapeno. He indicated the food with a tip of his chin. "Spicy. Just like the woman who made it."

"You already had sex, stop with the flattery. And not all of those assholes would care to have anything to do with me or my burrito, despite how delicious my burritos are." She winked and grabbed her keys as they headed out the door.

He took another bite and groaned. "Babe, my family loves you. The ones who count anyway. I hate that this makes you so upset."

"Get over it, Galen. Two of your siblings hate me along with about a third of your jamboree. I'm a cat-stealing human bitch, remember?" She shrugged, but he wasn't fooled by her nonchalance.

Some days he really hated the politics he had to deal with. "You know that's bullshit. It doesn't matter what any of them think. I love you. I'm *with* you. That won't change." He looked at the spot on her shoulder he'd bitten less than an hour before. It lay beneath the soft sweater she wore, but they both knew it was there. He'd marked the other shoulder the last time and it was still there, fading but clear. After he marked her that way, she'd draw her fingertips over it, as if reliving the moment he'd given it to her. That simple gesture was more than if she'd tattooed his name on her forehead.

"That's all that matters to me." And she meant it. The weight lifted and he brushed a kiss over her mouth.

"Good."

It wasn't until they parted at their front stoop, her going one way and he another, that he remembered her call from the night before.

"Renee!"

She turned around, smiling, glowing with magic and love.

"You wanted to talk to me about the wolf? I'm sorry I forgot to ask you about it earlier."

She skipped back to him, kissing his mouth. "You were kind of busy fucking me instead. Which, given how much you know I like that, is A-okay with me. I'll talk to you about it tonight. We still on for date night?"

"You sure? I'm sorry I forgot. I came in so late and then this morning, well you distracted me with all that naked skin." Need for her hit again and he pushed it away, focused on whatever she'd wanted to talk about. "I want to hear it."

"I know you do." Her smile softened to one he saw rarely, tinged with sentiment he knew was genuine. "I know you do," she repeated. "But right now I've got to get to work and so do you. It's not urgent. I just wanted to bounce a few things off your super brain."

He hugged her. "I'll be home by six or so. We can talk while I'm making dinner."

"Good. And then you can tell me what the hell is going on with your family that you wake up tense. Since it has to do with me and all."

He knew she'd be back to that at some point. She was a bulldog about that stuff. "I'll see you tonight. Be safe today."

"I make coffee and smoothies, what could possibly happen?"

"I don't know. Darlin', you know I love you, but trouble finds you wherever you are. I just want to be sure to be there or have you surrounded by people when and if it happens."

She rolled her eyes and flipped him the middle finger as she blew him a kiss with her other hand and sauntered away. "I love you too. Don't look at my ass, pervert."

Chapter Five

"Running late this morning?" Susan/Phoenix asked as Renee came in through the back door. She was actually half an hour early, but that wasn't the point at all.

Instead of the retort burning her tongue, she ignored her stepmother and began to set up. Which of course wasn't what Phoenix wanted so she came over.

"You can't just come and go as you please, you know. Just because you're my daughter you can't get away with this sort of thing."

Renee looked up after she'd set the first carafes of coffee to brew. "Why are you trying to pick a fight? In the first place, I *can* just come and go as I please. I don't work for you, I rent space from you. In the second place, I'm not late, I'm half an hour early, something you'd know if you showed up here before eleven every once in a while. Lastly, you are not my mother. Now, kindly get the fuck out of my face."

Phoenix paled a bit, not used to Renee defending herself, especially not via the F word. "I've told your father we were too permissive with you. You don't show any respect for all I've done for you. Your *mother* didn't raise you, I did!"

"What do you want from me? I am grateful. I appreciate all you've done. But that doesn't give you a license to attack me when you get bored. I've never done anything to you. I always behaved. I got good grades. Nothing ever seemed to make you happy."

"You didn't always behave, did you?" The menace in Susan/Phoenix's voice shook her, gripped her somewhere deep and she felt lost for a few moments. Until the anger rushed in to replace the fear.

Renee tried to calm the storm of emotion riding her system, especially when the books on a nearby shelf began to shake and the window to her right began to rattle. Times like these, she realized she was more than just a woman who knew the phone would ring. And times like these, she hated that she didn't understand it, wanted to be normal, to have a normal life.

"Get yourself under control. The devil has you, Renee. You get it from her people, I know. Resist it."

That was all Renee needed to hear to come back to herself. She sighed and looked back to her stepmother. "Go away. Oh my God! I don't want to deal with you. You got what you wanted, I'm upset. Happy? Go away! I'm going to have customers soon and I need to get things prepared."

Her stepmother huffed a breath to let Renee know just how abused she'd been, and stomped off. Probably to call Renee's father, who wouldn't stand up for Renee. She knew he cared about her, knew he did what he honestly thought was best in getting a woman to take the place of her dead mother. But it wasn't enough. It wasn't the same as a mother who loved her. Susan hadn't even really been a very good babysitter, though Renee didn't want to believe the woman hated her or wished her ill. But to Susan, Renee was just in the way.

Rather than wallow, she just got on with things and moved beyond those people and events she couldn't change. She didn't remember a whole lot about her mother, but what she did, she cherished, held onto in her heart. That's what counted.

She had Galen. She had Galen and his parents, both of whom were so very good to her. Loving and kind and made it clear they knew she was good for their son. The rest of his family and the other cats in the jamboree fell all over the place. Some hated her, some loved her, most didn't care one way or the other.

It was enough, though. It was enough that she was loved and cherished.

And yet, there was an empty space inside her.

Luckily, the day was busier than most, leaving very little time to obsess on her stepmother's outward aggression. As she worked, Renee figured she had that month's expenses now taken care of, which always gave her a sense of accomplishment. It seemed to please Phoenix to make cracks about Renee being a kept woman. And while Galen's salary made hers look like pocket change, she paid her own damned way in the world.

She wondered, idly, while she sliced bananas for a smoothie, where Jack might be that day. And then felt guilty that she'd been thinking of him. She loved Galen, so why was she even thinking about anyone else? It wasn't as if she planned to do anything, wasn't even as if she *wanted* to do anything. It was a crush maybe. Something riding the line between like and crush. That was it.

She really wished she'd had the chance to run all this by Galen. Certainly, his way of spending their time before they both had to rush off to work was far more enjoyable than a discussion would have been. She smiled as a shiver worked up her spine at the memory of his teeth on her shoulder, marking her.

She touched that spot, the first place he'd ever marked her two years before. Each time he did it, it lasted longer. Now that they'd imprinted, the mark would last at least a month before beginning to fade. The mark wasn't a casual sex thing, he did it, the same way all male jaguar shifters did. He did it to claim her, to imbue her with his scent, the tattoo of his bite. When they

60

were with his family, she wore sleeveless dresses or shirts, to show it off, to let them all know who she was to him.

What she felt when he marked her that way wasn't something she could easily put into words. It was a wedding ring, a declaration of his connection and commitment, it was sexy and caveman all at once, wrapped up in caring. It made her feel cherished and cosseted. Possessed but not owned.

She could think about the deliciousness that was Jack Meyers all she wanted, but she knew that's all it would ever be. Flirting and thinking. Never doing. Never, because she had everything she wanted and would not jeopardize it. Even if she had the very strong feeling he was connected to something bigger. What or why, she didn't know.

As if her thoughts had conjured him, she looked up and caught the light glinting off the blond hair. Their gazes met and he smiled, sending heat to her toes and a fresh wave of guilt rolling through her.

"Good afternoon, Renee." He approached and she saw the similarities between him and Galen right off. Both had that predatory walk. They appeared laid back on the surface, but the eyes took in everything, the muscles coiled just so, enough to spring into action when and if needed.

She fought her blush at the not so very idle thought of what those muscles would look like naked.

"Afternoon, Jack. Your smoothie is coming right up. How about apple, mango, banana today?"

"Do I have to? How about some coffee instead?"

"You are *such* a baby. Fine, get scurvy. See if I care when your teeth fall out and your muscles won't work. You won't be nearly as pretty that way."

He laughed, surprised. "Pretty huh? You noticed." His look was smug and she rolled her eyes as she scooped the fruit into the blender.

"You sell coffee, how can you be anti-coffee?"

"I'm not anti-coffee. I love coffee, have it every day in fact. But I'm looking at you and I bet you've been up since before dawn and I also bet you've had at least three cups by now. So I'm saying have some fruit." She poured the smoothie into a cup and pushed it his way.

He sipped so cautiously she wanted to laugh. "You're a werewolf, how can you be afraid of fruit?" She kept her voice low.

"You never did tell me how you knew that."

"I saw your other self." She shrugged, noticing Phoenix watching from the other end of the store.

"It'd be a lot easier if you'd come out to lunch with me so we could speak privately."

"That's not going to happen. I told you. I'm taken."

"I have so much to say to you. So much I need to explain." He leaned in, earnest look on his face. "But you've got observers. Your boss keeps watching."

"That's not my boss," she said, annoyed. "That's my father's wife. She owns the shop, but not me or this cart."

His hand tightened on the counter's edge. "Are you not welcome here?"

In the light, his wolf shimmered briefly and she drew a deep breath. Not from fear, but from fascination. He was beautiful. And fearsome.

"It's family, family is always complicated."

He moved his hand, just barely touching hers with a fingertip before drawing away. "I don't like to think about anyone harming you or making you sad."

She swallowed, hard. "Why?" Her whisper held her angst at how much it meant to her that he'd say it, her confusion and no small amount of fear. Not of him, but of what he might mean to her.

And then something else, something warm and soft rushed through her system. She looked to the door and saw Galen standing there, looking so handsome and slightly angry, she wanted to fan herself.

Instead she watched, unable not to, as he stalked over, his eyes never leaving hers.

Galen let out most of his tension when he saw her, when he took in how she responded to his entrance. This was not a guilty face, this was the woman who loved him, who made him blueberry pancakes with that flax crap she didn't think he knew she added. The woman whose body welcomed him any time he wanted or needed it. This was his woman.

But the man standing at her cart, that was another story altogether. That man looked at Renee with not just hungry eyes, but with eyes that said mate. That simply would not do.

He stalked right behind her counter and pulled her into his arms where she willingly went, her body fitting to his, just as it had that morning, just as it always had. Her head tilted back to look into his face, her expression pleased but surprised.

He kissed her and she hugged him tight.

"Hi there, to what do I owe this visit?" She smiled, the dimple just below the apple of her cheek standing out, drawing his finger to slide through the dent.

"Got a call, said I needed to come by because you had a visitor." He cut his gaze to the wolf, who met his look with one of his own. Well now, an alpha werewolf too.

Renee looked around him to Phoenix, who had been the one to call, telling Galen a man had been coming in the shop to flirt with Renee. Phoenix had made it sound like something far more had been going on. He knew that part had been a lie, Renee was too honest to do anything behind his back. But still, something was going on. The energy crackled between them, all the magic they held buffeting, sliding, caressing and arcing.

"Did you now?" Renee's voice had gone down an octave and a wave of her power spread outward. He reminded himself to get on her again about seeking out training to use her magic. She had so much more power than she realized and one of these days she'd end up hurting herself or someone else if she didn't learn to channel it correctly.

"Babe, chill. I'm here." He spoke softly, drawing his fingertips down her neck to the spot where he'd marked her earlier that day. Her breath hitched and he smiled. "She's a busybody, but you have to admit, this wolf right here didn't drop by just for a smoothie."

"I'm Jack Meyers. I think we should all talk."

The man was good looking if you went for that tall, blond, blue-eyed surfer thing. Which he did. Who wouldn't? He also clearly had a thing for Renee, which brought Galen's cat very close to the skin.

"About what, wolf? She's taken and I'll rip you to shreds if you try to change that."

Wolf bled into the other man's eyes as Galen's cat showed right back. Renee slapped a hand down on the counter just hard enough to make both men jump, breaking the spell.

"Enough. This is my place of work. I have a customer on his way back here right now so hold it together." Renee smiled over Jack's shoulder to an elderly man Galen recognized from the neighborhood.

"Busy today, sweetheart?" the man asked, his hat in his hands as he smiled.

Renee laughed. "Never too busy for you, Mr. Sherman. The usual?"

"Yes please. You know me so well. Today, can you add a little something?"

Renee paused as she steamed milk, looking him up and down. "Hmm. For you, I think today is a cinnamon day. What do you think?" She held up a cinnamon stick and a grater.

She chatted with him and Galen watched the old man fall under her spell. She knew about his life, the details of his family, asked after his daughter's new baby, how his garden was doing. She cared about him and he saw that. When Galen looked up, he saw Jack understanding her too and something more than outrage spilled through him.

Phoenix began to hover as Renee blew a kiss at Mr. Sherman and he left, grinning.

"I see you came by." Phoenix spoke around Renee, addressing Galen. He should have called Renee first, but he'd let himself get spooked and rushed over. Phoenix would see that as taking her side and for that, Galen felt badly.

Not one to be cowed, Renee sent her stepmother a look so frightening he took a step back, resting a hand on her hip.

"You and I will talk about this later." Renee turned her back on the other woman, cutting her off before she could speak. Her look at them wasn't much better. "And you two. If you start marking things with pee, I'm out of here. I'm pretty open-minded and stuff, but I do have limits. Jack, this is the husband I've been telling you about, Galen de La Vega. Galen, this is the wolf I've been *trying* to talk to you about."

They looked each other up and down, Galen's heart beating faster at the threat to his mate, to his life. But...also something else. It was hard to think there in the enclosed space, with Renee in between them, the scent of her magic on the air. It mixed with his, with Jack's and Galen didn't know what to think, how to deal with it.

Jack exhaled, hard, and Renee looked back and forth between them.

"We can't talk here." She took Galen's hand, bringing it to

her lips. "We don't have to talk anywhere. It's totally up to you."

Jack ground his teeth together, impotent rage coursing through him. The other woman had made Renee angry, had upset her. It was simply unacceptable to see her treated so badly.

This other male, Jack sighed, he could see the connection the two of them had. Just as Lia had told him earlier that day. Galen had imprinted on Renee and she clearly accepted that bond, felt it, returned it. Jack knew she was drawn to him, he saw it, heard it in her voice, scented it in the way her body warmed when he came into the shop. There was no mistake, Renee was his mate. *Too.*

He'd argued with himself all day, wavering on whether to come to the shop again. Renee wouldn't be the only female on the planet who he'd be able to share a mate connection with. It didn't work that way. If there were only one person they could mate with, their race would die out. But none of that meant as much as the way she'd barreled into his life. There was no escaping the very real sense of fate at play, of his being meant to make these choices. Who was he to argue with fate?

Lia had explained that they could *share* Renee through a bond. The jaguar via his imprint on her and Jack through his mate bond. But did he want that? It wasn't usual. Male wolves were exceptionally territorial and possessive about something as easily replaced as a jacket or a house, they were a thousand times worse when it came to their mates.

Still, as he'd paced and growled at anyone who came near him, he couldn't stop thinking of her. Didn't want to. He wanted her, wanted to wake up next to her every day. Wanted her scent on their sheets. Wanted to bury his face in that glorious hair.

All his life he'd settled. He'd lost his own family so he'd been fostered by Templeton Mancini and his wife within the National Pack. He'd accepted his lot in life and he'd been happy with it.

But he didn't want to walk away and wait to see when he'd find another woman he could mate with. He'd *found* this one by total happenstance, he'd bumped into her without expecting it and that was how it was supposed to be.

He wanted her and he damned well would find a way to have her or at the end, he'd know he did his all out best to make it happen and would walk away with no regrets. Jack Anderson Meyers was no fucking quitter and he wasn't going to start now.

In truth, he wanted to rip the cat's arm off, as craving for her intensified and he couldn't touch. But there was something else. Something holding him back. He didn't know why or what, but he had to talk to her alone, away from this place and that woman near the counter trying to overhear everything they said. His wolf approved of how the cat moved his body in between the women, shielding Renee.

And he liked, even as he wanted to howl, the way Renee reassured Galen. That sort of loyalty was rare. He knew she felt the same pull to him as he did to her, but she put her man first. Once he was her man, too, or instead of Galen, *whatever*, he knew she'd show the same kind of loyalty and constancy.

Constancy. What an old-fashioned word for something he considered more important than just about anything else on the planet.

Renee waited as the two men sized each other up and then looked back to her. Galen brushed a kiss over her lips again before looking back at Jack.

"Are you free tonight? Perhaps you can come to our house for drinks. Nine?"

Jack nodded once and his eyes found hers, warming. She smiled in response, feeling that pull again. But nothing could happen here, nothing could be said here, especially with Phoenix hovering. Any minute now, she expected her father to show up, Renee was sure he'd been summoned.

Galen wrote their address down and Jack took it with a nod. "I'll see you both tonight."

Before he turned, he took her hand, kissing her wrist where he had before. Her heart sped. Galen still had an arm around her waist, his body pressed to her side, his muscles tightened and something without words happened when they all three touched. Everything inside her surged and broke over both men. A warm flow of magic came from her gut, surrounding them. She heard nothing but three heartbeats, smelled nothing but Galen and Jack. The taste of honey, the scent of amber, of sunshine and forest all mixing on her tongue as they remained locked for long moments.

It was only the ringing of the chimes over the front door that broke the spell. Her father stood there, shocked and then pained.

"What the blazes is going on?" He didn't even sound like himself. His voice was a stranger's voice, a man totally untouched by emotion.

Jack turned, shielding her with his back. Galen put a hand on Jack's shoulder, uniting the three again with that touch.

Things began to tumble out of control and her head swam. "Jack, we'll see you tonight. Galen, I'm going home now. I'm done here for today. I want to go home."

Galen looked to her. "I'll deal with him. Clean up and I'll get you home. Jack, go on now or this will explode and the one hurt the most will be Renee," he said in an undertone.

Jack nodded and left, sending a narrowed glance at Phoenix as he did.

Galen had a hushed, but firm conversation with her father and Phoenix as Renee cleaned up quickly, putting everything away and locking the cart up. She'd done it so many times it was simply routine at this point.

When she walked out, it was without a single word toward her father or Phoenix, Galen's arm around her, anchoring her to his side, to the world, in every way that counted and she needed.

Chapter Six

She remained silent until he'd locked the door and she'd hung up her things. "Galen, do you think I was doing something wrong with Jack? That I was hiding something from you?"

She looked so sad, it pulled at his heart. He hugged her first and then kissed her temple. "No. I didn't come to the shop because I thought Phoenix was telling the truth. But I admit it, I got jealous that anyone would be there trying to take you from me. Stupid and immature, I know. But it wasn't about you." He tipped her chin up. "I love you. I trust you."

"I would never, ever betray you. I need you to understand that." She took both his hands in hers. "I'm yours."

He closed his eyes a moment before speaking. "I do understand that. If I didn't I wouldn't be standing here right now. Babe, you wear my mark on your skin, you smell of me, you're my mate and as far as I'm concerned, my wife. This thing with the wolf, it's big, I can feel it too. But I know you didn't try to hide anything, that's not who you are."

She nodded. "Good. I'm so glad. When I saw you come in I was worried that you believed her." She took a deep breath, pressing her lips to his neck, over his pulse. The scrape of her teeth across the skin there brought gooseflesh and a ragged moan.

"I believe you. I believe *in* you." His breath caught as she bit, just hard enough to make her point. He tipped his head back a bit, submitting. Her hands, sliding up his sides, trembled.

"You're the only person in the world who understands me. That's...I can't tell you how much that means to me. It's precious." She stepped back and began to peel off her clothing. Rooted to the spot, he watched the unveiling as need pounded through his veins.

"You're a gift, Renee. Do you understand that? Before you, there were just a whole bunch of days and experiences, some really good ones, but none of them half as special as what you do for me."

Naked, the pale sunlight washing over her skin, she stepped close again, reaching to ease his tie off and unbutton his shirt. "I love that you're like this behind closed doors when out there you're snarly and hard." Her smile held secrets only he knew. "Do you need to go back to work?" She kissed his chest, tiptoeing up to reach his collarbone and the sensitive skin at the hollow of his throat.

He had a shit-ton of work to do, but none more important than this. Than her. His own need echoed from hers. His possessive urge calmed by her touch, by the way she'd deferred to him with the Jack situation.

The Jack situation. What a fucking ball of complications that was. But she was here. With him and she wanted him to know that. Not just standing there, but there, in *their* hallway, with her hands on him, taking care of him. She made clear with everything she was that he was her choice. No matter what Jack meant to them, the relationship between Renee and Galen was safe and solid and nothing would change that.

That reassurance was exactly what he needed. She hadn't done it to be calculating, he knew. She simply understood what he needed and provided it. That she seemed to have no idea of how important that was, when she did it for him every day, sent him reeling. His beautiful witch.

"No. I'm where I need to be right now. I love you so much." He groaned when she got to her knees, undoing his belt and trousers, easing them off after he'd gotten rid of his shoes and socks.

Like a cat, she rubbed her cheek along his thighs and over his cock, licking his belly, the seam where thigh met body and finally his cock. Just a quick kiss and she was gone again.

She gave herself to him so openly, so freely and with so much joy, he always found himself utterly destroyed and remade every time they were together.

"Wait," he managed to gasp. "The floor is hard here, come back to the bedroom where you can lay down or at least use a pillow under your knees."

Her eyes rolled up, her gaze meeting his as she took his cock into her mouth, as far back as she could.

"Christ."

She let go, licking across the head and crown before saying, "Sometimes a girl likes it hard."

Well, he was a goner now.

Renee loved this, loved being on her knees, loved pleasing him. He tasted just right. She dragged her nails up the backs of his legs, up hardened calves and powerful thighs, up to gentle and then cup the spectacular ass, pulling him closer and deeper.

The floor beneath her knees was hard, yes, but on some level she sort of liked it, liked that she needed his cock inside her in some way so badly that she couldn't wait, didn't want to wait to get to somewhere softer. And like she said, sometimes a girl liked it hard.

As if he read her thoughts, he tangled a hand through her hair, holding tight enough to sting a bit, but not hurt. Shivers ran through her, tapping into a place a little bit dark. And that was okay because with him, the darkness was safe.

She knew it was when they were so connected, when she let go this way, that her magic would seep through her pores, filling the air. It had never happened with anyone else. The warmth of it washed over her, swirling around them both.

Dimly, she heard his intake of breath, felt the change in the grip in her hair. His control slipped, delighting her. He was close.

The hands in her hair began to guide her more as he thrust, at first haltingly, and then, he gave up the reins and let himself go. He'd never hurt her, not as a man, not as a cat, they both knew it and so he let go, rolling his hips, his breathing coming faster.

"So good. This is, fuck, fuck, *fuck.*" He pressed deep as she breathed through her nose and reveled in the sensuality of that moment, of the raw heat of the way he filled her, filled her senses in every way.

He let go and went to his knees in front of her, embracing, skin to skin, his hands sliding into her hair again. His mouth found hers and locked on. Sure, aggressive, his tongue swept over her lips, and she let him in, opened her mouth and he groaned, the rumble sliding down her throat.

A quick yank of her hair and her head tipped back, exposing her throat. She went still, limp, submitting, and the sound he made was more cat than man, a growling grumble that echoed through her bones straight to her clit.

His tongue swept down her neck. She nearly came when he stopped where neck met body. He was going to bite her, mark her again. A whimper, not of fear, but of need, slipped through her lips and he braced one arm around her waist, holding her there.

Electric pleasure, brilliant shards of it, burst through her as he bit down. An orgasm, cell deep, rolled from pussy to her scalp as she cried out, holding him to her, her nails digging into his biceps.

The grumble he gave as he released her from the bite was nearly a purr, utterly satisfied predator.

She was still panting from the bite when he laid her back on the entryway floor and loomed over her, parting her thighs with his body. He licked over each nipple until she panted, not even bothering to stop the entreaties for him to continue downward.

"Please, if you don't put your mouth on my pussy I'm going to die."

He chuckled against her nipple for a moment but after a hard nip of sharp, white teeth, he obliged, kissing and licking downward. Thank God he didn't tease, instead he gave her a long lick, swirling his tongue around her clit before sucking it into his mouth. His hands held her thighs open as he set about eating her pussy until she shook from head to toe.

Her muscles, just moments before, had been fluid, relaxed after the bite, but now they tightened, reaching for peak, readying for climax and when it hit, the breath whooshed from her, her spine arching, leaving the floor beneath her back. On and on it went until she went limp.

He laughed, kissing her belly. "You taste so good. Come on, lazy witch, let's snuggle on the couch for a bit." He picked her up easily and she snuggled into his body, the heat from his skin comforting. The grumbling purr returned as they settled in, her still in his lap, his arms around her body, cradling.

She'd been alone for a very long time and he'd come, just when she was sure she'd be that way forever. He took one look and there wasn't any way he wouldn't have her. The rush of that, of the attentions of a man like Galen had made her giddy, even as they'd started a flirtation of sorts.

He hadn't touched her for months. Instead, he called her, wrote her letters and cards as he traveled with his favorite brother, Armando. They'd left two weeks after she met him, on a trip to Spain to visit family. He'd sent her postcards with colorful stamps, the precise handwriting bringing a thrill to her every time she opened her mailbox.

By the time he came back, something had taken root, something so deep neither of them had ever questioned it. The first time they made love, hell, the first time they fucked, it had left them both with scratches, bruises and her a bite on her inner thigh. They'd lain in his big bed panting for breath as the sun rose. She'd never left and he made sure she knew he never wanted her to.

"You're thinking." He said it with his lips against her temple, she felt the curve of his smile on her skin.

"I was thinking about the postcards you sent me from Seville, of the pink and orange stamps bearing the faces of long dead kings." She still had them. Every single letter and card he'd ever sent her lived in her top drawer.

"It was hard for me to leave once I'd met you. I knew what you were to me that first night we met. But when I returned and you stood there waiting on the other side of the customs area, I knew you felt it too."

"You think I'd have just let some hot Spaniard slash Jamaican get away? I hadn't even kissed you yet, hadn't seen you naked, though I sure as hell thought about it every five minutes. I had to snap you up before some ho got to you first."

He laughed, holding her tighter.

"Thank God for that. You protected my virtue, babe."

"It needed protecting apparently. That is, if the looks I've been getting for years are any indication of how friendly you were with the ladies before I came along. Men too." Some women would have been put off by that, by the fact that Galen had been with both men and women before he met her. She just found it hot.

He never gave her any reason to feel like he wasn't satisfied with her so why should she be threatened? Shifters had a totally different attitude about sexuality; many of them considered themselves bisexual and they loved where they found that connection. She'd met many of his former lovers but they all knew the difference between what they'd had with Galen and what she had with him. As long as none of them ever messed with that, whoever he was naked with before she came along had nothing to do with her.

"I sampled a few flowers until I found the right one," he teased.

They snuggled for a while longer, until the sun disappeared and long shadows painted the walls.

With a sigh she got up and stretched. "Want some tea?" She padded toward the kitchen to light the burner under the kettle.

"Yes please."

She touched the mark on her neck, pressing just a bit, enjoying the soreness.

"Got carried away," he said, putting his shirt over her shoulders. His expression was one of utter satisfaction and she had to laugh.

"I'm not complaining." She paused, watching him move around the room, totally comfortable in his nakedness. "You want to talk? About the Jack situation?"

"What is he to you, Renee?"

"I don't know," she answered truthfully as she scooped loose tea into the cache within the ceramic pot before pouring the boiling water in. "I think he's not someone to me, but to us. There's this pull between us. More than attraction. I see gorgeous men every day, Boston's full of them. No, it's something else. But when you came in, when the three of us touched? Something happened and I don't know what it was. I just know that I've been on edge, waiting for something and I think he's it. What, I just can't say."

She put two mugs out and turned back to him. "But I need to say again that I'm not going anywhere. You and I are solid. I'm with you forever, no escaping for you, mister."

He leaned against the counter and she couldn't help but notice his cock showing some signs of life as she bent to grab the sugar. "Why would I want to escape this? A sexy witch who makes me tea and fills out my shirts in a way I'm certain to remember when I'm in court and I have to hold my briefcase in front of my lap? Sounds pretty fucking perfect to me."

She put sugar in his tea, one heaping spoonful because he was a sugar-whore. "Cookie? I made gingersnaps."

"Mmmm, makes me want to fuck you right here and now."

"Clearly I underestimated how much you like ginger." She winked and put some cookies on a plate and poured his tea.

"Back to the Jack thing. I agree we need to hear him out, to see what he's got to say. I'm intrigued enough to follow this up some. If we don't like whatever he proposes, we kick his ass out." He shrugged. "No harm done in either case."

She hoped so.

Jack walked up the block. Without really looking at the address, he knew the way. Her scent hung on the air, calling to him. He only lived about five blocks over from their street, had passed this way hundreds of times while jogging or heading to the library.

His experience with her, and with Galen earlier that day, had shaken him deeply. He'd left and walked aimlessly for an hour before ending up at home, looking at the phone, looking at his computer, walking through the space he'd never thought felt empty before and today it did.

He raged about that as he'd paced. He didn't want this whatever it was. Had never imagined he'd have to *share* his mate. And it was clear that was the choice with her. It wouldn't be some situation where the cat came around to see her from time to time. This male was intertwined with her. Whatever else he may feel, he could see the connection between Renee and Galen from the moment Galen had walked into the shop.

Cats didn't have the same sort of mate bond as wolves, yes, but he'd seen the mark on Renee's neck, knew that wasn't casual, knew she had imprinted on the cocky jaguar as he so clearly had with her. Jack also understood, though he hadn't known her long, his mate was not a woman who made shallow allegiances.

He hated that connection. And yet, it made him crave her even more. Loyalty was an important quality as far as Jack was concerned. To have a woman like that at his side, a woman who placed value on people and her relationships with them was powerfully alluring.

He wanted to talk to Grace about it, but there was enough complicated emotional stuff between them and he didn't need what she would offer. She was his friend and, yes, she wanted what was best for him, but there was jealousy when he'd spoken of Renee earlier that day, enough to put his guard up. Jack needed to talk to someone who would know what he felt, what he was up against.

So he'd picked up the phone and called Gabe Murphy, an old friend who now had a tri-mate bond with another man and woman. Instead of being an anchor bond to a mated couple, Gabe had ended up mated with both Tracy Warden and the male she'd already bonded with, Nick Lawrence. If anyone could give him advice, it would be Gabe.

He listened to Jack explain the situation so far.

"I can only answer for me, Jack. I didn't go into the negotiations where I met Nick and Tracy thinking I'd end up in a permanent ménage. But the magic is the magic, right? There's nothing to say when you're up against that." He paused for a long moment. Knowing Gabe was a man of few words, Jack waited until he found the right ones and finally continued.

"What is it you want? You know she's your mate. You know she's imprinted with a cat, which means she's married to him. You can find another woman, you know that too. You haven't claimed her so there's nothing more than attraction holding you to her right now."

Jack shook his head and groaned, knowing he couldn't be heard doing that. "No. It's more than that. More than attraction. It's like...it's more like all the potential is there, welling up between us. All the what-can-be draws me to her like nothing I've ever felt before. I don't want that with anyone else. I'm...I can't explain it, but I know I'd never have this with anyone but her."

Gabe laughed. "The first time I saw Tracy I couldn't quite understand why I'd be looking twice. She was so beyond not my type. But once I touched her, once I touched Nick, it just changed. I know what you're saying, Jack, because I've felt it. I know it. Yes, you can, and you would have a happy life with another female next year or in five years when you found her. But she's not Renee and Renee is what you want and who you're *meant* to be with. And if you're meant for her, it means you're meant for Galen too. It's not like you haven't been with men and from how you're talking, they both sound pretty easy to look at." Even though Jack couldn't see Gabe, he knew his friend shrugged.

"It's not a date. Yeah he's hot and yes, I'm attracted to him too. It's a lot to take on, a man and a woman? Another shifter with their own rules. It's going to be hard to work out."

Gabe snorted. "Don't lecture me on what it is or isn't,

asshole. I live it. It won't be easy all the time. But Tracy and Nick are worth it to me. Our children are worth it. Fate brought you this gift in these two people. Of course, as you well know, Fate's a tricky thing. But if it's meant to be, it's meant to be."

"You know, I'm about done with all this complicated life lesson shit. You know? I've done my time." Jack pushed out of the chair he'd dropped into just moments before to begin the walk to the front windows and back, over and over.

"I've never known you to be a quitter, Jack. Or a whiner. Life's handed you some challenges, yeah? So what? You think that makes you special? You got out. No matter how you got there, no matter what you endured, you live in an expensive condo with a view of the river. You have people who love you, people who care and now you've found your mate. So it's not easy and that sucks and all. But you have this thing we are bred to crave. She's right there within your reach. So grab, or don't, but don't you fucking why me over it." Of all the people walking the earth, only three would have ever spoken to him that way and walked away without some damage. Gabe was one.

He was right too.

So Jack found himself standing there, hand resting on the ironwork decorating the top of the short brick wall framing the front of the brownstone. He heard laughter, scented garlic and the sharp bite of greens.

Their door gleamed, beckoning his hand as he rapped, using the old-fashioned knocker fastened to the shiny red wood.

He heard the laughter as she approached, knew her footfalls as she descended an inner staircase. And then she was before him, her smile tentative but genuine and he knew, trouble or not, that he'd cleave himself to this woman until he drew his last breath.

"I'm glad you found us without any trouble. Come in." She stood back and waved him in, the bracelets on her wrist catching the yellow glow from the streetlamp just feet away.

The front hall was invitingly warm. Hardwood floors with richly colored rugs led into the heart of the house. "It was a duplex. Galen and I bought it and rented out the other half for a year. And then we thought it would be nice to expand, use the whole space so we started a remodel that following spring."

She held her hand out for his coat, which he gave to her keeping. A slice of her belly flashed as she stretched to hang it. When she turned, her mouth had crept up on one side into a saucy smile.

"It's beautiful. You two must have worked pretty hard to get it this nice."

"We learned an awful lot about sanding and stains and how to lay tile. I figure if the law ever turns into a bust, I can lay floors." Galen strolled out. Renee looked to him and there it was, the warmth of their connection as it flowed between them.

He stood on the edge, just outside the glow they made.

Renee reached out, touching his hand with a fingertip. The jolt he felt wasn't static electricity. It was connection of the metaphysical and magical kind. "Would you like to come through for a drink? I've just made a batch of margaritas. Galen made some snacks you shouldn't miss. He's a really great cook."

Galen put an arm around Renee, kissing her quickly before turning his attention to Jack again. "Come on in, let's talk."

If the hall and the rooms he skirted past had been lovely, the kitchen was a monument to people who loved to cook. He knew he must have looked like a total hick, but he couldn't seem to stop the openmouthed wonder propelling him through the large room. The center island had a large indoor grill and double sinks. Another range, with a huge oven and a built-in microwave dominated another wall. The fridge, a gleaming Sub Zero, made him weak in the knees.

"This is, Christ, I don't think I've ever seen a kitchen this fabulous. Not in person anyway. This is magazine spread stuff." Jack turned in a circle, stopping when Renee pressed a chilled margarita glass into his hand.

"Galen loves to cook these big fancy meals. I love to eat them. It's a good thing."

Galen waved a hand at the nearby table. "Sit down, Jack. If you're hungry, please do have something."

Well this was awkward.

But hot damn did he look good there sitting at their kitchen table. Gah, why! Why did he look good and why was she noticing this way?

She busied herself, filling a plate with the delicious little appetizers Galen made like they were toast instead of mini-gourmet miracles. Maybe if she kept her mouth full of food, she could avoid saying something bad.

Great googly moogly this was good. She grabbed another few little turnover dealies and tried not to shove them all in her mouth at once.

Galen watched, amused and proud she liked what he'd prepared so much.

"Okay, okay, so I never claimed to have any self control when it comes to anything deep fried or in pastry."

He laughed. "One of the many reasons I love you. When you like things, you *really* like them." Cheeky.

She put some bits and pieces on a plate and put it in front of Jack. She'd already done that for Galen.

Jack nodded his thanks. "I don't even know where to start. My resume? I'm healthy, Enforcer in the National Pack. In my

Pack, two wolves share the second in command position—
Enforcer and Mediator. I don't know if you know about how
Packs work. Single. Forty. Boston born and bred. I feel like I'm
babbling, I guess I am. I don't normally babble. I've been told
I'm scary and smooth and all that jazz." Jack stopped speaking
to take a bite.

"How about you just forge ahead? You're not being graded
or anything." Galen spoke to Jack, but held a hand out for
Renee to take, bringing her to sit next to him, placing her
between him and Jack.

She leaned into Galen a moment, needing the contact,
knowing he did too. When she turned her head, Jack was closer
than she'd remembered. It...she wanted to say alarmed her, but
it wasn't that. It wasn't fear, it was unexpected, different than
she'd ever thought she could feel about any person other than
Galen. But there it was, that anticipation, the depth of need, a
sort of fascination. It all bound together, hanging just out of
reach but never out of her thoughts.

He met her gaze, a smile hinting at his lips. "I'm just going
to cut through the bullshit, okay?"

"Please do." Her heart sped, her skin warming. She licked
her lips and his breath caught, his pupils swallowing the iris of
his eyes for a moment.

He gulped down the margarita. The alcohol wouldn't last
long for him so she put the bottle and a shot glass within his
reach. Galen surprised her by taking a shot first and then
pushing a full shot toward Jack.

Their fingers brushed, just briefly, but wow, the chemistry
there wasn't something she imagined. Though, so okay she
wasn't above imagining it—*hello,* the idea of the two of them
naked and sweaty, hands all over each other—wow. Where had
that come from?

She gulped the shot herself and refilled it. "Sorry. Do go
on." They wouldn't get tipsy for long, but she wasn't a shifter so

she could. Of course, Galen could eat eleventy million calories in one day and not get fat either. There were definitely plusses to this whole shifter metabolism thing.

Jack looked at her, and laughed. "Nervous?"

"Are you fucking kidding me? Of course I'm nervous. I don't know who you are or what you mean to me or my life. I don't know why I can't stop thinking about you or why the way you smell makes me sort of forget what I was saying." Whoops, tequila setting in.

Jack leaned in and took her hand. "Sweetheart, there's no easy way to bring this up as we sit here at the table you share with your husband and all." He looked to Galen for a moment and then back to her. "I'm your mate. That's why you can't stop and neither can I. That's who I am and what I mean to your life. I don't know how else to say this." He looked to Galen and she turned her head to see. Challenge hung in the air, but it sharpened into expectation.

"*I'm* her mate." Galen didn't raise his voice, didn't get up. He sat there, very preternaturally still for so long she began to wonder if she could see him breathing. His gaze locked with Jack's as they stared each other down. Galen put his hand on top of hers in a gesture, an underline to say she was already taken.

"You are. I don't dispute that. But there's more." Jack leaned closer, his scent drawing her to lean in, taking Galen with her.

The tension between them rose, tautened so much she felt pulled by a pretty leash. At the same time, her connection to Galen glittered between them. Laced her to both these men in a way that had she been standing, would have driven her to her knees.

It was as if she couldn't breathe once she was close enough, his scent was the only thing she was aware of. It ran riot through her system, jangling nerves, scrambling thoughts.

"You call to me, Renee." Jack slid his thumb over each of her knuckles, sending shivers through her.

In her ear, Galen purred, tugging on her consciousness. Goddess knew there was no way to hide how aroused she was right then. Her nipples pressed against her shirt, her pussy slicked, her clit was swollen to the point that each move she made sent ripples of sensation outward.

"Babe, you're throwing off some serious magic just now and your pussy smells so fucking good it's taking all my control not to toss you on this table and eat you right this moment."

Renee closed her eyes a moment, trying to keep control.

And then Jack reached out to touch her face.

Galen's hand shot out, catching Jack's before he could touch Renee. The circuit they made, the three of them in that moment, brought a moan from her lips and a half growl from both men. She couldn't stop it. Something within welled up and began to flow out. Magic. Shit. So much magic her skin pricked where it brushed against her.

She turned, letting go of the sight of Galen's hand holding Jack's. Of the way the grasp had turned into something else. She turned and Galen's eyes moved to her face, roving over each of her features before settling back to her gaze. His lips parted, breathing sped. His cat lurked right there, a shadow just below the dark skin.

Slowly, knowing what he was, she moved closer until making contact, rubbing her cheek along his arm, chest and to the hand caressing Jack's hand. His growl turned into a smooth purr again, his cat realizing her bond was safe.

"Babe," Galen murmured, gasping as her tongue darted around the fleshy tenderness below his thumb. "This is going somewhere you need to be sure you understand."

The moon was high overhead, heavy with its own magic. That magic called to both men. She sat back but didn't break contact with either man.

"What does this mean?"

"I don't know what it means on top of whatever we have right now." Galen didn't look at her though, he stared at Jack.

"My bond with her won't erase yours. She'll still be imprinted with you. I can't say I love the idea of sharing, but—" he turned to face Renee, "—but I want you so much I can't think straight. I want to know you. I want to be with you. We can work the details out. I'm not here to try to break anyone up. When I come inside you, our DNA will change, forging a bond only death can break. It's forever."

"Come inside me?" Renee struggled to get her head clear. She moved back, trying to break contact, but both men hung on. "I don't even know you."

"Don't you?" He stood, bringing her to his body. Full contact from head to toe and she drowned in him. All she wanted was to touch him, to taste his skin, to be naked beneath him.

"Holy crapdoodle," she mumbled, pushing back, moving away before she did something stupid.

He moved with her, Galen right behind. They hunted her, she felt that very clearly. Even knowing that, she found herself responding, even as uncertainty and confusion overwhelmed her. Sexual male scent hung in the air, thick and alluring. The chemistry they had thrummed between her thighs, coursed through her bloodstream. She wanted to lay back and let it take her wherever it wanted to go.

She pulled at her arms to free herself, but both males truly thought they were protecting her and held on to prevent her from falling. "Stop! Stop. Both of you, just back off. I can't think. I need to think."

Galen bent, looking at her carefully. She saw the strain of his control, his muscles tensed, his breathing quick. He warred with his cat, with the beast inside. "Babe, take a deep breath."

She stumbled back and this time, they both let her. "What is *going on*?" It all felt so right that she didn't trust it. This was *not* how she was. Things were happening so fast. She wasn't fast. She was slow and measured. She made choices she'd given a great deal of thought to. The edge of the thrill, the idea of something utterly meant to be, but so outside the realm of what she could believe was laced with concern. At the same time, she did believe in *meant to be*. Was this such a thing? Was this moment meant to be and if so, which direction was she supposed to take?

The two of them there so close to her intoxicated her, muddled her senses with exquisite ferocity and sensuality. Before it was only Galen who did that. Now Jack did, as well. Her heart sped as she struggled to not just jump on them.

Galen licked his lips. She knew he wanted them on her and she wanted that too. Instead, he held back, his voice taut. "Renee, it's the mate bond. I'm afraid Jack is right. I can see it when I look at him, I can feel it inside you now. Your connection to him is forming."

Jack allowed himself a small bit of relief. Galen supported it and that meant he had a chance, a real chance. He knew Renee felt the same attraction, but she was loyal and constant. She would not allow herself to entertain the mere idea of this threesome unless Galen was supportive of it. Even better, the attraction wasn't just between two of them, all three of them had amazing chemistry.

For the moment, he had to help her get past her fear, he had to get her to trust him.

Renee shook her head as she looked back and forth between them. "Connection is doing what? Well I don't want it to! Who said that's what I wanted? Who said I'd be *fucking* anyone else?" Hysteria crept around the edges of her voice. He sent a look to Galen as her need crawled into his gut.

He felt sorry for her as she struggled. He only wanted to love her and he said so.

"I'm already in love with someone. I'm already mated! I'm a married woman and I don't cheat!"

Jack never took his eyes from hers as he fleetingly brushed his fingertips over the soft skin of her temple. Her shoulders let go of a bit of tension. His wolf was so very close, the moon called that magic, mixed with hers until his hands shook from the need to touch her, to comfort her. He hated the panic on her face, but was relieved to see no fear there.

"Renee, you know me. You've *always* known me. It's hard when one of the mates is human, it'll be even harder that you have imprinted with Galen. I know this is a lot to take in. I know you love Galen. I respect that. If you tell me to go away, I will. I'll walk out the door right now and never come back."

He paused, taking a deep breath, only to be swamped with her as his hormones surged even higher. "I want you more than I can explain." He held his hands out. "I'm shaking, I want you so much. But I want you to want that too."

Galen raised his hand, slowly, giving her a chance to move away, but she didn't. He tucked a curl, those gloriously riotous curls of hers, behind her ear. His voice was soft, gentle. "What is it you want? Tell me and I'll make it happen."

She shook her head, dislodging the curl Galen had just put back in place, before plopping back onto the couch. Galen followed, sitting so that his side pressed to hers. Jack watched as the calm slid through her, as she let Galen's presence soothe. She looked up to him. "Jack, why don't you sit, too?"

Galen handed her a glass of water and Jack sat on the coffee table, his knees nearly touching hers.

Renee turned to face Galen more fully. "What is it *you* want, Galen? I love you and I'm having a hard time here. I...I want someone else in a way I'd be devastated over if the situations were reversed. What do you think of all this?"

Galen sighed and Jack hoped like hell this would go in the right direction. He would leave if that's what she wanted. But *he* didn't want to. He wanted to stay. With her.

"I'm not human. I know what it means to live as other. I know what it means to have more than one nature and I *know* what it means to find that person who fits into the empty spaces inside. You're that to me. You make me whole, Renee."

She nodded, tears gleaming in her eyes. Jack realized that up until Renee, he'd found himself attracted to or romantically involved with women who weren't overly emotional. Well, amend that. Certainly Nina and Grace Warden were emotional women, but more on the fierce side. Renee wore her feelings on her skin. It fascinated him, touched him to see the emotions play over her face the way they did. It only made her more beautiful.

Galen looked to Jack and then back to her. "But you could make him whole too. You aren't a shifter, but you know there's more out there—" Galen indicated the world around them with the sweep of his hand, "—than most people imagine. I know my cat responds to you on a level only an *other* would get. Your magic calls to me, your heart holds me. I'm yours. Period." He shrugged. "But his wolf is the same. I see how he looks at you. This isn't some game he's playing. I can scent the truth. I can *see* how you respond to him. I can see your magic envelop him like it does me. I'm not noble. I'm not good. I want you all to myself, but the truth is, you're his too. Fate, the goddess, God, whatever you want to call it, has brought the three of us here to this moment right now. What I want is for you to be happy and to fulfill your fate. I think that fate includes Jack. Whether I like it or not, that's the truth." He paused.

"And? I can tell there's more," she said.

Galen looked Jack up and down before the left corner of his mouth lifted and Jack felt a shiver of desire up his spine as he wondered what that mouth would taste like.

"I'd be lying if I said I didn't find him sexually attractive. I'd be lying if I didn't admit thinking he makes you safer, this makes my nest safer, my mate safer. This makes some part of me I can't even define very satisfied."

She blushed, but didn't hide her smile. Jack couldn't find himself bothered by Galen's attraction, probably because he felt it too. The possibility of what this could be stunned him.

"What do *you* want?" she asked Jack.

It was a dangerous question. He wanted everything. Instead he said, "I'd really like to be touching you right now. Would that be all right?"

She looked up with a small smile, but one he needed. She patted the couch next to her and he moved. Barely, he held back his need to fully rub against her, instead content to sit with part of his leg along hers.

"I know you don't come from this background. You're not a shifter, but you're something more than human too. What I want is to be with you. I don't want to date you. I don't want to only see you on weekends. I want you to be my family. And with you, Galen too. We can make a family."

She took his hand. "Before this goes any further, you have to understand something. Family is incredibly important to me. It's not a joke or a way to get around my trepidation over this."

"My parents abandoned me. My birth parents. My mother was a wolf, my father apparently human. He couldn't handle what I was so they dumped me at the hospital and I spent the early part of my life in and out of foster care and group homes. When I was eight, a man showed up at the foster home I lived in. At the time I had no idea who he was, but he was a wolf too. He'd seen me on the playground, knew enough to know there weren't any pack families in that neighborhood so his wife asked after me. We don't achieve our first change into wolf until right around puberty. They knew I'd be doing that alone and afraid and they stepped in. He and his wife became my family.

They brought me into their home and into their Pack. Family means everything to me, Renee. When I say I want that with you, it's anything but a ruse."

Sorrow washed over her face, followed by contrition. "I'm sorry. About your parents and also about misjudging you."

Galen interrupted. "I ran a background check this afternoon. No criminal record. Owns his own condo. Has a car, motorcycle and a boat. No outstanding debt. Pays his bills, lives within his means. Has a lot of ex-girlfriends."

Jack meant to be pissed, but *he'd* done the same thing with *them* just that morning. And the smile on Renee's face wiped it all away.

He gave in to his desire to brush his thumb over her bottom lip. "What are you smiling about?" Again she shone with her emotions, teasing his senses.

"Galen checking up on the man who wants to share me with him. You having lots of ex-girlfriends." She looked him up and down. "Like *that's* a surprise. Galen's got scads of them too, both genders and they're all ridiculously gorgeous." She frowned for a moment and then laughed again. "The total absurdity of this moment makes me feel like I'm watching a Tim Burton movie."

"It's certainly not what I imagined my mate bond would be like. I figured it would be easy. Of course when it came to my friends finding their mates, none of them got easy women. Even Grace, who's small and quiet like you, takes all Cade's energy to keep from being steamrolled." Jack nearly cringed at the mention of Grace, especially when Renee's eyes narrowed ever-so-slightly. He'd meant to bring it up in a more finessed way.

The Grace discussion would be a whole new conversation, one he imagined would go slightly better than the tales of when Grace and Nina Warden met for the first time. Grace meant something to him. He loved her, and up until the moment he'd met Renee, she'd been the one woman he'd never been able to stop loving when he put his mind to it.

"*Christ.* Pour me another." Renee waved a hand toward the bottle of tequila and Galen got up to retrieve it for her.

"You sure about this?" Galen asked as he handed the shot glass over. "You're the definition of lightweight," One corner of his mouth quirked up and she rolled her eyes in response. She knocked it back and poured one more. Jack looked to Galen briefly, reassured by the other man's expression. He looked far more amused than worried.

"Think I can manage it." With a snort, she got up, moving past both of them, heading to the stereo. Galen watched her move with the same look on his face Jack imagined he had. He liked the way she walked, so very intent on her path. Jack also liked the curve of Galen's neck, wanted to see that body naked of clothes, glistening with sweat.

He sat back and pondered that for a little bit. He'd been with men before though nothing lasting. None of them had ever captured his attention enough to come back for more after a month or two. But Jack had a feeling this man would.

"Just wait," Galen murmured in a voice so low only another shifter would have heard. The sound brushed over Jack's skin like a caress.

"Don't think I don't know you're frowning," Renee called over her shoulder.

Galen snorted and shook his head. "Never say so, darlin'. I never frown when confronted with your ass. I'm always smiling and thinking about you naked."

"Is this...is this the Bee Gees?" Jack asked, though now he was thinking about her naked too.

"Renee loves disco music. And you thought she was all sparkly sexy magic and hot tits, huh?" Galen lifted a shoulder as he grinned. "Wait until we all take a road trip. Thousands of miles in the car and she gets to choose every third time. You can't even drink enough alcohol to make it okay."

Jack laughed. "I'm already invited on road trips?"

"We both know how this is going to go." As he spoke, Galen swiveled to keep Renee in his sights. It was clear to Jack she was thinking, turning things over in her head as she fiddled near the stereo.

Galen sighed, clearly contented, before speaking again. "Look at her and tell me, after you've felt that magic wash over you, after you've held her against your body that you're going to walk away."

It had been the most important feeling he'd ever had when he held her to him. "If she told me right now to go, I would. I'm not interested if she doesn't want me too. I don't want to force her into anything. And man, I can't believe you're not more territorial. I mean, it works out nicely for me and all, but you're clearly an alpha."

"I understand what it means to find home in another person." Galen faced him now. "I know if fate brought you to Renee and me, you're meant to be here. I also know if you harm her in any way, I will bring pain like you've never even imagined."

Before Jack could respond, Renee turned and his attention was captured again. God damn she was beautiful.

"You guys done talking about my boobs?"

Jack grinned. "I'm not even going to answer that."

"Pffft, you don't have to. They are pretty awesome." Her smile was lopsided, but genuine. The tequila had hit, her voice lost its edge, smoothing into not quite a slur, but she was definitely more relaxed than she'd been a few minutes before.

"He can duck out of answering, but I'll tell you straight, I'm never going to be done talking about them. I happen to enjoy your boobs very much." Galen smirked and she rolled her eyes. "Why you keeping all the way over there? That last shot leave you a little uneasy on your feet? Not that I'll be complaining about it, you're easy when you've been drinking tequila."

"Aren't you the comedian tonight? Hmpf. You know," she paused, looking both men over, "it just occurred to me that Jack isn't just my type, but your type too."

"What?" Galen asked, laughing, but not denying.

"Look at him. He's all blond and surfer boy good looks. Great body. He looks a lot like, what was his name? The one you were with before the woman before me. Not that I keep track." She burst into giggles and Jack shook his head.

"Come on over here and sit down, Renee." Jack patted the sofa and she eyed them both again, clearly sober enough to know they both had plans to get her naked. With a raised brow, she made her way over.

"Victor! That's it. Victor. The one who propositioned you when he thought I wasn't looking. As if I wouldn't be looking. Hello." She fell to the couch with a sigh, leaning her head against Galen's shoulder.

Galen had the same painful look on his face that Jack probably had when he'd brought up Grace some minutes before. "It was an invitation for three."

"Puhleeeeze. Galen, do you think I fell off the gullible truck? He is not interested in vagina. I bet he's never even touched one before. He likes cock. Yours, to be specific."

Galen struggled not to laugh. Jack liked their interplay. It was totally obvious they had love and respect between them. "Well, he was great fun to be with and that was one of his finest qualities. Still, I said no and that would be my answer if I saw Jack on the street without any context."

Renee frowned, fighting her own laughter. "Are you laughing at me?"

"Only on the inside." Galen winked at her.

She socked his arm and he caught her hand, gently,

carefully, bringing her fist to his lips to kiss.

"Do you like boys?" she asked Jack, bold as you please.

"How often do you drink tequila?" he shot back.

She rolled her eyes. "Like this? Only the times a ridiculously handsome werewolf tells me I'm his mate and he wants to come inside me to make me his mate and my husband seems to be okay with it. So up until now, only like twice a month or so."

Jack decided to move past talk and into action. He leaned in, his body just above hers, getting to his knees to get at that mouth. Galen's eyes went half mast; he made no move to stop Jack and neither did Renee.

In fact, her lips parted on a soft sigh as he loomed over her. When he slid his lips across hers, his body hardened, everything within him tugged, pulled to her, pulled to this woman he wanted so very badly.

Her taste was...right. So right he groaned, deepening the kiss until she opened to him, taking his tongue into her mouth, her own dancing along his. Her hands slid up, beneath the hem of his shirt, caressing his sides and then his back.

Need hit like a fever, like a balled up fist, and it sent him tipping into her, falling so deep he'd never be the same.

And he did it willingly, fell, let himself be consumed by her taste, by the scent of her skin, of her pussy and the honey between her thighs. Christ, he never wanted to stop touching her.

Everything within him wanted to howl. He'd found her. His whole life he'd known this moment would come, and now that it had, it was the best thing he'd ever experienced. Now that she'd submitted to him, his wolf wanted more, wanted all of her.

He hissed as her nails dug into his back, urging him closer. Her body molded to his, fit his just right. Each time she writhed, his cock ached a bit more.

"Are you okay with this? With *all* of this?" he managed to gasp as he broke his lips away. Jack couldn't believe he possessed the presence of mind to actually speak.

Her eyes opened. He'd never seen eyes like hers—honey gold. Her lashes were thick as she blinked up at him.

"Galen?"

"Yes, babe?" Galen leaned down to kiss her forehead, his face very close to Jack's. Without thinking, Jack turned, stretching until his mouth met Galen's. The contact went straight to his knees, to his cock, up his spine as it seemed to twine around where Renee had taken up residence inside him.

Galen nipped Jack's bottom lip as he pulled away.

"I was going to ask if we were okay with this, but I think I just got my answer." Renee's voice was thick and for all of Galen's sexual allure, he didn't begin to shadow what she was to him.

"Are *you* okay with that?" Jack indicated Galen with a tip of his chin, meaning the kiss and more.

"It feels good." She arched her back, bringing her body against his again and he groaned. "It feels right that this would be about the three of us. If it was me and you, and then me and you—" she indicated each man with the tip of her chin, "—it would bound to end up with people feeling left out."

"Yes," Galen whispered.

"This couch is too small. Come on through into the bedroom. I think our bed should do just fine." Renee scrambled up and held two hands out. Galen took one and Jack the other.

Chapter Seven

Okay then, so this was wow, so much more than she'd imagined that *something* to be. This was huge. Hot. Scary. Beautiful. She was utterly in over her head and she had no plan whatsoever to stop.

She couldn't stop. Her emotions clanged around inside her, driving her. She'd never felt her connection to Galen as strongly as she did right then. Each breath he took, each step he took, she felt. His desire, his need for her blanketed her skin, her senses. His love for her meant she could stand on this ledge and jump because it would be there no matter what.

If she overthought this, she'd do something bad like start to cry or laugh hysterically. It was surreal in the way it just felt like what they were all supposed to be doing. How odd, that it took this long in her life to really feel the hand of fate so strongly.

Their bedroom was lit by the streetlamps outside, and the moon overhead seemed to spotlight directly on the bed.

Before she could talk herself out of it, she pulled her shirt off, tossing her bra along while she was at it. Shimmying out of her jeans and panties took another half a minute and when she turned around again, both men stood side by side, watching her.

"Um, okay then. Here I am. There you are. Only I'm naked and you two aren't. It's okay that Galen is here, right? I'm babbling, oh my God, I'm babbling like an idiot and what are you two even doing here with me? Look at you!" She gestured at them both.

"Of course it's okay that Galen is here." Jack took the few steps he needed to get to her. "I'm here with you because there's no one on earth I'd rather be with. Naked is always a plus." He trailed a fingertip over her shoulder, across the spot where Galen had marked her.

A strangled gasp broke from her at that contact. Galen was suddenly there, turning the blankets back and helping to ease her onto the mattress.

"There. Pretty as a picture." Galen dipped down to lick over the spot on her neck where he'd bitten her a second time. She shuddered and squeezed her thighs together to try and ease the ache.

"I told you nearly four years ago and I'll say it again, you're mine. I take care of what's mine. I love you." Galen spoke as he pulled his T-shirt over his head, exposing the upper body she'd just rubbed herself all over that very afternoon. Her breath caught and he laughed.

Not to be outdone, Jack got rid of his shirt too. The pale gold hair on his chest gleamed in the low light and called to her hands. She got to her knees, sliding her palms up the flat belly, over the broad chest, stopping to kiss the scar on his right side.

"Why do you have a scar here? I thought you guys healed really fast." Behind her, she heard the jingle of Galen's belt and the *shuss* of jeans being shoved down and kicked off.

"Silver-tipped knives." His voice was thin with strain as he took her hand to another spot on his upper back. "Gunshot with silver ammo. Everything else heals just fine. And can I just tell you how pretty you are? Lay back, sweetheart, and let's get a look at you."

As she did, he got rid of his pants and boxers and stood for long moments, totally naked and obviously happy to be there, just looking at her.

"You're like the inside of a seashell, pink and fragile but so strong." He took her ankles in his hands, trapping them with his grip before slowly sliding them up her legs.

"I don't like that someone tried to hurt you."

The idea of him being in danger made her slightly ill. Galen brushed the hair back from her face and took her mouth in a kiss meant to reassure but quickly began to seduce, to cajole and possess.

"He's dead and I'm here with my hands on the most beautiful woman on earth. I think I got the better deal. It's part of my job, being attacked." He laughed softly and she did not feel like joining him.

The sight of his olive-toned skin stretched over the wide shoulders—shoulders holding her thighs apart so he could, *yesss*, take a long lick from her gate to her clit and back again—was almost as sexy as the way his hair felt on her belly, against her pussy.

"She tastes like the sea with an edge of sweetness," Galen said and Jack hummed his agreement. "Do you like that? Does his mouth on your pussy feel good? You look so sexy right now." He traced his finger around the bottom curve of her left breast and then around and around her nipple.

"By the way, she comes fast and hard," Galen managed to say right as Jack began to suck her clit in and out of his mouth. Stars painted her vision as she arched, fingers digging into the blankets.

Her pussy still clenched, wanting to be filled, when he was there, his cock nudging her open.

His struggle to take it slow showed on his face. One lock of hair slid down over his forehead. "Please. I need you now."

"Yes, yes please, inside me." She squirmed to get more as

he began to press inside. It felt so unbelievably good it was almost too much.

"Once I fuck you and the Claiming is done, we're going to take our time and do this all over again." Jack's voice had gone low, his wolf in every word.

She opened her eyes again once he started to thrust, sensation lighting up her body with each press. His cock touched parts of her Galen didn't, just as Galen's cock had that swing to the left and nudged her just right.

"Okay, I may need to soak in a bath of Epsom salts first though." She laughed and Galen curled around her from behind. She snuggled into him even as Jack began to stroke harder and deeper. "Yes, like that. Harder. I won't break."

The sound Jack made nearly made her come again.

"You like it hard?" Jack thrust, jiggling her breasts.

"Yes, yes, yes. I do." She gasped when Galen pinched her nipples in time with the thrusts.

"Me too." He grinned and began to fuck her in earnest, hard and deep. The bed squeaked a bit.

Galen's cock, hard at her back, was just out of her reach. God she needed it, she needed him too. All that naked skin, two cocks, four hands, two mouths, the idea of it was enough to make her want to giggle.

Instead she cried out as a hot rush of climax filled her and then teeth, *two* sets of teeth, sank into her skin. Galen on her shoulder and Jack, on her side, just below her left breast. He came inside her and the world tipped on its side as her cry of climax became a sob, a sob at the wonder of how it felt to be there right at that moment.

So much magic! It flowed from her until she wasn't sure she could hold it together. Dizziness hit and she smelled forests and fur, heard the growl of big cats, the howl of wolves.

Galen laid there, Renee in his arms, Jack leaning against

them both, all three panting. Galen had never seen anything like it. She was so powerful, she had no idea, he wagered, just how much raw magicks she poured out. It wrapped around them, made him feel safe as his cat recognized her taste and approved of the new flavor. Jack.

He *felt* her. Before that moment he'd been connected to her. He understood her without her even having to speak. He knew her bond to him was made by choice and by pleasure. But right then, they'd all three clicked together in a way that felt as natural as breathing.

He felt Jack's wonder, his fascination and adoration of their woman. Jack was a powerful shifter, Galen's cat approved because it meant she'd be safer too. The scent of sex hung in the air, teasing him, bringing his need back even though he'd had her only hours before.

"Wow," she mumbled, her eyes still closed.

Jack petted her hip. "Are you all right? I know the Claiming can be really difficult for human women."

"And you did it anyway? Without saying?" Galen wasn't quite ready to be pissed yet, but it was there, drawn out by any threat to Renee.

She looked up at Galen, seeking to reassure him. "I think my connection to Galen made it okay." She sat up. "I can feel you." She touched Jack's chest and he leaned into her touch. "I feel you in my head and in my heart. And you." She swiveled to speak to Galen again. "I feel you too, in here." She pointed to her belly and heart. "You were there before, but this is different. This is deeper. I've never..." She started to cry and both men, distressed and confused, rushed to comfort her.

"I...please don't cry. I don't want you to be sad. God. I've never in my life felt so happy. I've been so lonely at times. I suppose I thought it was normal so I just accepted it. But now I feel home. I feel full. I feel like I belong and that you and Galen belong to me."

"They're good tears. This is good." She cupped Jack's cheek and then Galen's. "I'm overwhelmed, but not sad or scared."

"Oh. Good. I'm glad. How do you do it, Galen? How do you keep your hands off her?" Jack looked around Renee to ask.

"I have four bite marks! Does it look like he keeps his hands off me?"

Galen laughed, pulling her to him and opening his arm wider, inviting Jack. The three hugged, with Renee's sweet curves in between them. Galen hungered for her with a ferocity no amount of Epsom salts could cure.

"I want you so badly. But I've had you twice today and Jack once." As he said it, his hand, dark against her belly, slid down, his fingers gently brushing through her pussy.

"Mmmm. Good thing I like sex or you two would wear me out. Forget about my ass, buddy." She grinned. "But I need you. I need this." She reached down and grabbed his cock, sliding her fist around him, pumping just the way he liked. "I've been with you thousands of times and I still haven't gotten my fill."

Bending, she began to lick around the crown. Jack reached out and grabbed Galen's cock, holding it for Renee. Their gazes locked for long moments before Galen was drawn, as always, back to her.

He adjusted himself, putting pillows behind his back so he could lean and watch her as he reclined. His beauty, as she crouched between his thighs, her mouth on his cock, her hands on his body. Each knob of her spine pressing against her skin called to his hands, his mouth, each brush of her nipples against his thighs brought a twinge, a deeper need for her. Her scent, her skin, the honey between her thighs, mixed with Jack, hung around them, comforting as it excited.

Jack sat next to where Renee knelt, his hands on her, stroking, touching, caressing like he couldn't get enough and Galen knew the feeling.

Her mouth was hot and wet, the heaven he daydreamed of a hundred times a day. Her tongue knew all the best parts of him, pressing just hard enough, swirling, licking fast and hard, slow and gentle. She drove him higher and higher, sucking his cock, cupping his sac, occasionally scoring, ever-so-gently over the sensitive skin there. Her middle finger extended to play over his asshole. He nearly laughed, remembering her stern warning away from her ass. He knew, when her hand left his balls, that she was reaching down to her cunt, bringing her lube back up. He groaned when the fingers sliding over his rear passage were hot and slick. Even harder when she pressed inside, deeper and deeper, widening gently by scissoring her fingers. When she brushed against his prostate he nearly wept with joy, it felt so fucking good. Something she kept mindful of as she sucked him deeper with just the right pressure and speed.

"Damn it, I'm not going to last," he managed to gasp out, right before orgasm barreled through him and into her.

It dizzied him, her love, the way she touched him, the way she knew him and yes, those pale blue eyes watching him as Jack caressed Renee with one hand and Galen's thigh with the other. He let his eyes close, fell back to catch his breath and just let himself enjoy the moment.

When he was able to open his eyes, he saw Renee kiss his belly and look to him with love and acceptance.

"I love you."

She rolled over, dropped a kiss on his lips. "You'd better. Be right back."

She headed into the adjoining bathroom.

"You all right?" Galen asked Jack.

"I've never been this all right. I...well, thank you. I know she wouldn't have done anything with me if you hadn't supported it, even if she wanted to. She would have chosen you and your bond."

Jack flopped next to him.

"She'd always have missed you if I had sent you away. She'd have wondered and I'd always worry that I stepped in the way of fate, endangering her or you, by not accepting what is so very plain. You're our mate. If I hadn't supported it, I'd have missed that too."

Jack's laughter shook the mattress a bit as Galen watched her silhouette in the doorway to the bathroom. She nearly glittered she had so much magic flowing. He sat to get a better look.

"Jesus. Babe, you're like gushing magic. I've never seen anything like it."

"It's beautiful," Jack murmured.

"It's a bit scary, sort of like I feel after two glasses of champagne. I don't know what to do with it."

"Come to bed." Jack held a hand out and she moved to take it, getting in bed between them, and Galen realized how utterly and totally satisfied he was at that very moment her body slid against his.

"We'll figure it out."

"Don't you have a coach or something?" Jack pulled on one of her curls and let go.

"No."

Galen wished she'd open up about this whole thing. He knew enough that her stepmother, despite owning that shop, didn't believe in magic and had made Renee believe she was unnatural and wrong. There was more there, something dark, but for years Renee had refused to go into it so he'd let her. He'd tried to research her mother's family, but had come up empty. In fact, their lives before they'd come to Boston seemed a mystery. Her father wouldn't speak about it at all. He barely tolerated Galen as it was and he didn't know Galen was a shifter. He did know Galen had dark skin and was a lawyer and that had been two strikes already. The stepmother liked him well enough. He kept Renee out of trouble as she saw it. He'd never say it to Renee, but it was also that the woman felt like with Galen around, they didn't have to do anything for Renee. She saw the expensive suits and figured he'd be a source of financial support, despite the fact that Renee had supported herself since the age of seventeen.

If she hadn't been so stubborn he'd have purchased her a permanent space for her juice bar as far away from that shop as possible. But she wanted to do things her own way and he respected that enough to stand back and help however she'd let him. For the time being, but after that scene with her dad and stepmother that afternoon, he doubted it would go on much longer.

"No?"

"It's not a complicated answer. No."

Galen laughed, he couldn't help it, she was so full of shit.

Jack snorted. "There's a story behind that, I can tell. Just so you know up front, I'm nosy and I like to take care of people. It's what I do and who I am." Jack sighed and Galen grinned in the dark.

"Good luck with that," he mumbled and Renee huffed, reaching across his body to turn on the light. He grabbed her and she laughed.

"Punk. Let me go."

"Not ever."

Her annoyance melted and she smiled, that sweet, crooked smile reserved only for him. "Just cause you're all hot and hard and you have a big cock doesn't mean you can boss me around."

"Oh, my sweet beautiful witch, of course I can boss you around. You like it."

"I like it when you're fucking me. Or licking my pussy.

Something useful. Not when you're poking at me on this magic stuff. I'm just a girl with some interesting talents. Nothing special."

Jack growled. "You're special, Renee. Don't ever talk like that about yourself. Sweetheart, I don't know a lot about witches and magic, but even I can see you're powerful. If you don't have a teacher, we'll get you one. I have no idea how we'd find one, but we will. I'll get my people on it when I go back to work."

"You can stay, can't you?" Renee looked to him, her lashes fluttering, and Galen bit his lip to keep from smiling. She didn't want to talk about it and she'd make sure Jack forgot. He could never stand against her when she truly wanted something either.

"I'd love to stay." Jack moved to snuggle in on her other side.

"We'll have to figure out the logistics of all this." Her voice was sleepy and Galen knew she was tired. So much had happened that day.

"Tomorrow." Galen let drowsiness claim him, satiation, satisfaction. Life was very good.

"Are you off tomorrow?" Renee asked Galen.

"I am. But I ran out on a few things earlier. I need to put in a few hours but it can wait until the afternoon."

She kissed his side before turning over to face Jack. "You?"

"I don't have days off. Or I didn't. I guess I will now, or I'd better because you and I have a lot of time to catch up on. I need to go in in the morning though, to explain things to Cade and Grace. They'll want to meet you. You'll be officially accepted into the Pack too. But that's not anything we have to deal with right this very moment."

"The alarm clock is on your side." She leaned over Jack to get to it. "Hmm. I realize I'll be giving up having a side of the bed now. Unless you two want to sleep next to each other."

"Not that I mind sleeping against Galen, but I'd rather sleep against you. This place is nice. We might need a new...okay well we can talk about all this over the weekend. Set the alarm for seven please."

She groaned and Galen decided he'd let Jack figure out just how much she hated mornings on his own.

"Done." She sat. "I'll go set the coffeemaker." She bounced off, happy, and Galen grinned.

"You don't have to do that. I usually eat at Cade and Grace's." Jack got out of bed to follow her.

"Well, now you're mine. I feed you." Renee began to pour water and measure coffee, pushing buttons on the coffeemaker and setting it to start brewing right before they woke up.

Galen pinched Jack before he spoke again, shaking his head hard, telling him to shut up. Renee may not be a shifter but she was not a woman to be messed with, especially when it came to taking care of her people.

"All right." Jack yawned.

"Good answer." Renee turned to them with a smile. "Now how about some snacks and a movie? I don't have to be up early."

Chapter Eight

Jack woke up to the scent of his mate on the pillow. Utter satisfaction left him totally relaxed, happy. When he turned, he grinned at the sight of Renee face down, blankets up over her head. One of her arms lay over Galen's belly while the fingers of her other hand curled around Jack's shoulder.

God, she was beautiful.

He kissed her shoulder and she burrowed deeper. Her skin, God, her skin was so pale and soft. Needing to see more, he pulled the blanket back, exposing a perfect back leading down to the dip at her waist and a very gorgeous ass.

"Mmmfph."

The alarm sounded and he rolled to turn it off.

"This thing is like the fucking space shuttle. How the hell do I turn it off?" He poked at a few buttons that seemed to do nothing.

His annoyance melted when a sleep soft and naked Renee leaned over him to turn the alarm off. He hugged her, rolling his hips to emphasize just how happy he was to see her.

"Anngaahahah."

What that meant he didn't know. But she tried to burrow back into the covers, which would *not* accommodate morning sex.

"How can I wake you up with my cock if you burrow back

in there?"

What he got was a snarl, a snort of disgust and his hand slapped away.

Galen seemed to find this all very funny.

"What?"

"While you'll find our lady to be sweet and accommodating in many ways, she's not a morning person." Galen laughed as he got up. "Babe, I'm turning the heater up and I'll close the bathroom door for you." He looked back to Jack. "She's not a shifter, remember? She gets colder than we do. I've found," he said, continuing into the bathroom to flip on the switch to heat the room, "that she's much more amenable to lots of things if she's had a hot shower."

Renee grumbled something into her pillow, deep inside her blanket nest. Jack pulled the blanket away from her face just a bit, enough to see her. "What?"

She rolled over and he saw her breasts in the light for the first time. He swallowed and wet his lips.

"*I said*, don't talk about me like I'm not in the room or worse, that I'm mental."

He kissed her and she might have been annoyed, but she put her arms around him anyway before swatting him away and rolling out of bed. "I'm taking a shower. Coffee is already brewing. I'll make breakfast while you get your shower."

And just like that, she disappeared into the bathroom after a lingering kiss for Galen.

"You okay this morning?" Jack asked Galen. "I mean, with everything?"

He tossed Jack a pair of sweats. "If you want. I think we're the same size, my closet is here and the highboy dresser is mine. There are underwear and stuff." He pulled a pair of pajama bottoms on but stayed shirtless. "And yeah, I'm okay this morning. You?"

"I feel," he paused as he pulled on pants, "satisfied." He shrugged and followed Galen out toward the kitchen.

"I'll need to tell my family today, and the rest of the jamboree." Galen poured them both a cup of coffee.

"I'm mated to you too."

Galen looked up. "Yes. Is that a problem for you? With your pack?"

Jack laughed. "No. One of my best friends has a tri mate bond. It's a sort of mated threesome. Under normal circumstances, any female mated to a wolf would need what we call an anchor bond. Another male to take on part of the bond should the male die. Gabe, my friend, thought he'd anchor another couple and ended up mated to both." He shrugged. "So threesomes are not unheard of."

"So, when were you planning on telling me I had to have an anchor? Because I'm not going to do it." Renee came into the room smelling better than anyone had a right to. Her cheeks were rosy and her skin gleamed like a pearl.

He shook himself out of his fantasy when she poked him while walking past to the fridge.

"You won't need an anchor bond. I asked. I'd have told you. It's a big deal and I'd never have not mentioned it before the Claiming." There was something truly wrong with him that he found her so sexy, even when she was pissed at him. He needed to tell her about Grace, but he wasn't sure how. He knew the longer he went without telling her, the worse it would be.

Effortlessly, she moved around the kitchen preparing breakfast. He sipped his coffee while Galen made some calls and checked his email. Things were easy between them, the silences comfortable, the conversation natural.

"Are you going to move in with us?" she finally asked as she put a plate heaping with bacon, eggs and hash browns in front of him.

"Do you want me to?" He forked some food up and sighed happily. Galen sat beside him and blew her a kiss when she gave him his plate.

She took a deep breath. "Okay, you don't know me, I get that. But I'm a pretty straightforward person. We're mated, right? Did you think I'd kick you out today? Or move in with you and leave Galen? Share custody of my pussy? What? I wouldn't have opened my heart and my bed, hell, my life to you if I didn't plan to let you in all the way." She sipped her coffee as she nibbled on toast. "You're mine, Jack. Ours. Of course I want you with me and Galen."

He knew it, felt it through their link, but it sure felt good to hear it. "Will I fit here?"

Galen slid a hand up and down his back. "We'll make it work. Unless your place is bigger?"

"No. I like it here." And he did. He liked the feel of the space.

"Settled." She bent to rummage in a drawer and pulled out two keys. "Here, this one is to the outer door and this one is to the front door."

They chatted for another twenty minutes or so, but he had to go back to his place first to change before he went to Cade and Grace's.

Renee walked him to the door. "I'll see you later then?"

He put his arms around her and she moved to him with a happy sigh. The kiss she gave him rocketed him straight back into that place where need clawed his gut.

"Wow, that's, wow." Her voice was shaky. "I can feel it, the way you need." She slid the robe she wore off her shoulders and it fell to the floor with a whisper of fabric. "I'm here and awake."

With a strangled moan, he moved her against the wall at her back. "What you do to me."

She opened herself, tossing a thigh around his upper leg and grabbed for his button. Then of course, his phone rang, Cade's ringtone.

"Please don't tell me you have to take that," she said, reaching into his jeans and finding his cock.

"I won't." He ignored the ring and picked her up to get her cunt where he needed it. Cade would just have to understand, it wasn't the urgent ringtone so Jack was going to fuck his mate right then and there or die trying.

She shuddered and moaned into his ear as he lowered her onto his cock. "Love that shifter strength," she murmured. "Hard and fast, I know you have to rush off." She bit his earlobe and he growled, thrusting deep, just like she'd requested.

Her nails dug into his sides as he shifted her to rest more against the wall so he could reach her clit with a free hand.

"Glory hallelujah and all that stuff. Your cock feels so good inside me." The nails scored his skin and he wanted to fall to his knees it felt so good. Her words drove him higher, the clasp of her inner walls pushed him closer to the edge. Her clit was hard and slippery against his fingers and when she came, her body tightening around his cock, the sensation, the pleasure rushing through his body, white noise in his ears and her name on his lips, he did drop to his knees as his orgasm hit with such intensity he could barely draw breath.

She sat astride him, smiling down, the morning sun coming through the window just above their door, lighting the wine and gold in her hair. Magic coursed around her, ebbing and flowing. Within, his wolf stretched and quieted.

"I love you. I know we just met, but I do."

She moved to the side and grabbed her robe as he got up too. "I know. It's big and scary, but it's true. The love is there for me too."

He kissed her again, hating that he had to go. His phone

rang again and he groaned.

"I'll call you later, okay?"

She nodded and stood in the doorway, watching him leave as he answered.

Renee had walked with Galen to his office, pretended to be nice to Beth, who always seemed to be lurking like the stupid bitch she was. Ha, bitch! Well, bitches were just dogs? So would any of Jack's females in his pack be bitches in the figurative as well as literal sense?

Good gracious, well that was a lot of mental rambling! Not that she wasn't amused by it, Beth was a cow. But as she was pregnant, all Renee had was mental slapping since the physical kind would be frowned upon even if it hadn't have gotten her slapped right back by a female jaguar shifter.

She grabbed some kisses and left after some I love yous. She knew him, he'd be there for hours. He was a busy attorney, one of the few specialists in employee-side labor law in Boston. It was all acronyms to her, but ERISA was a big deal to those people who needed a specialist and he was their man.

She was proud of that. Proud of how smart he was, of how hard he worked. Proud a man like him loved her. And now she had Jack. Who she didn't know nearly as well. She did hope his pack would accept her. She wanted, very much, to have the people important to him like her.

The last several days had been overwhelming on so many levels it was impossible to really get it all straight. It wasn't just Jack and her bond to him. The magic within her had grown. Grown so much it was impossible to ignore.

She knew she had a sort of special gift. Knowing the phone would ring or sometimes, she'd been able to knock things over. She'd noticed lately when she had been really angry or upset, she had made things shake.

But after the night before, all that sort of chaotic noise had smoothed out. She felt like what she had wasn't just about phone calls or having a way with people and animals. It was as if she perched in a sunny spot and her magic shone all around her. It felt big, like the ocean. Though she wasn't scared by it she was still wary and impressed. And lost because she had no freaking idea what it was.

Most of all, she really wished she could talk to someone about it, learn how to harness it.

She hopped on the T and headed across the river to an occult/magic type bookshop in Cambridge. She'd only passed by a few times on her way to a movie theatre she and Galen caught arthouse flicks, but she'd always wanted to stop in. Why not then? Maybe they could help her there, refer her to someone. Her men were off doing werewolf and lawyer stuff, her cart was closed on weekends and she had the time and the curiosity.

But at the end of the block, four doors down and the street jam-packed with students, she stopped, a cold sweat breaking over her. She was not supposed to be there. Why, she didn't know, until a man stepped out of the bookshop. She simply *knew* she didn't want him to see her.

Quickly turning on her heel, she mixed in the crowd and headed away, back toward the T.

The further she got from that street, the better she felt, but she wasn't going to stop until she got on the other side of the river.

Her phone buzzed in her pocket as she slid into a seat and tried not to be obvious about checking to see if she'd been followed.

"What's happening? Where are you?" Jack demanded when she answered.

As the train pulled away from the stop, she saw him, saw

the man from the shop standing on a nearby corner, looking around. She ducked, hoping he hadn't seen her.

"Nothing," she whispered, not sitting up again until she was sure they'd moved on and weren't going to stop and let anyone else board.

"Bullshit. I can feel you. I can feel your fear. Where are you?"

Her call waiting buzzed and she sighed. That would most likely be Galen. She bet this mate thing between the three of them had made him all sneaky Pete into her head like Jack apparently was.

"Galen is on the other line. I have to get it or he'll worry. I'll call you when I get home." She broke the connection over his growled curse and order not to hang up.

"Hello?"

"What took you so long to answer? Where are you?"

"Hey, handsome. I'm fine. On my way across the river back toward home."

"Why are you scared? What's happening?"

"I got spooked. It was stupid. I'm on a crowded train in broad daylight and I'll be home in ten minutes. Really, go back to work. I'm all right. Let's have pizza for dinner. I'll handle the details. I love you." She hung up and ignored the phone when it buzzed again. She needed to hold her shit together and talking to them wouldn't help that just then.

Of course when the train stopped and she made to get off, she saw Jack right away. Galen stood next to him.

Instead of being mad, she simply went to them and let them hug her, even as they chided her for not answering the phone.

It felt so good to be cared about, to be fussed over; stupidly, she couldn't hold back tears and it only made them worry more about her.

Jack looked around the outside of the house and went in first, giving Galen the all clear signal before they allowed her inside. Galen ushered her to the couch and they bookended her.

"I'm going crazy here, sweetheart. What the hell has you so spooked?" The tension rolled off Jack in waves. Even normally laid back Galen had been replaced by hardcore protector Galen.

She told them everything, from the way she'd headed to the shop as if by rote and then the way she got sick and sweaty and just knew the man she saw would bring her harm if she didn't get away from him immediately.

"Did he see you on the T today?" Galen asked.

"I don't know. I don't think so. But he was following me, looking for me. I know it."

"Why do you think he was following you? Did you speak to him? Know him from before?" Jack held her hand as he spoke.

"I've never seen him before. I'd have remembered. I was walking down the street toward the shop and I began to feel sick. It was wrong, the air. I can't explain it, but I just knew I shouldn't be there and when he came out onto the sidewalk I had to not let him see me." She shrugged. "I know it sounds stupid, but I just felt it. He was, there was something about him. I think he had magic. But not like mine. It looked, or felt different. I don't know! I don't know how I know, I just do."

Galen kissed her temple. "Babe, it's okay. We believe you. You practically glow with your magic now. Before I could sense it, taste it even. But last night, something happened. My cat, Jack's wolf...it was a full moon and we all connected, unlocked things within us all."

"You think maybe he saw it too? Like she's a front porch light and he's a bug? Great. Just great. Even better that we're responsible for making her less safe." Jack frowned.

She took his hand. "Oh for goodness sake. You can't be

responsible for everything."

Then of course, they began to speak as if she weren't even there. Being annoyed at them was better than being scared, she supposed.

Jack leaned forward, around her body to address Galen. "I don't like that at all. What would he want with her?"

"Nothing good." Galen's eyes shone with violence.

Jack turned his gaze back her way. "You aren't to go around by yourself for the time being. Got me? One of us will take you to work, one of us will escort you home. Until we figure out who this guy is and what he wants, you're at risk."

She counted to ten. She knew shifters were this way in general about mates, but in the face of a threat, they got even worse.

"I appreciate the protection and concern, I really do. But this is silly. You're not going to treat me like I'm five. I'm a grown woman. I walk around alone all the time."

"You did. And now you won't. This isn't about you being five, Renee, and you know it. This is a dangerous situation, we don't know enough right now. Until we know more, this is how it will be." Galen's mouth had set, that spelled trouble for her because she knew he wasn't going to give in when he had that face.

She narrowed her eyes. "This is ridiculous."

He shrugged, so gallingly casual. "Suck it up."

She slumped, knowing she couldn't get out of it and not really wanting to. She was still spooked and they made her feel safe.

"Don't you both have work to do?"

"Nice try. I finished my work and was on my way out when this all went down. I'm home for the day." Galen tossed his feet up on the coffee table and she resisted the urge to shove his feet off the wood.

She sent him what she hoped was a snotty smile, but he pretended not to notice. "Well then good, you can go to your Saturday rowing thing with your crazy assed siblings." The de La Vegas liked to row on the Charles every Saturday until the river began to freeze at the shore. Because they were all insane. In any case, it was nice to be able to get out of that because they all had superhuman energy and she, alas, was just a human. Ha.

"Not today. There's some thing for Beth and another woman who's pregnant too. My dad is off with Max to get wood for some construction project he'll fuck up and we'll have to call in a contractor. They're all busy and I'd rather be with you anyway."

Jack smoothed a hand down her back and she leaned on him a moment. "I spoke with Cade before I left. I have a few days off, but they'd like to meet you. They asked us all to dinner on Monday to officially welcome you into the Pack." He looked to Galen. "Both of you. There's an official ceremony, but we can do that whenever we're ready."

"I have no idea what to tell my father and Susan. Things are already really tense between us lately. I don't know what happened but in the last six months or so, she's way more condescending. Makes more comments about my mom and her family. We end up in a fight of some sort at least once a week. My dad has become more distant with me during this time too. I'm not ashamed of it, I just, I honestly don't know if they care or what."

"You didn't tell me it had gotten so bad." Galen sighed, still holding her hand. "Why don't you just take me up on the offer to lease the space in the lobby of our building? It's the perfect size for you. Easier to deal with than the cart. And it's not dependent on them. And, it's protected by my people. No one could get to you. I'd feel a lot better on a few levels if you moved."

"Because I can't afford to do that yet."

"How much do you need? Whatever I've got is yours." Jack squeezed in tighter and she found herself surrounded by them. Damn, that was just, wow, hard to think when all that gorgeous man was up on her.

Galen's voice cut through her tingles. "That's not the issue. I've offered to do the same. And she *can* afford it, but she has this notion that she has to put the exact same amount into the household as I do."

"I don't put the *exact same* as you do into the household! You put in a lot more money than I possibly could. I do all I can. You put in a certain percentage of your wages into things. Into the savings and utilities and the mortgage. All that stuff, vacations, whatever. I do the same. The increase in a lease or rental for my space is not in my budget. Right now, my schedule is my own. I don't have to work on weekends or at night. I have a leisurely life because of how much more you put into the budget than I do." His sister already thought Renee was a gold digger and basically dumb and shallow. Renee didn't care to deal with the fallout of letting Galen pay for that lease. He thought she was just being stubborn and because she didn't want to put him in the middle, she just let him think it.

"But I'll be living here too." Jack kicked his shoes off, putting them on the coffee table too. "So that helps, right? You should have enough to do it yourself in that case."

"The building is owned by my jamboree. All the business floors are anyway. We lease out the rights to the retail space in the lobby and one atrium floor to another company. That company requires the first year's lease fees paid in advance. I could, of course, intervene and ask them to make an exception for my wife. If my wife would allow me to do so. Which she does not. I could pay the first year's fees for her and she could pay me back monthly, if she felt the stupid need to pay me back in the first place. She also refuses that."

"Not that Galen's bitter about it or anything." Renee tried to get up, but both men held her fast. "I'm done with this conversation now. I'm not going to just let you give me tens of thousands of dollars! And I'm not going to use your family connections to get me a special deal that others don't get. I know I'm not a lawyer or second in command of a werewolf pack. But I have my own business. It makes me happy and it pays my bills. It means something to me that I do it on my own."

Galen hugged her. "I know, babe. I'm sorry. I just want to help you. I want to take care of you. I respect what you do, but can't we find a way, a middle way, where we can protect you and you can still manage your own business too?"

"Sweetheart, if you're in Galen's building, you'd be way safer. Let us help you with this. I know we'd both feel a lot better if we knew you were more protected. If you won't just take the money, you can pay us back, in installments or whatever you need."

"I appreciate your concern, I respect that you want to protect me and I appreciate that. I do feel safer knowing you two look out for me. But I'm done talking about it and we're going to move on to another topic." She totally sounded like a self-help book, she knew she did. But she wanted them to know she appreciated their concern and still wasn't going to let them take over her entire life.

She pushed hard enough that they finally let go and she stood, needing to be away from them right then. It was so easy to give in to all that love and protection. To let them take care of her instead of her taking care of them and herself. But she didn't want that, didn't want to be a freaking dependent. How could she respect herself if she just let them take over that way? How could *they* respect her in that case?

Jack was very nearly close to changing. He'd never felt so

close to the edge before. The first jolt of her fear through their bond had doubled him over. He'd been in a meeting with Cade, on a teleconference with several other pack leaders at the time.

He'd lurched to his feet, intent on finding her. This wasn't her being startled or nearly hit by a car or something fleeting. It hadn't gone away. It stayed. She was being terrorized and he wasn't there to protect her.

Grace had stopped him as he'd fumbled with his phone. She'd wanted to examine him but Cade forced her back, allowing Jack to call Renee's phone. She didn't answer right away and when she finally did she expected to just go on home and for him to stay at work?

And now this fuckall crazy idea of hers to not take the help they offered to get her out of what sounded like a very unpleasant situation and into a guarded building with more space?

"You can't just walk away from this," Galen said.

"I can't? And how do you think that? Thank you both for the offer. I decline." She continued on toward the hall opposite the bedrooms. A door slammed and KC and the Sunshine Band started up.

"I haven't heard 'Boogie Man' in a good long time." The '70s. Jack thought of that time when his life had been so chaotic. Absent any real connections to anchor him. He'd had a beer can novelty radio. He'd won it at some foster kid picnic and had listened to music long into the night, long after everyone else had gone to sleep.

"She's got a darkroom back there. Another thing I've encouraged her to do more of is photography. She's quite good at it. But she's been raised to think anything artistic is bad. Raised to think she was wrong for her magic. So she runs her own business, does very well at it and still gets to be creative in her own way. But she hides her photography by saying it's just a hobby. Stupid Susan, fuck! The woman owns a magic shop

121

and she's like the opposite of magic. It's nonsensical." Galen pushed himself from the couch and went into the kitchen. Jack followed.

"So I know more of the story with her family. What's the story with yours? Have you told them yet?"

"I used to think things would mellow out, and over the last three years, things have gotten better for the most part. Jaguars are insular. We keep with our kind most often. When we imprint on a human, they almost always take the change. She doesn't want to and I don't need her to."

"Your jamboree finds that insulting? A repudiation of what they are?"

"Some do, yes. More at the start. She's really hard not to like. Most of them have seen how much I love her and how much she loves me. They know her decision about the change isn't about them at all, but that she doesn't want to be anything but what she is now. I've known her long enough to understand how very important it is to her to be that. To affirmatively choose to be who and what she is instead of trying to change for others."

Galen began to rifle through the fridge.

Jack frowned. "But the ones who don't? The ones who think she won't change because she's some sort of human supremacist?"

"I've got eight brothers and sisters. Two of them don't like her. They feel like she's getting in the way of my choosing a woman in our jamboree or who'd change. They don't want me to have children with her. My mother was that way until last year. I don't know what happened, Renee won't talk about it. But whatever it was, my mother has been very supportive of our relationship and of Renee ever since. I thought things were okay, but given the way she reacted today, I'm beginning to think she's not telling me the extent of what's going on."

"So you haven't told them about me? About this?" Jack wasn't insulted, he just wanted to get all the details.

"I met with my father and my older brother, Max, and told them. I'm a grown man, a full member of the jamboree and third in line to take over. I don't need permission or a vote of support. I'll make an announcement of it at the next meeting, two weeks from now. I expect most of the jaguars there will support me. Some won't though. It's an old argument and things are changing. It's just slow." Galen handed Jack a soda and moved to stand next to him, both of them leaning back against the counter, staring out the large windows over the neighboring houses, of trees and gardens and beyond, the barest slice of river.

"Let me know what I can do to help." Jack cocked his head, looking at Galen, letting himself admire him.

Galen looked back. Neither of them spoke for long moments. Jack breathed in deep. That hit of recognition shocked through Jack's body. Connection. Deep arousal, attraction, need to protect and defend.

He turned, as Galen had. Where Jack's kiss with Renee had been sweet and sensual, this first kiss between Jack and Galen without Renee involved was hard, raw, a gnash of teeth and tongue. Hands pulling and yanking, hips pressing, cocks grinding through denim.

Galen's taste ran through his system, wild and powerful. His wolf responded, growling with satisfaction and challenge. Galen kissed down his neck, pulling his shirt open, the soft tear of the cotton wasn't louder than the sounds they made.

Mouth and teeth on neck and chest, over nipples, just this side of pain. Jack arched into Galen's touch as he managed to get Galen's belt undone and pants unzipped. His cock felt right in his hand, slick at the head.

Galen hissed, arching, pushing, thrusting his cock into Jack's fist. And bit him.

Jack cried out as Galen's teeth pressed into the flesh of his pectoral muscles, just above his nipple. So much pleasure rushed through him he nearly came from that bite.

Galen's hand worked its way around Jack's cock. "Give it to me, Jack," Galen murmured as he thrust against Jack. They were standing close enough that knuckles touched, angled cock to rub against cock, slick and hard.

Galen rested his forehead on Jack's shoulder, his neck so invitingly close. When Jack's teeth began to press into that beautiful, dark caramel skin, he growled, holding Galen in place as he came in a heated rush. Not too much longer later, a breath perhaps, Galen followed.

The silence after wasn't uncomfortable. Galen moved away, pausing to kiss the spot on Jack's neck just below his jaw. He handed Jack a washcloth to clean up with, but not before licking up Jack's hand, from wrist to palm. The gesture was tender, sexy and full of challenge. Loving Galen would be nearly as complicated as loving Renee. The two males were used to being in charge. The challenge of dominating one another would add spice and conflict too.

"I never expected this. I've been with men before. Loved men before. But this is so much more than what I've had in the past. You're beautiful, sexy, strong, all things my cat, and the man approves of." He paused for a moment. "When I met Renee there was nothing else. She owns my heart in a way no one could ever do. I need you to understand that. You are my mate, I believe that. The bites have tied us closer." Galen took a drink of his soda.

"But she's my first priority." Jack nodded. "And yours. I agree and understand."

"Wow, this week, I gotta tell you has been full of surprises." Galen shrugged with a laugh.

"Do you regret this?" Funny to ask, Jack knew, but he needed to know.

Galen shook his head. "No. Despite my inner cynic about most things, I do believe in fate. I believe this is meant to be. That you love her and want to protect her like I do means more because we have a connection to each other as well. Without her, there wouldn't be you. She's the connection, I can't regret her, or our connection to you."

"I agree." He looked back down the hallway where she'd retreated.

"We should get her out of the house tonight. Yes, it's exposed, but she's spooked and really pissed off. When she puts on Chaka Khan's 'I'm Every Woman' you better know she's still good and mad. If she puts on Patsy Cline, you need to wear a cup." Galen sort of laughed, but Jack knew their woman was totally capable of it.

The music halted between tracks and Jack wondered if he'd be hearing Chaka and running for the door. Instead a slow, sultry number came on.

Galen smiled. "Etta James. We've turned the corner. Next song will tell us if she's going to be our dinner date or if she'll be in there another hour." Both waited, continuing to look out the windows over the city.

Silversun Pickups came on, one of Jack's favorite bands. "'Three Seed'? Is that good or bad? This isn't a love song after all."

"'Three came from one little seed'," Galen said with a smile, indicating the lyrics. "Sounds hopeful to me."

The door opened, music flowed out and she followed, singing to herself absently as she looked at prints in her hand.

"Whatcha got there, babe?" Galen lit up when their eyes locked. A smile bloomed over Renee's features, making her so beautiful in that moment it unfurled something inside Jack.

She handed him the prints. Jack looked over Galen's shoulder at the black and white shots he'd laid side by side on the bar.

"My parents?" Galen traced the set of hands in the photograph. Clearly a couple, hands clasped easily, fitting perfectly. Perched between the feminine thumb and forefinger, the stem of a tulip.

The focus had been perfect, highlighting the connection of hand to hand and through that of the two people not in the picture at all.

"Yes. You remember that weekend we went out on Carlos's boat? It was just a silly moment. But they're so close, united, it's beautiful. I thought I'd have it framed for your mom's birthday next month."

Galen took her face between his hands. "Who am I that I'd be blessed to have you in my life? To see the world the way you do is to remember the magic all around us. Thank you. My mom will love this."

Jack looked at them, at the way Galen touched her so very gently, with tenderness and care. This was his family, the place where his heart lived.

They looked at the other shots. One of Galen and a man who had to be a sibling sitting around a fire pit. They leaned toward each other, sharing something clearly mischievous.

"I want to have this framed for you and Max. You two can put them in your office at work and then the next time you want to break his nose, you can remember this moment."

"God we're trouble." Galen laughed as he shook his head. "It's a wonder my mom never tried to sell us at a garage sale."

"She might have, but the neighbors would have known not to buy you, no matter how cute you were." Renee waggled her brows and Galen snorted, kissing her quickly.

The others were nature shots, beautiful, simple and he noted, from perspectives most people wouldn't have seen.

"You see a lot." He turned her toward him and she

automatically slid into his embrace.

"Meh. I like to take pictures. It's fun and that's about it."

He began to sway with her, slow dancing in the kitchen as Goldfrapp's "Black Cherry" came on. He didn't need Galen to interpret this song. She was everything.

"I love this song," he said, just being with her.

"Me too. This is a great sex CD."

He agreed.

"When you two recover from your interlude, you can show me."

"Our interlude?" Galen asked, still leaning against the counter, watching them, an amused smile on his lips.

"I know what pussy smells like after sex, and I know what the air smells like after you've come." She writhed against Jack and his cock quickly let her know he was just fine to go again.

"Does that bother you?"

She leaned back as if he'd dipped her, the long line of her neck exposed. His wolf approved mightily of the gesture of total sexual submission. The sound of her laughter, the way she glowed with pleasure and contentment, he knew the answer.

"No, gorgeous. Not at all. As long as there's a place for me I have no negative opinions of it at all. It's hot. You can let me watch sometimes though."

Jack laughed as she straightened again. "Galen and I think dinner out would be good. What do you say?"

"Don't you need to move some stuff in?" She got to her tiptoes to kiss him before twirling to the counter to get some tea. "Oh and I moved all my stuff to the closet in the guest bedroom. You can share the big closet with Galen. I moved my dresser in there too so there's room for yours. Oh, and I moved my stuff from Galen's office and put it into my darkroom area. I don't need it and you may."

"You moved that dresser? Damn it, Renee, that's a heavy piece of furniture. I could have done it."

Jack just met her smile with one of his. His mate, making their home open to him. "Thank you, sweetheart. I don't want to push you out of your office space."

"I have a really large space outside the darkroom. It's well lit and I have my computer in there anyway. I don't do a lot, not enough to need half of Galen's office. If you need, or want an office of your own, we have the guest room too."

"All I need is a space for a computer, a printer and a fax machine. A lot of my work is going to meetings and talking on the damned phone. I'm fine sharing with Galen if he is."

"It's a big space. Plenty of room for another desk. I've got a fax machine and a printer. Wireless through the house and my computer has teleconference capability, so you're welcome to use it too."

They discussed the logistics of all the stuff he wanted to keep and that he didn't really care about. He made some calls and arranged to meet with some friends in the morning to move the big stuff. He'd put the condo on the market in a few weeks after he'd gotten settled with them.

She flitted around, chatting with them, clipping herbs from the pots in the window, making more tea, filling the space with the sweetness of her energy. It made him so unbearably happy.

Galen smiled, his gaze tracking Jack's. "Yeah."

She turned to them, catching them both staring. "I'm starving. How about Serafina? I think something carb laden with extra cheese sounds just right."

"Good idea. Let me call and see if they can get us in?"

"I need to go by my place to get some clothes. I know where Serafina is. Call me and tell me when the reservation is and I'll meet you two there. If you don't mind, I'll take you up on the parking spot here."

"Not a problem. Why don't I come with you?"

He realized how much he wanted to have some alone time with her when her suggestion pleased him so much. Part of it too, was that she wanted to be with him as well.

"They can't get us in for another hour and a half." Galen hung the phone up. "I need to stop by my office. I realized I left my memory stick there and I want to work a little tomorrow afternoon. I'll meet you at Serafina."

"All right. Let me get changed and we'll head to your place, Jack. Do you mind?"

"Not if I can watch."

She laughed. "I'm pretty sure it's not very exciting, but whatever floats your boat."

"Be careful, babe. Listen to Jack when you're out." He stepped into his boots, zipping them.

"Damn you look handsome." Renee kissed Galen. "Yes, yes. I'll be careful. You too. See you soon."

Chapter Nine

Some time later, Jack and Renee headed to his condo. For the first time in his life, he was out and about with his woman. Not a woman he was enjoying or was dating, not with a woman who belonged to another man. Or at least not solely.

Pride warmed him as he led her into his place. It wasn't big, but it was his. A place he bought with his own money. Partly because he had to get out of the same building as Grace and Cade, but also because he'd never had a place of his own.

"I hope you'll bring the art." She walked through the space, taking everything in. It made him a bit anxious, knowing she'd see him so intimately as she traced the lines of a wood carving or read the spine of the book on his nightstand.

He grabbed a duffel and began to stuff some clothes into it. "I have to admit, I like this. You and me alone, one on one."

She nodded, picking up the picture frame on the nearby bedside table. "I like it too. I think we all need that. I want to know you. I admit, I'm hungry for details of your life."

Nerveless fingers dropped the duffel. He moved to her, loving the way she tipped her chin to look at him.

"There's this need inside me. It's got your name all over it." He cupped her throat, the feel of the thrum of her pulse beat against his fingers, settled within his head, a song just for her.

Her smile always made him want to give her one in return.

"You just *satisfied* your need with Galen less than an hour ago." She sighed softly as he began to knead her shoulders.

She had no idea, how could she not know what she did to him and to Galen? "I did. It was sexy and he's my mate. Touching is part of what shifters need. But you? What this is between you and me is something so deep it's in my bones. You rush through my veins, you make my heart beat. I never understood it. People told me. I watched my friends find mates and they all told me. I even felt a sliver of it when I became Grace's anchor. But to feel it? To have you inside me this way? It humbles me. It scares me. It calms and feeds me. You are something precious to me, in a way no one and nothing else can be."

She looked up, into his eyes. "I waited a long time for someone to see me the way Galen does. I never expected him. I never thought I'd be loved the way he does. I can't really do it justice, but meeting him, having a man like him love me is one of life's biggest blessings. And then you came around a corner and the world went upside down." She rested her head against his chest. "I don't know how it's possible that I'm here with you, when just five years ago I had no one. But whatever the reason, I'm glad. Now that you're here, I can't imagine life without you in it. I don't need for you to love me more than Galen. It's not a contest. I need for you to love me as much as you can."

He tipped her back so she fell on the mattress. "You have no idea. How can you not understand? You see so much, but not yourself?" He shook his head, unbuttoning her sweater only slow enough to keep from ripping it. The tiny bra with the bow perched jauntily between her breasts made him smile.

Her hand, the one that had been eagerly working to free his cock from his pants, suddenly stopped and moved to his chest where she shoved. Hard. "Wait. You're *anchored* to Grace?"

Oh, yeah.

"Yes. She's married to and mated with Cade Warden, one of

my closest friends. They have three kids together and if my suspicions are correct, another on the way. You'll meet her day after tomorrow when we go to dinner."

"Are you actually going to try to act casual right now? You should have told me." Her annoyance hit him, acrid and sticky.

"What else should I act like? Why are you mad? I anchored her before I knew you existed. You have another husband!"

She closed her eyes for a moment. "Get off me."

"Not until we settle this. Sweetheart, I'm here with you. I just told you how much you mean to me. This is silly. I've only known you a few days. This is the first we've ever been alone. When should I have told you?"

"Get off or I will knee your balls into your fucking throat." Anger coiled her muscles. His wolf stirred, agitated that she was upset, but undeniably attracted to a fully enraged, powerful female.

He rolled off to the side. "I can't believe this is happening. I tell you how much I love you, how much you mean to me and this is how you react?"

"You truly believe this reaction is to the very sweet things you said to me earlier? Really? I'm done now." She stood and straightened her sweater, buttoning up. It wasn't until she moved to leave the room that he realized done meant really done.

He jumped up, halting her progress to the front door. "You can't just walk away every time we get into a fight. You do this a lot I notice."

Her eyes narrowed, her hurt pricked him. Why didn't he learn from watching Grace and Cade fight? All his smart ways when it came to his job fell to the side when it came to handling this tiny woman.

"You notice? Really? Seriously, Jack, get the hell out of my way. I need to be not here with you right now. In your little shrine to Grace Warden. Christ, how did I not really notice?" She waved an arm around, indicating the pictures in the room. Two fell from shelves as the heat of her magic, the weight of her power throbbed in the room.

"Take it easy, Renee. You're going to blow the place up over something totally stupid. For fuck's sake! I'm with you. She's *married* with three kids. She's someone to me, yes. Special? Yes. But there's nothing more to it than that. You've got some nerve to judge me when you have another man in your bed."

She physically recoiled, her eyes widening. "Right. Yeah, I noticed you using that twice now. *You* came into my life, Jack. I told you the first moment you showed interest in me. I told you I was with someone. I told you I loved someone else. I never lied about my situation. I would never use this anchor bond thing to hurt you or her. But what? I can't ask a question? I can't feel anything about it when you hid it from me? I've got news for you, Jack. I don't regret loving Galen. You can never make it into a dirty thing. I won't allow it. You came to me. Over and over I might add. You came to me and Galen knowing what we were. You don't get to use that to hurt me or accuse me because I did nothing wrong.

"Had you bothered to share with me, I could have told you I have no problem with you loving other people before me. For goodness sake, why would I? That doesn't excuse the way you handled yourself just now. All defensive. It's unnecessary. I'm leaving now. I'll see you at dinner."

He didn't budge from his place blocking the door.

"You're right, I overreacted to your question. But it's not an excuse to go haring off on your own when someone may be out there trying to hurt you." He swallowed back panic at her leaving, annoyance with himself that he reacted the way he did to what he could see was a pretty mellow reaction on her part until he turned it into a fight. Still, the leaving thing didn't sit well. "I don't like it that you leave instead of stay to fight. Is what we have so fragile you can't test it with a disagreement?"

The blast of her anguish was enough to have him reaching for her. But she stepped away, her face flushed, eyes fever-bright. "I need to not be here with you right now. Period. If you don't like that I can't help it."

"This is ridiculous. Let's talk this through."

Her phone started ringing and she ignored it. She stood there so very still, her eyes focused on the floor. Her hands shook. Something wasn't right and he couldn't figure it out. He didn't know her well enough to understand if this was her way of dealing with upset or not. But it didn't fit.

He softened his tone, shifted his stance to seem less physically threatening. "Renee, please. Tell me. I'm sorry I reacted the way I did. We can't work it out if you're not here and you're not safe out there without me."

When she looked up, her mouth had hardened into a flat line. No emotion at all showed on her face and that hit him like a slap. "Fine. I'll sit here while you pack. Then you can drop me at home before you go to dinner."

This was worse than her anger, worse than her hurt. This was not his mate. She'd shut off, her emotions walled away even from the bond. He wasn't sure how she was doing it, but it was totally unacceptable.

"That's not going to happen. You're going to tell me what the hell is wrong and we're going to fix it."

Her phone rang again.

"For fuck's sake," she mumbled, pulling the phone out. "What?"

Galen demanded to know what was happening on the other end. Jack didn't even need shifter hearing for that.

"I've lost my appetite. I want to go to bed early. No, *not* like that. That's not going to be happening. *No.* I. Said. No. I'm not interested in a romantic dinner tonight. What? Why?"

Galen demanded to speak to Jack and he put his hand out, expecting her to put the phone into it. Instead she snorted and turned her back on him. "I'm going home. I'm not having this conversation with you. I don't *need* to explain myself." She snapped the phone shut and turned the ringer off.

He began to growl at her, but his own phone interrupted and he picked it up, grateful for Galen's backup in this, whatever it was going on between them.

"What the hell did you do?" Galen demanded without preamble.

"It's a long story. I'd be trying to fix it, but she won't talk to me about it. She's shut down now. Walled me out."

"What the fuck did you say, Jack? I'm going to kick your ass for this. I shouldn't have trusted you with her. She's not just any woman you're fucking you know. She's got wounds and buttons like anyone else."

"Why would you assume I would ever think of her like that?"

She took the phone from him. "Stop it! Oh my God, stop it! I'm not a bone to be argued over, nor am I to be talked about like I don't exist. I won't have you fighting like this."

Jack saw the cracks in the wall she'd built around her emotions, felt the strain she put into holding herself together. "I can't stand to see you like this." He took the phone back. "She's right, it's stupid to fight over her this way."

He didn't hear the door close.

Renee hit the sidewalk running, grateful she'd worn flats instead of the pretty high-heeled boots she'd nearly chosen instead. She was stupid to think she could ever make it work. She was a freak. Wrong. Weird. Men like Galen and Jack didn't need that. They had each other now. It assaulted her head, how wrong she was, how unnatural.

Her house was quiet when she burst inside. Even the way the banister gleamed from the lemon oil she'd used a few days before didn't please her.

Despite his clear belief that she was some kind of mental deficient, Renee locked the doors behind her. She wasn't unaware that there was someone out there focused on her in ways she couldn't understand.

She grabbed a bottle of scotch and headed for her workspace, locking the door behind her. She poured a shot while choosing some music.

Jack's voice changed every time he said Grace's name. It wasn't that he'd anchored her. It wasn't that he had loved people before her. The way he pretended to be so casual about something that clearly was *anything but* casual galled her most.

He hadn't told her before because Grace was something to him she couldn't be. Maybe he found Renee wanting. Maybe he regretted being mated to her. He'd been so lovely one moment and then things had gone to shit.

The little girl within shivered and a ragged sob escaped Renee's mouth, despite the fist clenched to hold it all in. Driven by the need to tuck away somewhere small, Renee gave in and took her blanket into the closet, settling in, letting the dark quiet calm her. Soothe the memories enough to keep them at bay.

The door downstairs opened. She heard two male voices, knew it was Galen and Jack.

"Renee!" Galen's bellow was sure to alert the entire street he was pissed. Great.

"Damn it, Renee, where are you?"

Steps coming closer. The wall fell apart and what was within consumed her, pulled her into the maelstrom of what had been once.

"I'm coming in there, now. You're worrying us, Renee." Galen blinked back the tears as a wave of terror and then pain swept through him. The hand on the knob of the door to her office space tightened, the metal groaning.

"Get in there. Something is wrong. Damn it." Jack kicked the door in, leaving the knob in Galen's hand.

Nothing. He looked around, dropping the doorknob on a nearby desk.

"She's not in the darkroom." Jack stormed back in.

Galen saw the closet door, knew she was in there. He indicated it with a tip of his chin and both of them moved to it.

"I'm opening the door. It's just me and Jack."

She was there, huddled in the far back, a blanket around her body. Ribbons of pain sliced at him the closer he got.

"Baby, what is it?" He spoke softly, but the tears thickened the sound. "Would you like to come out? Let us help you and then we'll leave you alone if that's what you really want. You can't be in this closet in the dark. That's not who you are."

"How do you know who I am?"

Her voice edged, honed and sharp with whatever drove her to this place.

"Is this why you run when we fight? Is this why you need to get away?" Galen coaxed the blanket back from her face. Her eyes weren't focused as she looked at something long past. It was like a scene from one of those horror movies she loved so much. A shiver of fear slid through his gut.

"I know you enough to know you're one of the strongest people alive. I know you enough to love you." Jack held a hand to her, but her eyes still focused on that far away thing.

Galen shoved the shoes out of his way and sat. "Okay then, we'll join you. No one needs to be alone in the dark when they're so beloved. By the way, there are seriously forty pairs of shoes in here. Is this your secret shoe stash?"

Jack shook his head when she didn't laugh or even roll her eyes.

"What led you here to this closet? Who did this to you?" Jack linked hands with her and she didn't pull away. She shook still, her skin clammy. His wolf wasn't pleased by the stink of her fear on the air, of the claustrophobic oppression of the small, cramped space.

Galen took her other hand and she whimpered. The sound ripped through him, the pain of it, the fear made him nauseous.

And then Jack stood somewhere else. The woman he recognized from The Willow Broom stood over a younger version of Renee. Those sweet curls were ruthlessly pulled back into a braid, her face was buried in her hands.

"I thought I told you to stop this. How are we supposed to have a normal life when you go acting weird again?"

"I'm sorry, Susan. I didn't mean to. It just happens sometimes."

"You've driven away everything kind enough to love you despite your freaky behavior. Your mother left you. Where's your father? He's not here. Left you with me. I'm all you've got, don't you forget it. The devil is in you; your mother poisoned you with what she was. You don't have to be that way."

Renee gasped for air. "No. Get out of my head."

Galen blinked, not trying to stop the tears.

She tried to pull her hands free from theirs, both men held fast.

"No. Renee, she's wrong." Jack's voice was choked with emotion. "You don't have to run from us. We're not going to leave you."

She groaned again and a wave hit, sucking them back into her memories.

A closet, roughly this size. She sat in the very back, her hands over her mouth. Her leg hurt, throbbed from a bruise on her thigh. Fiery welts peppered her calves. Blood ran from her palm where her nails had dug through the skin.

Somewhere outside, the sound of furniture being overturned. Yelling.

"How dare you embarrass me in front of my friends! Get out here and take your punishment."

The door slamming open, a hand in her hair, pulling her out into the light. She blinked up in time to see the fist headed toward her face and she opened up the rage, the rage she buried all the time. It boiled from her and Susan fell back, shock etched into her features.

"No. Don't touch me."

Susan snarled, her mouth twisted with dark emotion. "You broke a glass. They saw you. You weren't near it."

"You told them my mother abandoned me. She didn't. She wouldn't do that."

"She had to die to escape you. Your father works all the time. Anything to get away from you." She raised her hand and Renee stood on shaky legs.

"Never. You will never touch me again or I will break you too." She poked a tooth, now loose from how hard she'd been hit earlier once they'd gotten into the car and had driven away.

Susan knew she meant it.

"You'll kill everything you touch, Renee. Don't forget that. This is my house. Your father is with me. Don't push me or you'll end up in a home. All alone."

Something roared and Galen realized it was her. It was Renee shoving them both back, jumping over them to get out of the closet. Her eyes were no longer unfocused, though his were still blurry through tears.

Her chest heaved. She held her hands out to ward them off.

"Leave me alone, please. Please. I didn't mean to...that was my head, those are my memories. Mine." Bitterness, like ashes, bloomed through the link between the three.

"Your memories must have thought differently." Jack closed his eyes a moment and Galen knew how he felt. He wanted to storm out, to hunt Susan down and beat her until she wept like Renee had.

"I understand. I understand now why you need to leave when we fight." Galen didn't get up, not wanting to spook her. "I would never, ever reject you for being who you are. I love you. I love your magic. I love the way you are a total bitch until you've had coffee in the morning. I love the way you think I don't know you put protein powder in my smoothies."

"I know that." She exhaled hard. "I know that!"

"Why didn't you ever tell me?"

"Because I didn't want to see pity in your eyes. Like what I see now. I'm fine. She didn't know how to deal with my being different. She did the best she could. I wasn't easy to raise, you know."

Jack growled. "She's a bully, Renee. That's not about you, that's about her."

"I don't want to talk about it anymore. I feel sick."

Galen didn't know what to do other than to keep pushing, so he did. She had to understand they were with her for the long run; he had to get past the shit her stepmother poisoned her with. "Because you haven't eaten in hours. Because you've been upset for most of the day. Babe, come with us. Let us get you settled on the couch. Snuggle with Jack while I make some dinner."

"Please, please leave me alone."

She looked so lost, so terribly small standing there, her arms wrapped around herself, shaking. He felt as if something had been ripped from him. His cat paced, agitated, angry, needing to comfort and defend.

Jack fell to his knees before her, hanging his head. "I started this mess with my stupidity and selfishness. I didn't tell you and you got caught off guard and then when you asked for more info, I didn't really answer what you asked. I'm sorry. If I could take it back I would. But I can't. I can't and the damage has been done. You don't know how much I regret that."

She rubbed her face before sliding her fingers through Jack's hair. "You two are so much better off without me. You have each other now." Her voice was barely more than a whisper.

Galen stood. "Enough. This is total bullshit. Better off without you? So the last four years mean nothing to you? You think I've just been hanging out with you until a nice piece of ass came along to replace you? Is that how little you think of me?"

"No." She shook her head, taking her hand back from Jack's head. Jack spun, baring his teeth at Galen. Galen bared his right back.

"There's something wrong with me. Can't you see that? Your family can see it, Galen, why can't you?"

"So Beth doesn't like you. She doesn't like anyone. My parents love you. My brothers love you. I love you. Doesn't that count for anything?"

"I'm holding you back. I can't give you purebred children. I can't help you be the next leader of the jamboree. I'll never make the kind of money you do."

He grabbed her by the upper arms. This had to stop. She

was spiraling out of control, this vomiting of her memories had taken her into a dark place and she couldn't seem to get out. He worked very hard not to panic, but she was seriously scaring him. This wasn't her. She was not the kind of person who gave in to self-pity or bad thoughts, not like this.

"I've never seen you this way, babe. Come on now. Come back to me." He rubbed his face along her jawline, willing her to open back up to him.

"What's that?" Jack stood. "Do you hear that? Someone is pounding on the door downstairs."

Without waiting for permission, Galen gathered her into his arms and carried her out of her office and into the living room. "Sit here. Jack and I will be back. Don't let anyone in unless it's us."

She'd slipped away again, her eyes focused on something he couldn't see.

"I hope it's that bitch Susan or the asshole scaring her. I could use a really bloody fight right about now," Jack grumbled as they headed down to the outer door.

When they opened it, an older woman with striking features stood, her mouth in a hard line. Beside her stood a younger woman, perhaps two years older than Renee. She looked a lot like… *Holy shit.*

"Where is she?" the older woman asked.

"Who?" Galen demanded.

"Where is Renee? I know she lives here. I know there's something wrong with her. Someone is trying to harm her. *Where is she?*"

"Who the fuck are you and how do you know my wife?" Galen and Jack stood shoulder to shoulder.

"I'm her aunt, Rosemary. And this is Kendra, Renee's older sister. We're here to help. Please."

Renee's what? What the hell was up with the world all the

sudden?

"How do you know she lives here? Where have you been her whole life?" Jack wasn't budging.

"Our absence from her life was not my choice. My sister brought Kendra to me when she was just a baby. We knew about Renee, but she disappeared shortly after her mother was killed. Our family has been looking for her ever since. Someone is trying to harm her right now. Are you just going to stand there and let him burn her mind out?"

"I will rip out your throat without hesitation if you make one move to hurt her." Galen stood back to let them both enter. Jack stood aside, ready to move if or when he needed to.

Rosemary rushed up the stairs, Galen in the lead with the keys.

When he opened the door, it was to find Renee standing, her palms against the window panes, staring out into the night.

"Get her away from that window." Rosemary turned away and with Kendra, began to clear a space, pushing the couches back. Jack moved to help.

"Renee, honey? Visitors are here. For you. You're going to be so surprised." Galen edged closer, scenting the copper of her blood. Her palms bled, smearing the red against the glass.

"Get out of me," she whispered. "You can't have me. You can't have them!" she screamed and fell but he was fast enough to catch her.

"Can't have you?" Galen was very close to changing—his cat sliced him up to get out, wanting to defend her from any threat. But his cat couldn't help whatever the fuck was wrong with her.

"She means the mage who's wormed into her head. Put her here."

Renee looked, her eyes glassy, to the woman who'd just spoken. "Momma? Is that you? Have you come for me?"

143

Watching the scene continue to unfold filled Jack with so much bile and fear, so much adrenaline, he shook with it. He was losing her, he felt it deep inside and helpless rage rode him, turned his vision red with the need to fix his mate.

Renee was covered in blood as Galen attempted to get her back to the rest of the group. Their living room was a mess, the contents upended and shoved against the walls to make space for a ritual of some sort.

Jack wasn't even sure what to do, where to stand, much less what the hell was going on. He was entirely out of his element and it drove him to the depths of despair. He could rip a throat out, investigate someone, protect her from a physical threat but this? How could anyone stop this evil?

"Your guilt will not help her. Or you. Let it go." Rosemary, the oldest woman, the powerful witch who'd started drawing symbols with colored sand on their hardwoods, spoke to him without looking up. "Use your link to her. Bring her back. Don't let him win. He'll ruin her, ravage her and leave her a shell."

"Who and what is trying to hurt her?" Galen put her down where Rosemary had indicated and Jack reached out to touch her, needing the physical contact to better use their link, but also because he needed to feel her, know she was alive.

"Get her sweater and jeans off, she'll respond better skin to skin," Kendra said.

Jack made quick work while Galen took his own shirt off.

Continuing to work, Rosemary spoke, "She's got so much power pouring off her, she's made herself a target. The target of a man who steals magic instead of earning it. He's inside her now."

One handed, Jack tore his shirt off and pressed to her back as Galen did her front. They embraced around her, a solid unit. She was his and Galen's; no one else was going to take her and harm her if he could help it. "Come on, Renee, come back to us. Fight this bastard who's hurting you. You can't just leave, not when I've finally found you. If you go, I'll eat sweet rolls every day, no more fruit. I'll get scurvy."

Galen kissed the top of her head. "Babe, who will make my heart beat if not you?"

Galen and Jack shared a look. The man who did this to her had better get a good head start. They would hunt down and kill every fucking person involved in this if she didn't survive it. He might just do that anyway. *Yes, yes that sounded like a very good idea.*

Her head rested on Galen's shoulder, her skin was super heated, even to a shifter like him. This possession was like a fever.

Around them, the two women began to speak softly and slowly as they came to bracket Renee's sides so she was surrounded.

"Renee, I'm your Aunt Rosemary. I came a long way to find you. Your magic is very strong, so strong it called to me and finally led me here. I'd nearly given up hope. There's darker magicks at work here. Someone has found a way inside you, he's trying to hurt you and steal your life so he can have more. Fight him. I know you can hear me. Your sister is here too. She and I are here to help you."

"Renee, I'm Kendra, your big sister. I need you to build a wall inside. Can you do that? Go inside where he's leaking in and wall him out. You can do it. I know you can. Brick by brick, higher and higher. Just concentrate on that, we'll push him back too. Hold on to yourself, find that place you're connected to these men and open that. Close out the darkness and open yourself to their light. It's the only way."

Jack felt it, a trickle back through their bond. At first it started only to die off again, but then, she'd hold it for a little bit longer each time until she gasped, her head shooting back to his shoulder as it flooded through them again, that link between the three filled with the glory of their connection, of their bond. Brilliant and strong, it filled him like birdsong after a really long night.

She screamed, writhing, and then slumped against Galen, weeping.

"He's gone. His spell has been broken," Rosemary spoke. Jack had nearly forgotten she was there.

"I'm going to be sick." Renee stood and tried to run to the bathroom but her legs wouldn't hold her. Jack picked her up and carried her, but acquiesced once they got there, allowing her to push him out and shut the door in his face.

Her aunt stood with them, just outside the door to the bathroom. "She'll be filled with dark magicks, negative energy. It'll have made her sick. She's safe for now. Kendra and I are going to go and cast some protection around the outside of the house. I don't think he's been here. Something like this would have taken a few hours to feel the full effects of. You can tell me about your day when we come back inside." With that, she swooped from the room, Kendra in her wake, leaving Galen and Jack behind.

Chapter Ten

Renee opened her eyes, feeling like she'd been hit by a truck. Daylight filtered through the drawn curtains. The memories came back slowly, filling her with mixed emotions.

"Hey, there you are," Jack said, coming into her line of vision. Just seeing him, knowing he was there even after all he'd seen the night before, made her feel better. His smile was soft, worry clear around the edges. "How are you feeling?"

She didn't say anything, just held her arms open. He softened and got into the bed with her, holding her close. His scent comforted her, the way he felt, hard and strong, made her feel safe.

Words weren't where she thought they'd be. Instead, she took his hand and guided it to her pussy. She needed him, needed that connection, to lose herself in pleasure and know she was still in his heart the way he was in hers.

He groaned, moving his hand to her belly. "Oh, sweetheart, you've been through so much. Why don't you rest? We have time for this. Lots and lots of time."

"You don't want me?" Her voice sounded rusty and rarely used. She wouldn't blame him if he wanted to be free of her. The things she remembered from the night before made her want to weep. But she found herself unable. That well was dry.

The blue of his eyes deepened as he moved even closer. "How can you think that? I want you so much my hands shake sometimes. Last night we nearly lost you. I can't think about it too long or it makes me want to kill someone. You're healing. It can wait. I'll be right here when you're ready."

She turned to her side, curling into a ball. Right at that very moment, part of her wished the whole last week just hadn't happened. Everything inside felt jumbled, out of order and she couldn't quite grasp the context enough to put everything back.

"You're running again. I understand why. But don't. Don't run from me. There's no reason to." He rolled to curl around her, but she turned to him, burying her face in his neck, breathing him, needing him so much her head hurt with it.

He made a sound, trapping it deep in his chest, a sort of growl laded with so much emotion it tore into her gut. She gave over to that, to the feeling of being with him, of needing him. The rest would come later.

For then...

She got to her knees above him. His eyes locked with hers. His hands on her were gentle, but he didn't stop her from pushing his shirt over his head. Such a beautiful body. Tawny skin, wide shoulders, slim waist.

Kissing over his collarbone, she scooted down and licked over his nipples as she pushed his sweats down, exposing more of that honey dipped skin and a bare, hard cock.

Straddling his lap, she pulled her long T-shirt off before tossing the panties to the side. He slid his palms up her sides, caressing the underside of her breasts with his thumbs when he got there.

"Are you sure?" he asked.

No need for foreplay between them. She rose on her knees, angling him and sinking on his cock, not slow, not gentle. He arched as he freed that sound. The growl trickled from his mouth and wrapped around her. This is what she needed, it was what she needed before they got into that stupid fight the night before.

Each time she rose and then fell, she fell back into herself a bit more, took back control of herself, of her future. She claimed herself again, to rise and fall on her own mistakes and flaws. The bastard who'd gotten into her head the night before would never do so again.

"So beautiful. Strong." Jack arched into her, his hands all over her body, everywhere he could reach. His fingertip danced over her clit as she rolled her hips, undulating, grinding herself into him to get him as deep as she could.

She traced the outline of the mark Galen had made on Jack's side and he shuddered beneath her. What a gorgeous man he was. And his eyes held only her, even as her lids dropped as orgasm approached.

Bracing her weight by holding on to his biceps, she leaned her upper body forward so she could press back against him. Waves of sensation moved through her each time, wider and wider until she was pulled beneath willingly.

With a ragged moan of her name, he thrust up as she thrust back, coming deep inside her body.

He held her as she slumped forward onto his chest, his hands sliding over her back as she caught her breath.

"I'm sure," she managed to say, prompting him to laughter.

"Damn if I don't love you more every single second. I thought I was going to lose you last night." His hands never left her, as if he couldn't bear not touching her. And that was all right with her.

She pulled free and slipped into the space next to him. "I'm sorry about all that."

"Sorry for what?" He made slow circles up her spine.

"All the drama. You must regret this whole thing. I'm sure Grace and the other women you know aren't in need of saving all the time."

He tipped her chin, capturing her gaze. A grin made him look even sexier. "You and I need to revisit the whole Grace conversation later. Grace is married to one of my best friends. I don't want her, I want you. As for regret? Don't ever say that. I started that fight by being stubborn and stupid. What you did to fight for yourself, I've never seen anyone braver. You came back. You didn't let him win. And now I'm going to spend the rest of our lives proving to you how much I love you."

She blinked back tears and then sat up. "Holy crapdoodle! Did I hallucinate an aunt and a sister?"

"You didn't. They went back to their hotel after we got you to sleep. We invited them to stay here but they didn't want to impose even though we both assured them you'd want them here. Your aunt didn't tell us a lot, she said she wanted to tell it to you first. But she says she's been looking for you since before your mother died."

She swallowed the lump in her throat. "You know, I distinctly do not remember getting any fortune cookie saying my entire life would change totally this week. If there was a memo, I so did not get it. Where's Galen?"

"He went to get some food. I volunteered to stay here with you while he was gone. Not like it's a chore to watch you sleep. However, just for future reference, this sort of wake up is better than the one where you slapped my hands when I tried to touch your nipples."

She sent him a mock frown. "I'd been awake a little while. I needed you. I felt, well I didn't feel anything. I felt a lot of stuff, but nothing I could hold onto. I needed you to touch me, to fill me, to help me come back to myself. But don't get used to it, I don't think this will make me a morning person."

"Do you think it might make you a non Bee Gees person?"

She rolled her eyes. "I need to shower. I also need food and some coffee."

"Go on and grab a shower. I need to talk to the people who're supposed to help me move today. Cancel and reschedule."

She got out of bed, feeling distinctly bruised and battered. "Ugh, I hurt in places I didn't know I could hurt. By the by, you're not going to do that. Why would you? Unless you don't want to move in."

He got up, moving to her, and she got caught in the spell of how he looked just then—muscular, sexed up and totally naked.

"You have no tan lines," she said, gobbling up the sight of him. Maybe she'd need some assistance with back scrubbing. She looked at him through her lashes. She was sore, but she wasn't dead and *hoooo boy* did he look pretty all naked and golden there in her bedroom. It would be downright un-American not to take advantage of such an opportunity.

The door opened and closed, followed by the sound of Galen's footfalls into the kitchen.

"Of course I want to move in. But you need rest and quiet. Stop looking at me like that, you're playing with fire."

She laughed, kissing his chest and stepping back. "Okay, fine. I'll stop objectifying you. For now. I'm going to shower and get dressed. When will the moving peeps arrive?"

Galen opened the door carefully and then when he saw she was awake, moved to her quickly, pulling her tight to his body. "Babe, you scared the life out of me. Never do that again, got me?"

She hugged him back. "I'll keep that in mind."

"You're naked and soft and warm." He looked her over, his eyes changing, deepening in color and intensity. "And you smell like sex." He breathed in deep and she shivered.

"I am. You should take advantage of that."

He laughed. "Tempting, but we will shortly be invaded.

151

Take your shower. I brought back a huge amount of food and coffee is making. Your aunt and sister are coming over in a few and, Jack, I saw someone in a truck looking for a place to park. Dude looked wolfy."

Renee shrugged. "Guess that solves the issue of whether to call them or not. Okay, I'm going to shower. Be out shortly."

The shower was just what she needed. Time alone to rinse the night before from her skin. She felt violated, dirty and wrong inside and though it had improved some, the sense of invasion hung about her brain.

On top of that insanity, she suddenly had relatives to contend with. An aunt? A *sister*? How could she have a sister? Why hadn't her father told her? Why hadn't her mother told her? Why now after all this time? Who were they and what did they want?

She pushed back, trying to remember her life before Boston. What had her life been? She couldn't remember a single teacher, neighbor or friend. She'd been seven when her mother died, those were memories she should have been able to recall.

Trying to push too hard made her nauseated so she gave up for the time being. She needed to hold it together and get some answers.

She sighed, taking one last look in the mirror. She looked okay for someone who might have died the night before. At least Jack's friends wouldn't think she was a junkie or something.

The weather had turned cold, fall finally taking a solid grip on the weather, so she pulled on a sweater and jeans. The loft was always cold anyway, for Galen's and now she supposed Jack's comfort. But she drew the line at the point where she saw her breath.

When she emerged from the bedroom, the house was full of people she didn't know. Normally this would not be such a big deal, but wow, right then it made her want to run away.

Galen looked toward the bedroom door and stalked over, with eyes only for her. He wrapped his arms around her, burying his face in her hair. "Sorry, I had a moment when you came through the door...I remembered your face, the feeling of loneliness."

She hugged him right back. Needing that contact. "I wouldn't have made it back without you. But I'm back. I'm fine and he won't catch me unaware again."

"I'm going to kill him."

Renee didn't know how to reply to that.

"*Querida*, are you sure you want to do this today? Why not go back to bed? When Rosemary and Kendra arrive, I'll send them in."

She tipped her head back to look at him. They locked gazes, neither speaking but both understanding. "I'm fine. Really. Can I ask you a question?"

He smiled. "Always. Your tits look awesome, as does your ass."

She laughed, kissing him again for the simple pleasure of the moment. "Good to know. But the question is about Rosemary and Kendra. What do you think? Are they here for me or for money or what?"

"I didn't smell any lies on them. We're checking into their background, just to be sure. They seem to be the real deal. But I think we should be cautious until we know more. I know you're excited about having a sister, but I'll be damned if anyone else hurts you on my watch."

"I trust your nose and we'll wait and see. Who are all these people?" She looked around his body at all the faces.

"Jack's people. He ran downstairs for a moment, he'll be right back."

"Good thing I got out of bed then." She laughed, letting his presence comfort her.

He took her hand, kissing her fingertips. "I love it when you do that."

"Do what? Get all tingly cause you're putting the moves on me?"

He laughed, taking the tingles to a whole new level. "Well that too. I mean using the link, letting it help you. You used to hesitate."

"I know. I'm working on it. I believe in it, I trust it. But sometimes it's hard. I'm sorry if that hurts you."

"It's your way." He shrugged. "And before last night I understood and respected it. Now I understand a lot more."

"I can't talk about that right now." She scrubbed her hands down the front of her jeans, feeling dirty again.

"Whenever you're ready, I'll be here. Or if you want to talk to someone else, that's fine too. We'll get you whatever you need." He kissed the top of her head. "You sure you don't want to go back and lay down?"

"These people are important to Jack, so they're important to me too." Wow, wolves were a lot louder than cats. So much laughter and talking and they were all *huge*.

"Get something to eat. I put a plate for you in the oven." Galen took her hand and led her into the kitchen. She poured herself some coffee and looked around at her living room.

Galen put the plate on the counter and she smiled gratefully. "You went to the Mercado?" Her favorites heaped on the plate. Beans, fresh tortillas and eggs scrambled with chorizo and potatoes.

"Of course I did. Now eat."

Jack walked through the door, holding some boxes. He grinned at a group of men, tossing them the boxes. "Let's get this show on the road." She liked the way they responded to him, liked knowing he had people who loved him in his life.

He turned. "Hey, there you are."

She smiled and waved.

"Everyone, this is Renee." He moved to her side, hugging her. "Good to see you eating, sweetheart," he murmured briefly. "Grace and Cade couldn't be here this morning. They send their apologies and say they'll see us tomorrow night." He introduced her to the others, who all treated her with genuine friendliness.

Still, she was relieved when they all began to leave to get the move done.

"I'll see you both in a little while." She tiptoed up and kissed Jack and turned to Galen who shook his head at her. "What?"

Jack sighed. "He's not going anywhere. You think we'd leave you alone? After what happened last night?"

"Fine. Then I'll come too. I can help."

Galen shook his head. "Babe, he's got a dozen giant werewolves to help him with that. Your aunt and sister should be here shortly anyway."

"I hate being managed."

"I know. We'll be back in a bit." Jack kissed her quickly and headed out, ignoring the wrath of her frown.

"We're protecting you. Get that look off your face." Galen took her plate to the table and pulled the chair out for good measure. "Sit your pretty behind down and finish eating."

She would have glowered but, but, but chorizo. How could a woman resist handmade tortillas and chorizo in eggs? She was only human after all. She even liked that he pulled her chair out, not that he'd be able to get around her all the time by being all cute and stuff.

"Why didn't you ever tell me about what Susan did to you? Does your father know?" Galen sat as close to her as he could and still allow her to eat. She knew he needed the contact, she did too.

155

"Everyone has a bad childhood, Galen."

"Bullshit. I didn't. It's more than that and you know it. She *abused* you, mentally and physically. Does your father know?" The wash of his anger rolled over her, strangely comforting.

"He was gone a lot when I was growing up. She didn't have to marry a man with a kid. It was a huge job for her when she took me on. I wasn't easy to deal with. She didn't know how to process the magic stuff. She was trying to help in her own way." Mechanically, she kept eating, but it fell to her stomach like a rock.

"Why are you making excuses for her? She hurt you! It makes me want to rip her throat out. How can you be so calm?"

She stood, knocking her chair to the floor. "It's either that or let it hurt me more! Do you think I wanted that? I tried. I *tried so hard* to be what she wanted. Nothing I did was enough. I can either move on, or I can obsess about something I can't change. To what end?"

He stood, hugging her. "I'm sorry. I can still hear your sobs. Every time I close my eyes I see that closet. It tears me apart to know you endured that. To know I've had dinner with those people after all they did to you."

"This is why I didn't tell you. I don't want to burden you with this stuff. It's over. Past. You're my now, my future, my everything."

"And yet, you were in that closet last night, hiding. Do I scare you like that? Does Jack?"

She cupped his cheeks. "No. It was just, I don't know. I was upset. It was stupid. I just...old habit I guess."

The doorbell rang. "That'll be your aunt and sister. I'm staying in the room. We don't know these people, Renee."

No shit. She nodded, agreeing.

"Max is running a background check today. Until we know more, I think we should keep our guard up."

"Galen?" she called out as he neared the hallway.

He turned.

"I love you. You make me feel safe. Last night had nothing to do with you at all." She wanted to say it though she hoped he knew it anyway.

The smile he gave her smoothed away his frown lines and made her all warm again. "I love you too. And we're going to get naked and sweaty this afternoon when everyone is gone."

"I'm going to hold you to that."

She blinked, feeling caught between memory and the present, when her aunt came through the door. "You look just like her." Wonder warred with nervousness.

Her aunt laughed, rushing forward with open arms. Galen sprang into action, ready to knock the woman away if she proved to be a threat. It was sweet really, but unnecessary. This woman was part of her. Even if she hadn't shared any rescmblance with Renee's mother, she'd have known they were connected. She didn't know how or why, but she knew it just the same.

"I can't believe we finally found you. I'm Rosemary, your mom's older sister." She took the hand of the woman standing behind her, pulling her forward. "This is your older sister, Kendra."

Renee didn't know what to do. She couldn't stop staring. Tears burned her throat, anger churned in her gut, confusion ruling everywhere else.

"Look at you. It's been decades since I've seen you, and even then it was when you were a baby and a toddler. And yet, I've known you all your life." Kendra hugged Renee, who gave over to tears. She wanted it to be true so much she didn't trust her feelings. The chaos of the last week had knocked her off balance in a way she hadn't experienced in a very long time.

Lauren Dane

In the background, Galen's phone rang, "Imperial March" from Star Wars. His brother's ringtone.

"Please, come and sit down. Would you like some coffee? A smoothie? I got some blueberries at the farmer's market a few days ago." She moved from foot to foot.

"Please, it's okay. We're here to see you. We've wanted to so long. You look better, I'm glad you got some rest," Rosemary said, patting her arm and leading her toward the seating area.

"I'll bring you all some juice and a carafe of coffee," Galen called out.

"He's not hard to look at. How long have you two been together?" Kendra asked.

"Four years. He's the only person in my life who has always been there when I needed him. So you must understand this isn't personal, I am beyond excited to know I have other family out in the world. A sister. Oh my God." She took a deep breath. "I need to know why now? Why are you here now?" She twisted her fingers together. "I'm sorry. I know it sounds rude, I guess it is rude. But my mother's been dead twenty years now. My father told me he tried to contact her family when she died but none of them cared to have contact. He certainly never told me I had a sister."

Galen put a tray on the table between the couches and poured her a glass of juice she'd made just yesterday. *Yesterday* when she thought she was overwhelmed. Before someone tried to steal her mind and before her aunt showed up out of the blue.

Rosemary frowned, bristling with anger. "I can't speak to what your father said or did, but I can tell you what it is from my perspective. Your mother came to me thirty years ago. She had a baby, she was scared, worried for its safety. She begged me to keep her and raise her. Kendra was a week old. I tried to get your mom to stay, to call the police, to hone her magic enough to protect herself, but she was convinced the best thing

158

to do was run. So she did."

Renee crossed her arms across her stomach, nauseated. "Why?" She turned to Kendra. "Do we share the same father? Does he know?"

Rosemary answered, "Your mom met your dad when she was young. Away from home at school. She...she was sheltered in a way the rest of us weren't. She was sick a lot as a kid, so my parents were overprotective."

Despite her best efforts, Renee's foot started to bounce, a nervous tic. "I remember her. I was seven. I remember her voice. I remember the way it felt when she brushed my hair and when she whispered to me to keep my gifts secret. I remember she didn't come home and the police came to the door. Yesterday I remembered her death as something accidental. That's not true, is it?" Galen pressed the juice into her grasp and she drank it, needing something to do with her hands and taking the comfort he offered. Her aunt and sister had some coffee and began to nibble on some coffee cake Renee couldn't remember making.

"Yes. Or, no, she didn't die from an accident. She was killed in a mall shooting. Or that's the official report. Yes, he's my father too and yes he knew." Kendra's voice was small, filled with the emotion of a girl who'd been forgotten or ignored. Empathy poured from Renee; she knew what that was too.

A chill passed over her heart. Galen put an arm around her, kissing her temple.

"You say it like you don't believe it was what happened. Why?"

"I don't know what happened. Just what the report says. I have my own reasons for doubting much of what I've been told by your father and others." Rosemary crossed her arms over her chest, closing her body language.

Kendra reached out and squeezed Renee's hand. "We can

talk about all that later. We're not here to make you mad at your, um, our father."

Renee shook her head. "I don't understand! He knew? He knew she tossed you away and came back to have me? He never said anything? Never wondered where you were? Never told me? Why would he do that? Why can't I remember everything?"

"I don't like your father, but I don't know the whys and I don't want to put you in the middle. We just want to know you." Rosemary heaved a sigh. "We saw part of your memories last night, Renee."

"As for Susan, okay then, so you know it wasn't a picnic, being her stepdaughter. But I turned out just fine. She did the best she could. But my father is another story. Why would he abandon a child?"

"More than the horrible treatment by your stepmother, I saw places in your memory that were smooth as glass. Memory is like landscape, it's rarely flat. Something or more likely, someone, did that to you. I don't know what. I may know someone who'd have more answers though. I called and left a message. As for your mother leaving Kendra? She never told me what the story was. I asked her, many times, but she would get agitated, fearful, if I pressed too hard. The important thing was that she'd brought Kendra to me where she'd be safe. I figured he had threatened her or the baby and she ran. I didn't know she'd gone back to him for three years. When she had you, I got an announcement in the mail. She called from time to time, came to visit once a year but was always nervous."

"And when I was ten, she never came again. No calls, no letters." Kendra's lips trembled.

None of this made sense, damn it.

"Finally, frantic with worry, I called the house and he, your father, answered. I'd met him a few times. He made it clear he didn't think I was a good influence on your mother. Anyway, he hung up on me. But I knew something was wrong. Kendra's birthday had passed with no contact."

Renee noticed Kendra had some of the same physical tics she did. The finger twisting, the one shoulder shrug. Odd and comforting all at once. "Each birthday she sent me a new spell. We'd work on it when she came to visit in the spring. She didn't even call."

"My brother, your uncle Bill, he finally called the police station in Goleta and got the news that Karen had been murdered. Bill called Andrew back, thinking perhaps your dad would talk to him, but your dad refused to let us see you or to come to the funeral. We showed up anyway, I left Kendra with my mother because we didn't know what would happen and it was obvious your father didn't know about her. He had us thrown out."

Grandparents? Uncles?

"We got an attorney to work through the proper channels so that we could visit with you. And then you disappeared. He was supposed to go to a hearing and he never showed. His attorneys protected him at first, and then I think he ran from them too. We never stopped looking. Is he here? In Boston?"

"I have an uncle? Grandparents? I don't understand. Why would he do this? Why would he keep me from you?" It felt as if they all spoke another language. Nothing they said made any fucking sense.

"I have no idea other than his dislike. There were signs, with your mother I mean, that he hurt her, controlled her. But she never said so for sure."

Renee put her face in her hands, hunched over, reeling. What the fuck? Her father wasn't the most affectionate man ever, but he loved her. He'd married Susan to give Renee a mother figure. He'd tried. They'd moved all the way from...where? She pressed her fingertips into her temples. Memories slipped from her grasp as she tried to keep things straight.

Galen leaned down, putting his arms around her. "Babe, you don't have to solve all this now. We'll take it one step at a time. Max says Rosemary Kellogg is legit. She's lived in a far suburb of Nashville for thirty-five years. Your sister has been married and divorced. Her last name has never been Parcell. She's a—"

Kendra interrupted. "I can tell you all this if you just ask. Your name wasn't Parcell either. Not until you came to Boston. Your real last name is Langley. Our father's real name is Christopher Langley. Our mother's name was Karen, not Cindy."

"I won't apologize for making every effort I can to protect my wife." Galen looked so fierce just then she found it comforting and stupidly sexy too.

Letting the details she'd been given sink in, she bit into her bottom lip. The story got worse and worse. She needed to hear the rest, but she was afraid of what would come next.

"Okay then, Kendra, what else?" she asked, knowing Galen would correct any lies or omissions.

"I'm a third grade teacher. I was married for three years to a man who could not deal with who I am. As far as you and I go, I've wanted to know you my whole life. Mom used to let me hold you. We played together some when you were five and six. I used to write you these long letters, but we never knew where you were to send them. You have an entire family who's missed you every day for the last two decades. More than that, since you were born."

She scrubbed her hands through her hair, knowing she sent curls all over the place.

"I know this is a whole lot to take in at once and please believe me when I tell you we didn't want our introduction to you to be this way. At the same time, thank the heavens we were here to help last night. Will you let me check you over for any lasting effects? The magic he used on you is dirty, we want to be sure you're all clear of it," Rosemary said.

Renee didn't know why she trusted them, she just did. Maybe she missed her mother so much she lost touch with her common sense, but she had no fear of these two women. "All right."

Galen hovered, watching every move Rosemary made. Renee had been through enough and he'd do everything in his power to make sure no one ever hurt her again. He didn't smell lies on either woman, but his gut told him they were telling the truth anyway. What Max had uncovered said the same thing. Still, Galen had been practicing law long enough to see people flat out lie even when they look like they're telling the truth on every level.

However, if they made one move to hurt her in any way, he'd kill them both and no one would ever find the bodies. He'd had enough of this threat to her.

He watched Rosemary work, saw the way her magic fit with Renee's. There was simply no doubt in his mind that these women were who they claimed to be. He hadn't mentioned it to her yet, but Max was looking into Renee's father and any record of their past as a family before they moved to Boston.

That was the key. Why did Andrew Parcell stop any of his dead wife's relatives from seeing Renee when they'd wanted to so badly? Why had Kendra been turned over but not Renee? After living through the memories she'd nearly drowned in the night before, he had no positive feelings for either Parcell. Langley? The sheer amount of lies piling on top of lies lay heavily on his heart. This would hurt Renee and he couldn't protect her from that sort of heartbreak. She had to know the truth, but he knew quite plainly that the truth would harm her.

"You're fine. He's gone and there's no trace of his presence. We went through the neighborhood and around your yard." Kendra held up a drawstring bag of some sort. "We found some evidence that barter magic had been used. We cleared the spots and laid some warding around the perimeter. You really should have done that when you moved in."

An ache sliced through their link. Loss. Confusion.

"I-I don't know how."

"Renee was raised to believe her magic was unnatural and wrong. No one ever taught her anything but shame." Galen said it around his cat, who was far less patient than the man when it came to their woman.

"That's not fair. He didn't know what to do with me." Renee's hands went into action again, flying up in her defense. But it was half-hearted at best. She knew there was something very wrong going on.

He leaned over to kiss her. "It may not be fair, but it's true. He didn't do enough for you, Renee. We don't know the whys just yet, but the facts are the facts."

She sighed heavily.

"You never..." Rosemary's sentence broke off as she shook her head. "All right then. That's all right. You can learn. If you'll allow it, Kendra and I would love to teach you, train you to use your gifts. It would be my honor if you'd allow it. Your mother had a gift with green things and healing. She used to make teas and jams and all sorts of things for every imaginable ailment or situation." Rosemary smiled. "Are you perhaps a nurse or something like that?"

"I run a smoothie and coffee cart. I rent space from Susan, my stepmother."

Galen wasn't going to allow her to hide her light under a bushel. "And you make tea for people all the time too. You have all these custom teas and smoothies. You know when people are coming down with something." Galen liked this. He'd always known she was a nurturing person, but hearing this made it clear to her too, hopefully.

A bunch of noise sounded from the street. "Jack and his friends have arrived I think." Renee stood. "I need to put together a meal."

"Can we help?" Kendra asked.

Renee nodded and the ache in Galen's heart eased a little as he saw the way the sisters leaned their heads together as they worked and spoke in the kitchen.

"Looks like they're getting along well," Jack said as he finished installing the hardware to hang a large, framed photograph on the wall in the outer hall. They'd gotten everything moved in and the others had left. He and Galen had given the women some space to get to know each other better, but both of them never let her out of earshot.

Galen nodded, looking around the corner at the women and then back to where they'd been working. "We've been meaning to decorate this area out here and we got as far as paint and that's about it. And yes. They came along when she needed them most."

Jack liked how each bit of his they added to the space made him feel more at home. Clothes would need to be dealt with, but Renee had taken that over as she and her relatives had efficiently handled everything.

He lowered his voice, assured Galen would hear and insuring that Renee wouldn't. "To be honest, I think some of my friends weren't sure if they'd like her or not. By the time the last one left I heard nothing but positive things about her. She's recovering from last night and having her aunt and sister here are all to the good as far as I'm concerned. At least she's here and sort of resting. If not, I have the feeling she'd want to be out and about, getting into trouble. Now, what are we going to do about the father and stepmother?"

"If we could just kill them and eat them, things would be

way easier all around. Kidding. Sort of. She'll want to hear his side of this situation. She loves him. I wasn't surprised by the memories of Susan, but I have to admit I hadn't really thought Andrew capable of any of this. He's distracted and doesn't stand up for Renee like he should, but all this other stuff puzzles me. His name isn't Parcell. Not the one he was born with anyway. My brother can't find any records of his existence before they moved here to Boston. He's running checks with the new name now."

Jack put the hammer back in the toolbox. "Why doesn't Renee remember that? She was seven when her mother died. And they said murder! Had Renee ever mentioned that? Name changing or that her mother was murdered? I'd just gotten the impression it was a car accident or something."

"Earlier today Rosemary said she believes Renee's memory has been altered. She's got a friend looking into it." Galen reached out and slid a palm up Jack's neck, his eyes half closed for a moment before he leaned in and kissed Jack's lips.

Slow and sexy, Jack let himself fall into that kiss, taking Galen's kiss into his body, letting the simmer of their attraction heat into something more urgent.

"Sorry. I couldn't resist." Galen broke the kiss and stepped back with a sexy, smug look.

"Don't. Don't resist. If we didn't have company I'd have your pants open and your cock out."

They touched foreheads a moment, letting that intimacy between them settle before resuming their work. Jack wasn't just moving into their house, not just into a relationship with Renee, but with Galen too.

"I like the way you taste, Jack." Galen winked as he held the shelf in place for Jack to screw to the wall. "Back to the memory thing a second. Here's why I find myself having a hard time with this. Renee seems flighty on the outside, but she's amazingly detail oriented. She remembers the tiniest of things.

Just a head's up, she will kick your ass in an argument if you change your story." Galen laughed.

"Sometimes severe abuse can cause memory issues. If that's the case, well, we'll have to take care of it." Jack locked his jaw against the rest of what he wanted to say. She didn't need the stress of his upset, but her abuse made him want to kill. When he met Galen's gaze again, he knew he wasn't the only one.

Galen liked the fierce look on Jack's face, a look they shared there on the landing. The night before they'd both been scared to death, but they'd stuck together and they'd survived it. Not the ideal or usual way to start a relationship, but they were all far from usual anyway. Jack would die to protect Renee, that was the most important thing.

Galen and Jack puttered around, fixing things, putting things away, listening to music and falling into their new lives together. Sometime after ten, Rosemary and Kendra left with hugs and promises to meet the following day.

Her energy was good, her color better and best of all, the sparkle was back in her eyes. She was happy. Galen felt it through their link and saw it in her movements. She deserved it.

He pulled her into his arms, kissing her soundly.

"You taste like Jack." She licked her lips with a smile and then turned to Jack. "Come here and let me see if you taste like him."

Jack's heat met hers, and Galen held his place, putting an arm around Jack as he leaned in to kiss Renee. She arched, her nails digging into Galen's side as she broke off with a sigh. "Mmmm. Yes, you do. You both taste so good on the other's lips."

He wasn't sure what he'd thought she would say, but that nearly drove him to his knees.

Galen licked up her neck. "I think the same. Before we end up naked and fucking, finish telling us about Rosemary and your sister."

Neither male let her go, both holding her to them and to each other too. She drew their energy in, Galen felt her draw upon it, let herself accept that link between them. He smiled against her temple as he pressed a kiss there.

"Rosemary called my father. She wants to meet with my dad. Goodness knows how that's going to go." She shrugged. "He's my father, I just can't imagine him deliberately hurting me. But none of this is logical at all. I can't understand why he wouldn't let them see me. Who was my mother really? Are my memories even real? Do you know what that's like? I've always thought the same thing about her. She's my mother, she died when I was young. My dad, a grieving widower, heads east to make a new life, remarries, yadda yadda. Now it turns out it's not true. Or it is and he's not telling me something for some reason. I just don't know."

"Whatever you need, we'll make it happen." Jack kissed her forehead. "We'll work it out. We just want you happy and safe. As for happy, you've made me that way. Thank you for putting my clothes away. You know you didn't have to. The little stuff pleases me, I can't help it."

Her laugh was soft, echoing through Galen where he'd pressed to her.

"I liked it. Touching your things. Loved the way your scent clung to the fabric. It felt like each thing I put away was another step you took into our life. I like you here, in our lives, in our house. Making our own family."

"Wow, that was pretty fabulous as compliments and love words go. Thank you." Jack kissed her and then Galen.

Chapter Eleven

Jack woke at the sound of the shower turning on. All it took was a deep breath and he knew it was Renee. A glance at the alarm clock told him it was six a.m. What the fuck was his grumpy little cowgirl doing up?

He laughed at the last internal dialog, imagining calling her that just to see her reaction. Galen stirred.

"She can't possibly want to go to work today," Galen murmured.

"I find it illogical for a woman who hates mornings like she does to work a job that demands she be in so early."

Galen laughed, reaching out to turn the lamp on. "She makes good profits on that cart. She's crazy busy from the minute she opens until she closes at three. She doesn't work weekends but takes on a few fairs and festivals in the summer. She donates the profits to this amazing children's charity she loves."

"Lotta layers, our girl." An understatement, Jack knew. "I don't want her working anywhere near those people, Galen."

Galen propped himself up on pillows, managing to continue looking sexy and tousled at the same time. He noticed Jack's interest and laughed. "Don't get something started unless you want to finish it."

It was Jack's turn to laugh. "I'm fine finishing it."

Galen moved then, quickly, to cover the empty space between them, naked skin meeting naked skin. "That so?"

Jack rolled him over, laying atop Galen's body, idly stroking his cock.

A muffled jumble from the bathroom and a soft curse made them both smile. "Before she gets back out here, let's form a united front on whatever we're going to do. Then there will be finishing."

"You learn fast." Galen licked over Jack's left nipple before speaking again. "I don't like her at her stepmother's shop either. But a frontal attack will not work with her. She has a deep sense of honor and loyalty. She'll be struggling with that. I wish I could deal with it for her, but she won't allow it. She has to face this stuff with her father on her own terms."

"I agree. So how can we help her do that while keeping her safe and encouraging her to move to your building?"

Galen grinned. "I like the way you think. I have to go in to work for a few hours today. I left in a hurry on Saturday so there are a number of things I need to tie up. While I'm there, I'm going to talk to my brother and father about the results of the background checks I had run." Galen's strangled moan when Jack palmed his balls was enough to slow the moment down, load it with deliciously honey-thick sensuality. What he and Galen had was different, an ease borne from what they both did, who they both were and beyond an attraction for the other—their love for Renee. Jack had that level of intimacy with very few people and nothing like this with any other man.

Hard as it was to ignore the fist around his cock enough to speak, he managed. "Okay, good. I've got my people on it too. We'll have to schedule a time to debrief and share info. I've got some really good people working for me so they should have something for me by day's end. I have this week off, but I'll want to check in daily at the Pack house. I can take her with me when I go though. It'll get Grace and Renee together more and I like her being around my friends and family. I suppose I want to show her off. All these years my friends would mate with amazing women and I'd be so envious." He laughed. "And here I am and Renee is so special and beautiful and sexy, I want everyone to know it. There's no one like her."

"I know the feeling. I hope your pack is more accepting than my jamboree was at first. You'll protect her from hurt." It wasn't a question, it was a statement and Jack agreed with it.

"I hope so. We're not as insular as cats are. Her not taking the change won't offend anyone. I've petitioned for her to take on my rank in the pack. At one point, a human who hadn't taken the change wouldn't be considered a pack member. The Alpha of Cascadia pushed for that change several years back. Cade's her anchor and brother-in-law so he saw her perspective and agreed with it. Renee's being human won't be a problem. She's easy to talk to, she listens in a way that makes you feel like you're the only person in the room. She'll charm people." He knew she would. Renee soothed him, calmed him, made him whole. Shifter or not, small female or not, she was one tough assed woman. The last several days had been full of one shock after another and she persevered. He admired that and so would his wolves.

Galen moved, lightning quick, and pinned Jack, looming above him. "What's Grace to you, Jack? I know this was the reason for the fight you and Renee had on Saturday. If this situation is going to make Renee unhappy, I will kick some ass."

"I'm her anchor bond. There are complicated emotions between an unmated male and the female he's anchored to. In a way, they're mated too. When I volunteered to be her anchor, they lived in Seattle and I lived here. I thought it would be fine. But then they ended up here as Alphas in this pack. But when I Claimed Renee, when I sealed the mate bond with her, and you, it broke the most intense feelings I had for Grace. I care about her very much. I was in love with a woman I knew I could not have. I never would have acted on those feelings and she's head over ass in love with Cade."

Galen rubbed his eyes. "And how does Grace feel about Renee?"

"That's complicated too."

Galen groaned, sitting up. "Complicated? Like what people say at Facebook? Come on, Jack, what the fuck does that mean? This is Renee we're talking about. You have to be high if you think I'd allow you to put her into any kind of situation where she could be hurt by people."

"Hey, dickhead, she's my woman too. Don't you forget that. Do you think I'd deliberately set her up to be hurt? Grace is, at base, a good woman. She's intelligent and she loves her family. There's often a bit of drama between the anchor female and the mated female. Grace had a situation a lot like this one. It was rocky at the very start, but now she and her sister-in-law are extremely close. Shifter females are territorial. It's part of why they're so hot. She would have faced a lot of the same stuff from your jamboree, Galen. Renee is, you must have noticed, an awful lot like a shifter female, by the way. Grace is levelheaded. She and Renee will be fine. I'll see to it. It's not like Grace hates her, she doesn't. How can anyone not love Renee within five minutes of meeting her?"

Galen sighed and stood. "I'm not sure about all those explanations, Jack. I hope you're right. People tend to write Renee off, like she's stupid and flighty. She's anything but either of those things. She observes with such intensity that it seems like she's not paying attention. She won't take any shit. She'll be friendly and up to a point, she'll deflect tension to avoid a scene. But she has limits and I've seen her lash out so hard at a full-grown jaguar he fell off a chair and gave her his throat. It would be a mistake for anyone to underestimate her. Now, the water turned off and you got me all hot to fuck. I'm off to sully her before she gets dressed."

"I'll hang out with her at the cart today," Jack said as he got up. "What? You think I'd leave you to sully her all by yourself?"

Renee heard their laughter as she toweled off. It made her smile, the way they'd bonded. Then again, they double-teamed her now. As if she wouldn't notice? Hmpf, how could she not notice? One pushy man was more than a full-time job. Two of them meant she had to push back twice as often when they got up in her business. Just a few days in and Jack seemed to fit in with Galen on the pestering just fine. Good thing they excelled at other things like sex and being nice to look at and stuff or it would be too much for any mortal woman to take.

She snorted a laugh as she heard the door opening.

"Oh, just in time. I can never get lotion on my back." She tossed the bottle to Jack, who caught it without pausing on his way to her.

Galen, naked and happy to see her, stalked over. He played against the bite marks, licking, caressing, nibbling until she squirmed. She could never win at the playing at nonchalance game with him. Thirty seconds after he touched her, she was pretty much begging.

"Interesting technique," she managed to mumble when Jack began to apply the lotion with his upper body, sliding against her, heating the air and her skin as the soft scent rose.

"Always thinking outside the box." Jack took the opportunity to make sure her breasts had plenty of lotion as he knelt at her feet.

She closed her eyes a moment at the wave of feeling.

"That's right, sweetheart, just close your eyes and let us wake you up," Galen murmured as he nipped her earlobe.

With her eyes closed, she gave in to the experience. Though

she knew who was doing what, she let go, falling into the experience

Wet. Tongue sliding up her calf.

Roll and tug on her nipples.

The hard brand of a cock at her hip.

Cool softness of hair on her inner thigh.

Nip of teeth on ear and belly button.

Hands caressing.

Whispers against skin.

Fingertips on labia, pulling her open.

Whoosh of air as a mouth found her clit.

Tongue caressing.

One hand clutching the head at her pussy.

One hand wrapped around the cock at her hip.

Thrust. Thrust. Thrust.

Warm and sticky.

Breath at her ear ragged.

Whisper of a growl.

Push and pull.

Orgasm edged around the corners, flowing into her, filling her up with each breath.

Fingers pressing into her gate, stretching.

Mouth on clit.

Teeth abrade.

Gasp for air as it hits.

Sharp sweetness.

She opened her eyes, meeting Jack's as he moved behind her. "You taste so good."

A flex of his hips and his cock invaded her pussy slowly but surely. Unable to look away from his gaze, she gripped the counter and pushed back against him.

His nails raked down her sides, hard enough she couldn't ignore, but not so hard it caused her pain. "I love this tattoo right here." His thumb rode over the skin above her hip where the tiny G surrounded by ivy lay.

"I got it two years ago. Now we'll have to find a way to work a J in there." She reached down, between her thighs, sliding her fingertips up and down the slick line of his cock each time he thrust.

He growled and she watched in the mirror as Galen kissed Jack's shoulder before leaning down to kiss hers. "You look so beautiful here, bent forward, your breasts swaying. If I hadn't come already, with embarrassing quickness, I hasten to add, I'd have my cock in your mouth right now." He noted the position of her hand. "Greedy." Galen slid one of his hands down her belly, fingers joining hers, and the other hand down to grip the base of Jack's cock.

She moaned at the added sensation of his fingers on her pussy and at the idea of him holding Jack's cock. Each time Jack fucked into her, the knuckle joint of her middle finger slid against her clit.

Meeting Jack's pleasure-blurred gaze in the mirror, it pleased her to see his reaction to her. Pleased her to know she still did it for him. While she was glad he and Jack shared some amazing sexual chemistry, she'd be lying to herself if she didn't admit her relief he still found her sexy too.

"Can you come again? Hmm?" Jack increased the speed and depth of thrust as she answered his question all around his cock.

"Holy..." Jack growled, his head falling back, his fingers digging into her hips as he came.

She worked to catch her breath as she looked at the picture they made in the mirror. They may not have been the average romance, but they were love, and that made all the difference in the world. Despite the darkness in her life at the moment, she'd found something important and no matter what, she had her family. It was a shield between her and the worst of the hurt.

*
**

"Woolgathering?" Jack asked from his nearby perch on a wooden bench. He'd accompanied her to The Willow Broom that morning, not letting her out of his sight. Galen hadn't been any help, backing Jack up totally and really, Renee didn't disagree that she needed some muscle so she wasn't complaining.

Susan would most likely flip her wig when she saw him and there was no real hope she'd take the news of another man in Renee's life, especially another non-human male, well. No, there would be drama and woe. Right about then, Renee couldn't have cared less about Susan's feelings.

"Just wondering why you're here instead of sleeping in since you have the time off." She handed an orange mango delight to a customer and began to assemble the strawberry banana whip for the next person in line.

"Now I think this falls under the we-already-discussed-this category. Plus, if I was sleeping, I'd only be seeing you in my dreams. Reality is way prettier."

"This one's high maintenance. I can tell." Her elderly customer tipped her chin toward Jack.

She laughed. "Not really. Just nosy and bossy."

The lady nodded sagely. "Handsome enough to get away with it? My Royce was that way. A rascal! But we had forty-two years and three children. Eighteen grandchildren now and a great grandbaby two months ago. The bossy ones are good to keep you warm in the winter."

Renee grinned at Jack. "It sounds like he was a keeper."

"Oh he was, indeed." She laughed at some inside joke and waved as she headed away.

Renee picked up her phone again, dialing her father's house. Jack heaved a sigh, they'd already argued about her calling her father so often so he didn't say more than that.

She was surprised when her father finally answered. "Dad, I need to see you as soon as possible. I have to talk to you about some stuff."

"What's this all about, Renee? You aren't breaking up with Galen are you? Susan told me about this other guy who's been hanging around. Please tell me you haven't done something monumentally stupid."

"I'm not breaking up with Galen."

"Susan told me what happened before I got to the shop on Friday. I saw he was mad."

"Dad, that did not happen the way she's portraying it. Jack was here, in the middle of a shop packed with people, in broad daylight. Susan *called* Galen at work and told him to get over here immediately. He wasn't angry. Not at me anyway."

"Oh. Well then what is it? I have errands to run today and we're out tonight with some friends." How she'd always hated it that he brushed her off that way.

"It's about Rosemary Kellogg."

Silence. Well now, apparently that was an attention getter.

She knew he hadn't cut the connection, could still hear the harshness of his breathing. It was at that moment Susan decided to flounce into the store and, upon seeing Jack, headed in their direction in full make-a-scene mode.

"Dad? Are you still there?" She looked up at Susan. "Don't start."

"I won't have this in my store! This is ridiculous. What kind of whore takes up with a new man while she's with the old one? You'd dump a successful attorney with a bright financial future for this? Galen may not be, well, totally acceptable, but he's the best you'll ever get. Don't let the hair and the teeth fool you on that one." Susan indicated Jack with a tip of her head. "He's not all he appears at first glance." Susan had her hands on her hips, rings on every finger.

"You won't have what? And this is my workspace. I lease this entire area. I look the other way when you add shelving here. But you don't get to say who I can have here. It's none of your business. And if you call me a whore again, I won't take it kindly." She let the menace be heard loud and clear.

"Are you upsetting your mother with this talk?" her father demanded over the phone. He interrupted her right as she'd been about to demand Susan explain what she meant by her comments about Jack being not what he seemed and Galen not being totally acceptable. Still, she refused to be sidetracked with her father.

"I haven't even mentioned that to Susan. My mother, as you know, is dead. I need to talk to you. I want to hear your side of the story. I have so many questions about my mother's family. About what happened before we came here to Boston."

"That subject is closed. You're not to see any of those people, Renee. They're poison." Her father sounded so very casual as her reality crumbled around her ears and she still did not know what the hell was happening.

"Closed?" She flipped the sign on the cart and attempted to move away from the counter. If customers came by the last thing she wanted was to have this conversation with her father with an audience. Of course Susan had to come too, talking over Renee to her father. Jack moved, intercepting Susan, getting in between them.

"You can't *close* a topic like this. You told me I had no one. You told me they didn't care. You changed our name! My entire life has been a lie! There's no more closing of this topic. I'm on my way over right now."

"Don't bother, Renee. I'm not discussing it. I made decisions for you. You're fine even if you lack ambition and have a messed up personal life. I did my best by you and I won't have you questioning me. Don't bring it up again."

He hung up and she snapped her phone shut.

"This is not over," she said to no one in particular. "Jack, I'm closing for the day. I have to go to my father's house."

"We'll take my car."

"You'll do no such thing," Susan snarled, grabbing Renee's arm. "You'll leave it all alone. We gave up everything for you and this is how you repay me and my love for you? Another woman's baby and I raised you. Where was *she*? Where was your father?"

Somewhere inside, the words unlocked so much rage Renee had to step back to try and get herself under control.

Jack vibrated with anger. He put his arms around Renee and she leaned into him, letting him give her comfort, letting him protect. "You mean when she was in the closet with welts on her legs? Or did you mean when you told her she was worthless and unlovable? I have a few ideas on just how that should be repaid. Would you like me to share them with you? I've given them lots of thought since I heard what your brand of parenting entailed."

Susan's face paled as her lips tightened. Direct hit. If Renee expected that to bring some sort of apology or acknowledgment of mistakes made, she wasn't holding her breath. "I don't know what Renee has told you, she has problems with truthfulness. Regardless, it's none of your concern." Her gaze left Jack warily and focused on Renee. "Renee, you will not bring this up to your father and dredge up years of pain and suffering you've caused. I forbid it."

"Hold up right there, ma'am. Don't. Don't waste a single breath more on this line of discussion. I've seen the damage you and your special kind of care caused. You will not be doing any more. I'm here now, you get me? Galen and I are here and we know what you are. Back up." Jack turned to keep himself between them.

Renee blinked, trying to clear the ringing in her ears. "You? You? *You* forbid me from asking my father why he lied to me for over twenty years? Why he changed our names and hid me and the cause of my mother's death? I don't think so."

"Don't make him choose, Renee. You and I both know you'll lose."

"Lose? What am I missing? It's like I'm only hearing every fourth word because you aren't making any sense. Choose what? Why would you characterize me asking him about my own life, my mother, as him having to choose? What part do you play in any of this anyway? What's *your* interest in the silence?" She knew something. Renee was absolutely sure Susan knew something about this entire thing and was most likely as involved as her father was.

"Get out. Your lease is up." Susan crossed her arms over her chest.

"What?" She felt caught in some indie foreign film with grown men in diapers pushing a hoop with a stick and a single yellow duckling in the far corner.

"Your lease is terminated. You have 48 hours to clear this cart out or I'll have it taken away myself."

Susan's emotions slammed, only confirming her suspicion that Susan had known what was going on. Renee had the feeling Susan had been around longer than she remembered. Doing what? Why?

Whatever the case, Renee wasn't going to let the woman push her around ever again. "You can't terminate my lease with no notice. The contract says sixty days. What are you hiding, Susan? What are you hiding that you'd toss me out of my father's life, toss my business into the street rather than even discuss?"

"Get out! I'll gladly pay the penalty to get you out of here early."

Ice. Her rage cooled to something else, something deeper and more dangerous. She narrowed her eyes at Susan. "You're damned right you will. What did you have to do with my mother's murder?"

"You're crazy!" Susan's face got redder and redder. Renee wondered idly if she'd explode.

"No. We both know I'm not. You've spent a lot of time trying to make me feel that way. Which begs the question as to why, doesn't it? I'm not crazy at all. My aunt and sister are here. They have a vastly different story to tell than I've heard from you and my father."

Just then, Galen walked in. His fury washed through the room, raising the hair on the back of Renee's neck. He stopped, looking Renee over carefully. "We're leaving right now." He and Jack shared some non-verbal ordering around and Galen turned back to her, delivering a quick kiss. "This isn't going to continue. She's dangerous to your mental well-being. We'll get another spot for this cart. And you," he addressed Susan, "will get the penalty, that's two month's lease payments, in cash, to my office by five this evening or we'll tie this up in court."

"Fine. Whatever it takes. Don't come here again, Renee. You're not welcome. And leave your father alone. You've brought him enough pain."

Something just ripped free of the moorings within her at those words.

"*I've* brought him pain? I have? You can look back at what you've done to me over the years and say that? What have I done to cause him pain? When have I ever done something other than try to please him and make him happy? Please, do enlighten me."

Susan pokered up and Renee tightened her hands into fists, fists she wanted to use so badly she scared herself. "I don't have to have this discussion with you. You're making a scene. I suppose, given your background, you showing some class is impossible. But the rest of us have it."

She would have knocked Susan off her feet with that last comment, but Jack put his arms around her, holding her to his body. "She's not worth it, sweetheart. Come on, let's go."

"Go? Because she says so? I think not. I think it's high time she answers for what she's done." Renee knew she was getting shrill, but once she'd really loosed all her anger and resentment, it burned through her veins like a drug.

Jack turned her in his arms. "Do you think she will? Right now?"

"Why are you taking her side?"

"I'm always on your side. You know that. But she's not going to tell you anything and you're so upset I'm worried about your health. We will get your answers, I promise. But nothing good will come of this if we stay here."

"I deserve an answer! I've been living a lie! How can I just walk away now? I don't understand what the fuck is happening and I am done with that. I need to know."

Galen kissed her cheek. "Babe, she's not going to answer you. Not right now. Unless you want me to unleash some cat-style justice, we can't force her. Let's go. We'll regroup and approach from another angle. We'll get your answers, believe that. You're so upset, Jack and I hate that. Please let us help you right now."

Susan watched them carefully, her phone in her hand. Renee had never wanted to hit anyone more than she did at that very moment. She considered what cat-style justice would look like and then reminded herself of those few times she'd seen it. While Renee did want to hurt them for lying to her, she didn't have the right.

"This isn't over." She stormed out, taking a deep breath once she got to the sidewalk.

Jack followed her out. "That was close, eh, babe? You made the right choice. You wouldn't have forgiven yourself if you'd have agreed to shifter style justice." He hugged her quickly. "As for the cart, we can store it in my friend's garage. He's got a boat but it's still on the water, so he's got the space. I'll get it moved later today."

Galen took his time coming back outside. Amped up on adrenaline and anger, Renee impatiently began to walk home.

"Hey, wait up," Galen called out, jogging up the block toward her and Jack. "I was just underlining how much she needed to deal with your money and this whole situation."

"I'm sure that worked out well," she grumbled as she kept walking.

"She's hiding something. A lot of somethings." Galen glared back over his shoulder.

"No kidding."

"Left, sweetheart, left," Jack called after her as she turned right, heading toward the T stop to get to her father's house.

"I know how to get home. I'm not going home."

"Babe, think about this. Let's go back to the house and work through some contingencies." Galen sent her his most charming smile and she wanted to sock him for being so effective at it.

"Let's not. I thought you had work to do? You're going to be fired if you keep leaving to save me from myself."

"Stop walking for a minute. Let's drive over at least. It's safer and we can leave whenever we want." Galen put a hand on her arm. "I'm not going to get fired. I'm technically on vacation anyway. What else would I be doing but be here with you?"

"Don't you wonder that? Seriously." She shook off his hand. "I'm doing this. He's been hiding this from me for twenty years, Galen! I need to know why."

"Fuck you, Renee." Galen's face hardened. "No, I never wonder that except for those panic moments when you're sick or in danger and I realize how fragile you are and how I could lose you and then what? What would my life be without you is not a passing thought, it's my worst nightmare. So don't cheapen that with this bullshit rhetoric. It's insulting to me and what we have."

She inclined her head in shifter fashion, submitting to his rank as an apology. She had been wrong and she said so.

He rolled his eyes and kissed her briefly, only to start up again about going home.

The train approached and she hustled to catch it. Jack and Galen had to move their pretty little shifter asses to keep up.

"Don't." She gave them both the evil eye as they surrounded her. Jack hung the phone up.

"Just making arrangements to go down to the shop to meet some friends later. We'll move the cart this afternoon." Jack took her hand. "I'm sorry about that scene. She's out of line."

"Doesn't matter. I don't want to talk about it right now. I need to hold it together until after I've confronted my father."

They sat, Renee in between them. Galen made work phone calls, *vacation, yeah right.* Still, he held one of her hands, his thumb playing over her wedding rings. Jack, his arm around her shoulders, her body tucked into his side was warm and real. The scenery out the window held enough of her attention she didn't jump out of her skin. Everything was upside down. But it made a sort of sense too. She'd always felt like there was something she'd forgotten, something she'd missed.

"She'll have called him already." Susan wouldn't have

waited a minute after they left the shop.

"Most likely, yes. Renee, you need to be prepared for this." Galen said it like she hadn't ever considered the price. She had, over and over with every possible outcome, and still she knew it would be horrible. And still, she had to do it.

Renee stood, heading for the doors as they stopped. Funny, her dad and Susan had moved to a small house after Renee had moved out on her own for college. Not enough room for her to stay over. She'd had dinner there maybe three times over the last few years.

Those moments she remembered as she cowered in that closet weren't common. Susan hadn't beaten her every day. She never felt abused as a child. Lonely, yes. Different. There were times she felt like she was in the wrong house, the wrong body. Renee had just chalked that up to her own awkwardness. Despite her father's general composed demeanor, she'd never felt he didn't love her. Which is why this whole thing was so confusing.

She kept walking. Three blocks, three blocks over and a right, two more blocks and there they were. Susan's car was out front, but a brief touch to the hood told her it hadn't been that long since she'd arrived.

"Why don't you let me go to the door?" Galen asked.

"No."

She went up the front walk, stopping on the porch to push the bell.

Her father opened the door, looking like a stranger. It hit her, even though she'd been expecting something unpleasant. He blocked her entrance with his body. "Why are you here, Renee? I told you I wasn't going to discuss this."

"I'm here to talk to you. You're my father. You can't just refuse to explain why you changed my name and hid me from my mother's relatives for twenty years! What am I supposed to do with that? I'm sure you had your reasons. I'm not even mad, I'm just confused. I want to hear your side of the story so I can understand. These people want a relationship with me; if there's something bad about them, don't you think you should share it?"

"I don't owe you any explanations. I fed and clothed you. I did my job, Renee, and I think it's ungrateful of you to barge into my house, uninvited, to demand anything."

"I'm *ungrateful?* I appreciate the roof and the food, thank you. I've thanked you many, many times over my life. I haven't done anything wrong. What is going on? Why are you acting this way?"

He looked at her, his eyes flat, like she was a stranger. Her confusion bled into humiliation. He shamed her and that brought her back to her purpose as she did her best to slam the door on the wave of pain he'd caused. But he wasn't done. "You live your life like everyone owes you things. It holds you back. Look at you. Thirty years old, not married, no kids. You live with some guy and I hear you've got another one hanging around. Do something with your life, Renee. You're wasting it looking to blame other people for your situation."

Galen stepped up, towering over her dad. "That is *more* than enough." He turned to Renee. "Let's go. He's not going to tell you anything and all he's doing is upsetting you."

"Please don't leave things like this, Dad. Try to see this from my perspective. I just found out my entire life has been built on misinformation. She was my mother, I loved her. Out of nowhere people come to my house and tell me I have an aunt, and a sister but you've never told me I had a sister. You told me Mom's family didn't want to see me. You changed our name. You changed her name. And I don't remember half of it. I'm asking you to help me." She took his hand, but Susan appeared, slapping it away.

Susan practically sneered. "Get off our porch. You're not

186

welcome here anymore."

Renee had no intention of speaking to Susan ever again if she could avoid it. "Dad, I'm begging you for your help."

"I can't help you, Renee. Leave it alone or you're dead to me."

She didn't want it to, she wanted to be tough and beyond hurt. But she wasn't. It did hurt, it hurt so bad she had to hold back tears at the verbal slap.

"You can't be serious! You're telling me I'm dead to you if I don't stop asking about *my* life? *My* history?"

"We've said all there is to say. If you can't respect that, yes. If you have anything to do with those people, if you persist in asking about the past, don't bother coming around here or the shop anymore."

"This is insane." She tossed her hands up in the air. "Dad, if you're in trouble, I can help you. If you lied because you were afraid of them taking me no one is going to hate you or try to sue you or anything."

"Just go. After all these years your father deserves some time when he's not doting on you. You made your bed." Susan began to close the door.

"What are you talking about? Honestly, this is the most bizarre conversation I've ever had." Renee was upset, but also just completely confused.

"Come on, babe." Galen pulled her away gently as she stared at the door. "Let's go home."

"This is fucking batshit crazy. Something is going on. Maybe he's in danger. Maybe he did it because they threatened me or something." Even as she said it, she knew that wasn't it.

Jack sighed. "I don't know. I scented lies, but not fear."

They walked back to the T stop without saying much. What was there to say?

Galen guided her to a seat, fitting himself beside her, with Jack on the other. "Don't lose heart. You're not out of line, you deserve answers." Galen stroked a hand up and down her arm. "We'll get them for you. Just know they may not be what you expect or even want to hear."

"Welcome to my life. I'm supposed to see Rosemary and Kendra this afternoon. What do I say? Should I worry about them? Do you think they'd harm me?"

"I don't think so." Jack paused. "Part of why I'm so good at my job is instinct. I'm not bragging." He favored her with an arrogant grin and she found herself totally charmed, yet again, by this man who fell into her life without warning. Galen laughed at her reaction, leaning in to kiss her.

"You're a handful, aren't you?" She shook her head, looking up at all that blond handsomeness.

Jack laughed, not a blush in sight. "Well, I'd hope I'm a bit more than a handful. But my point is sometimes your gut tells you things for a reason. You know how your gut tells you your aunt and sister are safe and you can trust them?"

She nodded, reaching out to take his hand, needing the contact. He smiled, squeezing and kissing her knuckles.

"Yes. But apparently I'm not cut out to be a werewolf cop because I thought I could trust my father too."

"Step one is for you to stop taking on shit that's not yours to own. Do you know what I'm talking about?" Jack cocked his head.

"Well I'm sorry! It stuns me. How could I have never known?" This is what really bothered her the most. What had she missed? How could this all have happened without her never noticing? Did she notice and not remember now? Everything about her father, about her life as a kid was based on lies. How could she know what was true or not?

A sense of violation began to flavor her confusion. What

had been done to her and why?

Jack's voice broke into her thoughts. "Because you never had any reason to doubt it. Why would you? You didn't know any different until recently. But now, think about it. Do you trust him? Be honest with yourself."

She took a deep breath, thinking. "No. But I don't know if it's even real. I don't know anything. I know it sounds whiny, but it's like the ground is gone and I'm stumbling and falling. My foundations are gone."

"I know. I'm sorry. But listen here, curly, your foundations are right here on either side of you. Galen and I are your foundations and we will always be here to hold you up when you need it. As for everyday stuff, one of us will be with you at all times until we get this all figured out. Galen's jamboree and my wolves are investigating. We will solve this puzzle."

"Jack's right, babe. Beyond this stuff with your family, what is real is *us*." Galen indicated the three of them. "I know this has been a crazy week and things seem confusing—they *are* confusing. But I want to tell you how much I love you, and how much I know this hurts you. It makes me want to hurt someone in return. Jack and I will keep you safe."

"All of you. Your heart and your body," Jack added.

Renee woke up from her nap feeling better. Though it couldn't have been too difficult to feel better than the humiliated, confused mess she was just a few hours before. Thanks to a sleeping draught, her rest had been deep and gloriously dreamless. Her brain appreciated that respite, she thought, as she sat up and stretched.

"There you are." Galen peeked in, looking delicious. Just looking at him made her feel better, alive and very in need of some TLC. Lucky for her, Galen excelled at TLC.

"Here I am. Woefully clothed. I think that's a crime or something." She batted her lashes at him.

"I definitely need to correct that, hmm?" He leaned there in the doorway, looking indolent and arrogant—and ridiculously hot.

"I feel very neglected, you know. All alone here." She tossed her shirt to the side and lay back on the bed again. The panties she wore were his favorites, boyshort style, hot pink.

He grinned as he pulled his clothes off, moving to her quickly. "We really can't have that. How can I make it better?" His words were smooth, as smooth as the way he got onto the bed. But just beneath he was something else and it drove her hormones into a frenzy.

When he got to his knees over her this way, it sucked all the oxygen from her lungs. He was smooth and human but she never forgot the predator within, and the way he moved when she was the center of his sensual attention blew her away.

He was warm and smelled so good she had to lick up his side, over each rib.

His groan echoed against her mouth and she fell into him, opening up to accept whatever he wanted to give, however he wanted to provide it.

He looked down at her, cocky smile softening to something else.

"Jeez, I run out to be sure that cart is safely residing at Dave's and I miss the sex?" Jack came into the bedroom, looking windblown and sexy.

She laughed. "Hurry up then! We're just getting started. Get naked and over here. You have work to do."

Within moments, he'd joined them in bed and she gave herself a moment to just appreciate the incredible hotness of being sandwiched between two men who looked like hers.

They snuggled, kissing, caressing, simply enjoying each other as the heat built. She knew shifters liked touch. She'd learned when she first began to spend the night at Galen's that he liked to touch her, even when they were sleeping. At first she'd resisted, trying to tell herself she felt suffocated. In truth, she'd been so rocked by how deeply it had touched her, the comfort and connection she found in his touch, that she ran from it. Galen had patiently won her over.

Even in those early days he'd let her be who she was, flaws and all. How rare and wonderful he was.

"Thank you." She looked up at him.

Galen paused, her breasts still mounded in his hands. "For what, babe? Sexual services come with the package and I quite enjoy them."

"Well, that obviously. But you know, for being so good to me."

"I love you," he said like it was totally obvious, which she supposed it was.

"Yeah. And I'm blessed for that." She let that sink in, watching his expression soften. She looked to Jack. "You too. You both are good to me and I am thankful."

She needed this reconnection more than she'd admitted to herself. It was stupid to resist it, she knew. The way she was drawn to Galen scared her no longer. Still, it overwhelmed sometimes. But he always comforted with a touch, a caress, a kiss, even as he excited.

And now with Jack, it was twice what she felt before. More than twice really, because her bond to Jack and his bond to both her and Galen had created a level of openness between the three that left her completely exposed.

There was no escaping what she felt for these men. What's more? She had spent years and years running from big feelings except when it was unavoidable. She supposed she understood it better after the last several days, but she was done running. She planned to be thankful every damned day for her blessings.

"Despite all the craziness over the last days, I want you both to know how much I love you and how lucky I am to have you both in my life." She kissed Jack's shoulder and stretched to get Galen, but he sprang into movement, covering her mouth with his own instead.

She arched, letting him course through their link. He mumbled a curse into her mouth. "I can't hold it together when you're like this."

"What do you mean?" she asked, sliding her hands all over his skin, rubbing her ass against Jack.

"Inside you're so beautiful I can't put it into words." He slid two fingers between her legs, quickly finding her clit and then her gate, slowly circling. "Here, yes. But here—" Galen pressed a kiss to her forehead, "—you're all light and magic, warm, and there's nothing like it. Every time you let me in it feels so good I want to roll around in it. It's big and I know that. I understand you're choosing to let us in and I want you to know I understand it's a gift, especially how things have been with your family."

"You're going to make me cry." She reached back and grabbed Jack's cock while kissing her way along Galen's neck.

"Why? Renee, we have something wonderful and special and you are the reason. There's nothing to cry over." Jack got to his knees, bracketing Galen. "No crying. Well, not tears of pain."

"I'd cry because what we have is so special. It's a woman thing. Anyway, you're better than a trip to the beach."

He paused a moment, cocking his head. "I already forbade tears." He swooped down to kiss her and then leaned up again. "Beach? How so?" His hands hadn't paused, though. Nimble fingers rolled and tugged on her nipples as he waited for her to be able to form words and put them in order to make sense.

Like she could!

"You're sand and sun, you're the smell of coconut, of white teeth, of blue skies as far as the eye can see. It's sexy and it makes me tingly."

He said nothing. Instead, he took her hand, placing it on his chest, over his heart and she understood.

Not one to let opportunity just pass her by, she grabbed the base of Jack's cock, so close to her face, angling him to take a taste. Better than a bag of chips. She took her time and learned him. Learned what spots he liked best and how he liked it.

Galen watched as she sucked Jack's cock. He stroked his own, content to just look on for the moment. Right then it was like watching the best pornographic movie ever made. The pale, creamy skin Renee had against the golden limbs Jack possessed. From his vantage, he could see the curve of Renee's ass leading down to her pussy, dark from desire, glistening. He scented her and something within responded, knowing that scent, knowing she needed.

Pre-come beaded on the head of his cock and he slid a thumb through it, the pleasure making him shiver just a bit.

Jack opened his eyes and looked down at her, looked down at their woman as she sucked him off. Galen knew that, knew the feeling of it, knew the pride that this woman with all her power and allure would be on her knees before him.

Echoes of that pinged through their link, set Galen on fire, a fire he couldn't contain when Jack's gaze met his. He needed her, needed Jack, needed to be in them and against them.

He got to his knees behind her, kissing the small of her back and then the tattoo. "I can smell your pussy, babe. Sticky sweet."

She whimpered, arching to get more contact with him, which only made him crazier for her. He hadn't fucked her since the day before. Had come that morning as the three of them had been together, but he needed to be in her.

Her moan, low and laced with need, curled around his gut, pulling him deeper as he brushed the head of his cock through her pussy, teasing around her gate.

"Think you can handle this every day?" Galen asked as he began to press inside. Since he was the one close to coming about thirty seconds after he thrust the first time, he didn't have any high ground to stand on. Still, twenty minutes after he came, he'd want her again.

She braced herself better, widening her thighs, one hand holding Jack's balls, the other on his thigh to keep her balance as Galen seated himself fully and pulled nearly all the way out only to plunge back into that welcoming heat.

He kept his pace slow and deep, content to just be with her, content to climb slowly toward climax.

As Renee became softer, warmer and more relaxed, Jack's body tensed. His chest gleamed with sweat, his muscles tightening as he approached orgasm. Christ he was sexy. Galen felt the edges of what Jack did, wrapped in Renee's responses. Seen through Renee, Jack was even sexier.

"Yes, so good. That's, ahhh, yes, more," Jack said through a clenched jaw.

Galen knew Renee had taken him as deeply as she could. Knew the way it felt with his cock in her mouth, his balls in her palm and the soft stroke over his asshole. She threw her entire self into sex, especially oral sex.

Something in the way the three of them had bonded together had freed her magic in a way it hadn't been before. She gave off the warm rush of power and it built the longer they all touched.

Jack groaned her name like a benediction, his hand in her hair tightening. Her moan in response reverberated through

Galen as he knew Jack filled her.

Renee's head lifted and she looked up at Jack, who bent to kiss her and whisper how much he loved her.

Her body called to Galen, her curves, each dip in her flesh, every rise. She was not unknown territory, but he delighted in exploring her over and over. Needing to see her face, he leaned down. "Flip over so I can look into your eyes as I fuck you."

She reluctantly moved forward, his cock slipping from her body. The look on her face made him want to laugh. Like a toddler who'd had a doll taken away.

"Greedy," he murmured, caressing every bit of her he could touch.

"I am. Put your cock in me!"

Jack laughed, kissing her neck. "If he doesn't want to oblige, give me a few minutes and I'll take care of it." He winked at Galen, who put his cock right back where he intended to be.

"I think not. Try to step on my action? Pfft. You just had your cock in her mouth. I have her pussy." Galen arched his back, getting in deeper, moaning at how good it felt.

She laughed, one arm curled up and around Jack, her gaze locked with Galen. The edges of their uneven number smoothed then as they all fit together seemingly effortlessly. Though in fact, it was difficult sometimes to see her react to Jack, difficult to see Jack react to her. It passed as he realized they all connected, she still loved him, still trusted and depended on him. The way she leaned on him during all this family drama meant a lot to him—as a man and as a cat. He *needed* to keep her safe, to protect her. That she sought that out, trusted he'd do so, made him want to roar up to the heavens.

Instead, he leaned down and kissed her.

"I love you."

The breath of that against his lips caught him.

"So much," he added, speeding his pace when she lifted her

195

feet, changing the angle of her hips, gripping his sides with her knees.

"I can see his cock sliding in and out of your pussy," Jack said, watching avidly.

She nodded. "Yes."

Jack's breath sped, along with Galen's. He slid a hand down her belly. "Here, let me help you, sweetheart."

Her breath snagged, her cunt gripping around Galen's cock as Jack began to finger her clit.

"Ohmigod, like...that, oh yes!" She arched, her nails against Galen's thigh, her hips rocking to grind herself against Jack's hand, onto Galen's cock. The result obviously worked for her, as her pussy superheated to nearly scalding. All of which worked for him as he fucked into her hard and deep, heading into orgasm without brakes once she began to come all around him.

Galen moved to the side, one arm pillowing her head as he caught his breath. Jack settled in but not before leaning over Renee to kiss Galen. Her softness made room for Jack's edge, the coarse nature of male against male, shifter against shifter.

The kiss was a wrestle, a struggle to titillate, to taste, to mark, to possess. It did all those things in a gnash of teeth and tongue, of lips, and when they finally broke apart, Galen struggled for breath as he flopped on his back.

"Wow. That was." She fanned herself. "Beyond hot. If I could have that image put on every surface I'd encounter in my life, I'd be such a happy girl. Not that I'm not happy now. Despite all this crazy, I'm so happy."

Jack dried his hair, still smiling and relaxed from the sex they'd shared only hours before. His woman, so strong and yet small, her mouth on him, her heart opened wide, his man, adoring her and yet leaving space for Jack. Both to love Renee and to love Galen too.

Funny how that had turned out. When he'd found Renee he wouldn't have ever thought he'd end up with her *and* her man. He smiled as he zipped his jeans, doubly fortunate, doubly blessed. What they had was beyond his wildest dreams. Gabe had been right.

When he walked out of the bathroom she was there, in her closet, putting lipstick on. He'd never seen her with makeup other than some mascara. He liked how she looked with a bit of extra sparkle.

"You look very Fey right now."

He stood behind her, needing to touch her. That was something unique to his bond with her. While he loved touching Galen, he *needed* to touch her. Needed to rub himself along her skin, to mark her with his scent, to mark himself with her. That need to know she was there, solid, and to delight in everything she was seemed bottomless.

She leaned back against him. "Fey? In a good way? The Fae are an amazing people." She frowned, as if that didn't apply to her.

"And? Of course in a good way. You *are* amazing, silly woman. Do you think two men could adore you as much as we do if you weren't?"

She shrugged. "I don't know. The bond to you is not something you have a choice over."

"That's not true, sweetheart. I did have a choice. Yes, I was attracted to you because you were capable of being my mate. But other women could have been if I'd wanted to look and find them. It's not one-person-on-earth rare, though it is about genetic compatibility as well as magic stuff. I *chose* you because you are the one person on earth I wanted. I wanted you, Renee, and I still want you. Sure, our mate bond means I can feel your emotions and being a shifter means I seek to touch you to comfort myself and you. But what we have isn't something I was forced into."

She turned in his arms. "I'm sorry, I know it seems silly."

"Nothing you do seems silly." He shook his head and hugged her. "You're not a shifter so how can you know? Never hesitate to ask or talk to me about something you're unsure of or bothered by. I love you and the more I know you, the more I love you. More importantly, I like you, I respect you. You and Galen are my family."

She chewed on her bottom lip a moment.

"You're going to eat your lipstick. Just say it. I'm never going to judge you like that." He realized he wanted her to share, to give him more of herself.

She paused and then forged ahead. "I'm nervous. About meeting Grace. I wish I wasn't. But I am."

He let himself relax, but chose his words carefully, not wanting to upset her or bring on another fight. "You know she's important to me and you know why. More important, you and I are solid, important. What we—you and me—have is totally different and far deeper than what ties me to Grace and Cade. She's curious. Because she loves me and she wants me to be happy. Loves me but not like you do, okay? *You* are important to me because you make me whole. You are important to me because you're my everything. You and Galen are part of me, in every breath I take. She'll see that and things will be fine. I've told her this, told Cade too. Told my friends and my pack because it's important."

Some of the tension left her spine and he breathed a bit easier.

"I don't have to rumble or anything, do I? None of this fucked up shifter political crap, right? Because I could tell you some shit about what my first year as Galen's girlfriend was like."

"What? Galen's jamboree hurt you?"

She shook her head. "I'm sorry, nevermind. It's silly and I'm talking out of school."

He shook his head right back at her. "It's not silly and you're not talking out of school. You're sharing something about your life with your mate. Please, share with me."

She licked her lips and nodded. "Okay so no. Not exactly. Jaguars are so, gah, they're incestuous! They're constantly up in each other's business and there's all this hazing for humans who join the jamboree. I have always sort of felt...nevermind. It's dumb."

He took her hand and drew her into the bedroom. Sweeping her up, he sat on the big chair near the window and settled her on his lap. "Tell me." Damn she felt good there, warm and substantial, all his.

"They're all sleek and beautiful. Well educated. Many of them speak three or four languages. All his siblings are lawyers. His mother is a judge. They adore Galen and he loves them too. But I'm not what they wanted for him. I feel short, fat and dumb. Human. Weak. I can't shift into a five-hundred-pound predator with razor sharp teeth and nails. I can't run more than a few blocks without begging for death and they're rowing and jogging and sporting it up for kicks because they're all insane. I don't fit and they know it. Some of them take time to remind me of that. Not all of them. I don't want you to think they're all mean to me. Most of them are really sweet and supportive. I suppose I hadn't really given them enough credit until more recently. It's my fault for being myopic. His father is a sweetheart. His older brother is my biggest defender other than Galen. You'll love Max, it's impossible not to. He's got seven brothers and sisters, by the way. Five of them like me, well, six if you count Galen. I can't complain about the odds really. Most of the rest of the group fall into the 'she's not bad and he loves her' camp."

"But not all?"

"Not all. I understand their perspective. I'm just a human. He's one of the alpha cats in the jamboree. When I have children, they'll be mixed. This weakens their genetics. Makes the jamboree less strong."

These people had done such a damned number on her. He wouldn't show her any pity, she'd hate it, but she sure deserved a fucking break.

"Bullshit. When you have our children, they'll be shifters. It's the dominant genetic trait. Cats, wolves, whatever. You're a powerful witch, our children will be stronger for it, not weaker."

She smiled and it made him feel like he was ten feet tall.

"That's what Galen says. But it's hard when his sister comes to my cart to tell me she's doing the right thing for her family with her pregnancy and if I wasn't just with him for money I'd let him go and be with one of his own kind."

He sighed. "She sounds like a twat. The mother?"

She rolled her eyes and he wanted to laugh.

"His mother is a stone cold bitch and I love her to death." She snorted. "She *hated* me for three years. Every time I'd come in contact with her, she'd give me company manners. For her, that was a slap, you know? The other wives and husbands don't get waited on, they get their own iced tea or whatever. For me, she'd offer. Underlining my difference."

He didn't feel too kindly toward Galen's family at that moment. "So what happened?"

"She came over here to bring food for Galen. Another slap. Like I couldn't feed him after all that time? So I taught her that just because I'm quiet and don't make a scene didn't mean I was a pushover. I have my limits and she reached them. We had a discussion. I cleared up her misapprehensions. She's been very good to me ever since. I can get all morose sometimes, but in truth, his parents are very wonderful people

200

and the majority of his family and jamboree are accepting of me."

He grinned, liking how spunky she was when she needed to be. "I know this makes me a pervert, but that's a hot story about his mom. I like the idea of you getting up in her face to set things right." She blushed and shrugged. "You're not a pushover. Not a gold digger. You're not *just* anything, much less human. You strengthen us, Renee, not weaken us. Anyone who says different will get a mouth full of my fist."

"He didn't know. Galen...I don't want you to think he stood by when this stuff happened. He knows some of them don't like me, but they rarely mess with me if he's around and after a while, he realized I was uncomfortable with some of them and he made sure to be around. I honestly don't think he knows the extent of it. The hazing period has passed for the most part. There's no need to dredge it up again. From what I understand, it's part of the process, that sort of hazing. I dread it though. But you're worth it."

Jack hugged her, breathing her in. She'd been with her sister and aunt for the last several hours and the spice of her magic painted his senses. His wolf loved it. Her power drew him, both parts of his nature.

"Curly, being worth it is great and all, but it's unnecessary past a certain point. Anyway, sharing part of yourself with me isn't dredging. It's good for me to know, so I can understand you better and so I know what the situation is. I would never think Galen would sit by while anything bad happened to you. That's not who he is."

"Not who I am what?" Galen strolled in with a huge bouquet of wildflowers. Renee saw them and shot up with a squeal of delight. He handed them to her with a kiss. "I picked them up on my way back from the office. I deposited the check Susan had sent over. I'm glad you like them." His grin told Jack Galen knew exactly the reaction he'd get.

"You know I love them. Look at these poppies! Bluebells and cornflowers too. So pretty. It's like a party in my hands." Galen laughed as she yanked him down to kiss him a few times. "I'm going to put these in water. We should get moving soon so we're not late. They have kids so I don't want to mess up their schedules." With a flash of color and her smile, she spun and left the bedroom.

"What were you two talking about? I'm not who?" Galen walked past Jack and into the bathroom where he washed his face and brushed his teeth.

"She told me some of the difficulties she's had with your jamboree. She was reassuring me it wasn't stuff that happened in front of you, that you'd not let her be abused and insulted and just stand by." Anger rushed through his veins at the thought of how alone she must have felt. "I told her I knew you wouldn't have. She stuck with you because she loves you. Your sister, the pregnant one? She should count her lucky stars she's knocked up or I'd be on her ass demanding she apologize for her insults."

Galen turned back to Jack after he'd dried his face. "Do *you* think I'd let my family treat her badly?"

"I just said I didn't. If I did, this would be a different conversation. But your sister and some of your jamboree have used her being human to manipulate Renee into thinking she's a gold digger or a pollutant in their precious genetic stream."

Galen froze. "What?"

"Told her if she had kids with you it would damage the strength of the jamboree, and you in the bargain. That she was only with you for the money. Said if she truly loved you, she'd let you mate with one of your own kind and leave you alone."

It was clear to Jack that Galen had no idea the level of nastiness that'd been aimed at Renee and Jack regretted not being smoother in his delivery. He should have been sure she was okay with him sharing. At the same time, it needed to be said and they'd deal with the other stuff later as they got used to each other.

"She knows you wouldn't let her be hurt."

"Oh for Pete's sake! Jack, what are you doing?" Renee came into the room again, looking mightily annoyed. "I can't believe you. You should have left it to me if and when to tell him. What on earth was the purpose?"

He resisted the urge to hang his head. Only barely, because she was right to be mad at him for not asking her if he could share the info with Galen. "I'm sorry. He needed to know, sweetheart. I'd want to know if our situations were reversed."

"Listen here, you two, neither of you get to make that choice for me. I know you're protective alpha shifters, blah blah. But I don't recognize your sovereignty over me. Got that? As for the issues with Galen's jamboree—it's over. Most of it anyway. I love his mom, she loves me. We're good. It's only two siblings and no one has partially shifted and menaced me with a claw in a long time."

Galen's eyes widened. "What! Who the *fuck* did that? Tell me right now, Renee."

She sighed dangerously, narrowing a glare at Jack before turning back to Galen. "No. Now come on. We have a dinner to go to with Jack's sort-of-wife. Joy!"

"Renee, you can't just walk away from this." Galen followed her out into the living room. Jack joined them.

"Galen, what on earth can you possibly do at this point? If you had stepped in it would have only made things worse. They already think I'm weak for being human. If I needed you to protect me all the time, they'd never have accepted me. Cats don't embrace the weak. You know this better than I do. They hazed me. I survived and did so without running anyone over in my car. I think that's a win."

He took her by the upper arms, pulling her close. "Babe,

you are *mine* to protect. That's part of what I am. What they are. Who did the partial shift?"

"It doesn't matter. Please, Galen, please respect my need to have handled it on my own. I had to do it my way, on my own. Don't pretend you don't understand that. Other mates brought into the jamboree deal with the same sort of stuff."

"Who? Renee, it can't stand that you were threatened that way. Yes, there's some hazing, but there are lines. Also, you two go on ahead because I need to stop in at my sister's house on the way."

Renee widened her eyes, surprised and then annoyed. "It's like I'm not even speaking. Are you thinking about sports right now instead?" She spun, turning her glare to Jack. "And *you*! I shared that with you for entirely different reasons than why I didn't tell Galen myself. You had no right to do that. You had no right to disrespect me the way you did. How can I trust you to tell you things now?"

She had a point, and he knew this would come up again many times in their future. She was a woman who liked to handle her own shit. It was a quality he respected. But.

"Sweetheart, you are mated to two shifter males. It's who we are. You're ours to protect. To keep happy. I'm sorry you're upset and I agree, I should have brought it up better, or at least told you I planned to discuss it with Galen. He had a right to know."

Galen smoothed down the front of his pants. "Jack's right, babe. I'm not mad at you. I understand you wanted to stand on your own two feet with my family and friends, but we have rules and it's clear those rules were violated."

"Well jeepers, silly me! I'm *so* glad you're sort of accepting of my feeble female notions about standing on my own and proving to your family—who already think I'm a horrible choice for you—that I am not. That I love you and when I need to be strong, I am. You don't know what it's like. But what does that matter as long as you two get to protect me? Who cares if your sister thinks I'm fucking you for your paycheck? I'll just let you two handle everything because thinking is so hard."

Jack sighed. "That's not what we're saying and you know it. It's one thing to stand up when you're being tested. It's another for a shifter to bring about a situation where a human could be infected without their consent. More than you being ours, more than you being disrespected in your mate's jamboree, I'm a lawkeeper, this sort of thing is my job. It can't go unaddressed."

She looked at them both and shook her head. "That settles it, huh? This is all about you and your cocks. Why should I bother, you know, actually trying to solve problems and stuff, after all, I'm just a human and you are a werewolf FBI agent and he's a jaguar super hero. *I am not your job, Jack.*"

She threw her hands up and stepped back, grabbing her bag. "I'm not going to talk about this anymore. Let's get this over with please. I don't want to be late."

Galen clenched his fists and tried to relax, but Jack felt his tension, his anger and need to comfort. They echoed his own. On the other hand, Renee was *pissed off.* His wolf liked that, but the man had been around enough women to know they'd be paying for this for a while longer.

"We're not going anywhere until we get this settled. When anyone in my family or jamboree harms you or threatens to harm you, I expect to be informed immediately."

"Same here. Wolves used to be a lot more hostile to humans, but over the last several years, it's eased up a lot. But you're my mate, which means you carry my position in the pack. I've explained already that you have chosen not to convert and no one seems bothered. Any wolf who doesn't show respect will get the shit kicked out of them via my boot."

"Why bother even speaking, I wonder? Do either of you even listen to me or, for fuck's sake, yourselves? When it comes to physically protecting me when I'm threatened, I accept and am grateful for your help. I understand who you both are and I make lots of allowances for that. For instance, if human men said and did the crap you two have in the last twenty minutes, I'd have gone after them with the kitchen shears. You notice they're right within my reach. My, how very rational I'm being. Still, this experience has left me running low on calm just now and I can see you don't take me seriously because, after all, you're giant male predator shifters and I'm just a little human woman."

"If you expect me to back off on this, Renee, you're wrong. And it's not because I think you're weak." Galen shrugged and Renee rolled her eyes. He did like how she got up in their faces without fear. Having her fear him would be his undoing.

She grabbed a coat from the peg and went to the door. "We going now?"

"Fine. You know I love you, you know I respect you and you know I'm not going to let this go. So, you two go on to dinner and I'll join you in an hour or so. Please send my apologies for my being late. I'll go to my parents' house and speak to them about all this." Galen stalked out the door without another word.

"He did *not* just do that."

"I think he did and I don't blame him."

Her eyes widened and then narrowed as he felt the heat of her anger through their link.

"I think I just officially lost my appetite. You go to dinner. Tell them I'm not feeling well. Or you can tell them you and Galen injured me when you both tossed your dicks around. Whatever."

"That's rude to Grace and Cade. They made preparations for this dinner. They've invited a lot of the pack over tonight just to meet you. This is my family and I'd be really hurt if you insulted them to punish me."

He clearly struck a nerve and knew he should feel bad, but he wanted her at his side. Wanted to show her off and yes, he wanted her to meet the people most important to him after her and Galen.

She went still for long moments and finally made an agitated sound. "I can't believe you're playing it this way. This isn't over, Jack. You will have a bill come due for this crap." She buttoned her coat with shaking hands, slapping his away when he tried to assist. "God forbid I ever fucking do something for myself. God forbid I insult them when neither of them could be bothered to come here to help you move your stuff. God forbid I have feelings or opinions on anything."

She left him to lock the inner door and grab his coat to dash after her. He locked the outer door and caught up to her at the corner. "Don't run off like that. This freak is out there."

"Jack?" She smiled up at him sweetly, but he wasn't fooled.

He put his arm around her shoulder and she stiffened. Too bad.

"What is it, gorgeous?" He walked them toward Cade and Grace's.

"Fuck off. I'm not playing right now, understand? I'll go to this dinner because you're right, it would be rude of me not to go and despite my wanting to twist your balls off right now, I do care that the people you love, love me too. However, you need to give me some credit and not treat me like I'm dim." She pinched him, interrupting the protest he'd been about to give. "*Don't* patronize me. You used that crap to manipulate me. I don't like to be manipulated. Makes me feel like never sucking your cock again."

Wisely, he shut up, but kept his arm around her as they walked over. It wasn't far and the night was chilly but clear and the air smelled good. He had her at his side, they'd survived a disagreement and she hadn't killed him or yanked off any of his favorite body parts, so he considered that a win.

Chapter Twelve

Galen was so angry he had to pause at his parents' front gate before going inside. He knew she'd been hazed a bit, but the level of detail had made him sick. How dare they treat her that way?

He understood she wanted to stand on her own. Respected that about her. She was right that they'd gain respect for her when she handled things without going to him. But there was way more than the usual silliness. This was a serious offense against his mate and a breach of jamboree protocol. He was angry at them, and at himself, for not knowing.

It still felt like home when he entered the cluttered entry. Pictures of all eight de La Vega children and their parents filled the wall space. More pictures, more and more with added husbands, wives and children, sat in frames on shelves and tabletops. A discarded pair of rollerblades rested under a bench near the door.

His mother stood in the kitchen, her glasses perched on her nose, watching his niece April scoop cookie dough onto a baking sheet.

Galen smiled, kissing April's cheek before hugging his mother.

"What a lovely surprise. What brings you here tonight and where's your wife?" She looked around him, toward the doorway he'd come through.

"What am I? Leftovers?"

She shrugged. "I like your wife, what can I say. But you're always my boy."

"She and Jack are on their way over to his Alphas' house for dinner. It's a big deal." He smiled, knowing between the two of them, they could probably manage to keep Renee out of trouble. Or, well at the very least, alive. Jack's entry into their life hadn't been expected, but Galen was thankful for it nonetheless.

"Nanna's got the cookies now, sweetie." His mother shooed his niece out and slid the baking sheet into the oven. "Now, you want to be telling me why you're here and not there?"

"I found out today that some cats partially shifted and threatened Renee. I also found out my sister called her a gold digging whore and told her if we had children they'd be weak. I know you and Renee had a rocky start, but this isn't right."

She pursed her lips and took a deep breath. "Our rocky start was really about me. You know that, right? She and I are fine now. She set me straight. Your wife is a strong, powerful woman. That she's as well liked as she is by most of this jamboree is a testament to that. It took a while, longer than most, but she's settling in. Or I thought she was. Did she tell you which of us threatened her?"

"She won't tell me. She'd told Jack some stuff. I guess she was nervous about tonight and revealed some things about what she'd experienced here. But when I found out, I demanded she tell me so I could deal with it. Mami, she's obsessed with standing on her own two feet or some such bullshit. I appreciate that she wants to be strong, but how could she not tell me? Didn't she trust me to protect her?"

"I suppose you shared with her that you felt her wanting to stand on her own two feet was bullshit?" His mother gave him a close inspection. "Though I don't see any missing limbs. She's more patient than I'd be in her place, Galen. As for the rest, of course she trusts you. If she didn't, she would have run to you the first time it happened rather than working through it on her own. If she'd been in real danger, she knows she can count on you. Imputing anything else from her actions is silly. She's human, Galen. Fragile. Breakable. Easily injured. But she held her own with fully grown shifters. She proved something to the jamboree and to herself. She's a powerful woman. She didn't tell you because she loves you and she knows how much this family means to you. She didn't tell you because she *needed* to do this herself. And she did." His mother shrugged.

"So we'll just let it slide that one of our cats unsheathed a claw at my mate?" Galen's anger tore at his gut.

"You're the one who brought home a human, boy. Did you think that would be a cake walk? Really? If so, you're not very smart. As for the unsheathing, what if it was Beth?"

"What if it was? Mami, she went into Renee's shop and told her she was pregnant. Not to celebrate with her sister-in-law, but to lord it over her. To use a wonderful thing to make my wife feel worthless. This is not acceptable. That's beyond Renee and whatever her personal stance is. This is my sister, a subordinate in this jamboree, deliberately trying to harm my mate."

"The punishment for unsheathing a claw at a human is beating. Your sister could lose the baby. You're willing to do that? Because of something she might have done two years ago?"

"Stop with the devil's advocate stuff!" He slammed a hand down on the counter.

She narrowed her eyes at him. "I know you did *not* just come into my kitchen and raise your voice to your mother. Renee may be patient because you're so pretty and all, but I've got eight kids and a pretty mate, I know your game."

He hung his head. "I'm sorry. It makes me angry. She's the best thing I've ever known. This is bullshit. My family should
210

love her. How can they not? Instead, she comes here with an open heart and she gets shit on. How can I ever feel right in bringing her here ever again?"

"Of course it makes you angry. You wouldn't care if you didn't love her. You wouldn't be scared if you didn't understand possessing the most wonderful thing in the world also means you can lose it. Each time one of you took the first step I worried. When you went out into the world. When you began to bring dates home." She gave him that infuriating shrug of hers. "Your family *does* love her. So Beth's a fool. So Carlos is a fool. Six out of eight is good odds. This isn't solely about us being shifters. All families deal with this stuff. Who doesn't like who, who is dating what person. Imagine what it will be like when Papi gets old enough Max will take over. Oh the fighting! But it's our way. Renee knows this. She knows she's loved and while I know she wishes she and Beth got along, it's never going to happen. I've already counseled her on this topic. Your sister is stubborn and myopic. She loves you, but she can't see that if she gave Renee a chance, things would go much better."

"Did you know Beth is the one who unsheathed a claw?"

"Your father found out. Not from Renee, but from someone else who'd witnessed it. Your father disciplined her. That's all you need to know. It's done and as far as I know she never did it again."

"And no one saw fit to tell me?"

"To be honest, I figured Renee would have by now. It was eighteen months ago. She would have been well within her rights to do so. As far as Papi telling you, why should he? He runs the jamboree. He took care of a problem. There's no need to make this worse than it was. She took her punishment in flesh."

"I have to go. This doesn't sit well with me. I can't bring her around if it's unsafe. My cat..."

"Your cat knows she is safe here. If you stop bringing her

around the only person who loses is Renee. Everyone will think she ran to you. She'll lose all the ground she's won. She worked hard for that ground. Harder than I ever imagined she would. But she did and I'm telling you right now, you go to her and tell her you're sorry and buy her something. Don't mess this up."

He groaned.

"I'm right about this and you know it. Go on. Papi will be back soon with pizza and several grandchildren. If they see you, you'll never escape." She grinned.

"So I just walk away from this? My woman has been threatened and disrespected for four years and that's just fine and dandy?"

"Your woman came here the first time and said four words. Her eyes were so wide I thought she might have passed out from shock. The last time she was here, she was positively covered in children and your siblings who adore her. All this other stuff is meaningless. This is our world, Galen. She knows it and you know it. She stands where she is, not for any other reason than because she made it happen. So no, it's not fine and dandy she was threatened and disrespected. But that's not how it is today except for two exceptions and a few old school cats from the jamboree who'll be dead in a few years anyway, so who cares? I watch out for her. So do many of your siblings and their mates. She is one of us, even if she has no fur. She has power and, as I told her on the phone yesterday, if she singed a few cats who got out of line with her magic, she'll be even more fine."

"You talk to her on the phone? What ever happened between you two?"

"Of course I talk to her on the phone. Several times a week. As for what happened, none of your business, boy. Now go on before I maim you for being impertinent."

"You're bloodthirsty." He smiled, for real this time. He would take care of the Beth situation. Carlos was in Costa Rica, but when he returned, Galen would rip him a new one. He'd never take his eyes from her at a jamboree gathering again. Still, his mother was right about most of the situation. Renee had stood on her own and proven herself a powerful mate. He would have to remember to compliment her on it. Only later when she wouldn't assume he was patronizing her.

"I am. Where do you think you get it? Your papi is mellow. He's a poet who practices law. Me? I'll rip throats out and then read poetry. Now go to her. We'd like to meet Jack too. I'm interested to see what this bond you three share looks like. I can see it on you now. I was concerned about you, about you having to share someone you so clearly adore. Things are good between the three of you?"

"Mami, that story is very long. I'll tell you when we go to breakfast on Thursday. For now just know I love them both and they both love me. I don't feel threatened, which I worried I might. It's early days, I'm sure we'll have our rough spots, but I think we've got a concrete bond and real respect. We can make it through whatever gets thrown at us. Rosemary told me she came by and warded the house."

"She did. And they went to the office and warded the entire building including the parking garage. They want to be sure anywhere Renee will be, will be safe. This mage sounds dangerous. We'll be watching."

His stomach clenched a moment at the memory of what Renee had suffered. How she'd been during the attack.

"What she remembered..."

His mother hugged him. "Is past. You're here with her now. Get going and tell Renee I send my love."

Remnants of her anger still clung to Renee as they approached the big building he told her was owned by Cade and Grace. Strong emotion pulsed through her veins, from Galen

213

Lauren Dane

doing God knew what at the de La Vegas' house to her own upset. Jack, she'd begun to realize, was hard to shake. His attitude was one of utter calm and total efficiency.

"Here we are. Let's go through the front so I can introduce you to the guards. I want everyone to know you on sight. It'll be easier for you to come and go if they know who you are."

Oh how she wanted to stomp her foot and make him drag her in! But she was a big girl and she knew how important this was to Jack. She'd make him pay for being a dick later. Since she was there anyway, she really did want to meet his friends and she'd be lying to herself if she didn't admit, at least in her head, that she was dying to see what Grace was like.

Two ridiculously gargantuan males stood just inside the doors. At first glance, the place appeared to be luxury condos, but once she got inside, she saw it was far more than that.

When the guards saw who it was, they stood at attention.

"Hey, Jack! You finally brought Renee to meet us." The male speaking was gloriously beautiful. Tall, lithe, his brown eyes missed nothing as he inclined his head. A river of straight, fragrant hair the color of darkest sky, slid forward.

"Akio, this is Renee, my mate. One of them." Jack laughed.

She shook hands and tried not to blush. "It's nice to meet you, Akio." She grinned. "By the way, Southie?"

Akio nodded. "You're good with accents."

"I volunteer at a community center there. I teach classes on photography. When I'm there for a long time, I pick it up and my Boston thickens."

"I used to think it would lessen. The longer I lived out this way, it should soften up." He snorted. "Not so much."

"Ha! So you say. When I first met you I had no idea what the hell you were saying about a third of the time. You're way better now."

Another male stepped forward and bumped hips with Akio

214

to move him aside. "I'm Tony. Jack won't shut up about you so I feel like I know you already. Welcome to the pack."

Tony was built like a tank. Short, red hair, freckles and an easy smile hid the predator just beneath the surface.

She took the hand he held out. "Nice to meet you."

"Go on through. Belly was shouting for you about five minutes ago."

Jack turned to Grace. "Belly is our nickname for Annabelle Warden. She's the middle kiddo and a holy terror. She's four so she knows everything and as long as it's all about her, things are good to go."

Renee smiled back, squeezing his hand. It was hard to stay mad at him when he was so very sweet. But she managed. There'd be an ass kicking later.

"Ready?" he asked quietly. "They're going to love you. How could they not?"

"A question for the ages I'm sure. Come on then. Let's get this show on the road. God." She froze. "Should we have brought something? Flowers? A dessert?"

He pulled her through some double doors and the whole place opened up. They'd taken half the building's apartments and gutted it, apparently to make one open three-story living space.

"This is fabulous. Absolutely breathtaking." The view was of a rambling garden just beyond the windows and then down to the water and the cityscape beyond.

"You must be Renee."

She turned and *holy wow*. This had to be Grace and suddenly Renee wanted the ground to open up and swallow her. Petite, elegant and beautiful, she was everything Renee was not. How could she compete?

"You must be Grace. Jack has spoken of you often."

Oh yes, this wasn't awkward at all. She wanted to roll her eyes or punch Jack, maybe both. Instead she shook hands with a woman Jack had loved for years and pretended this was all totally normal for her.

"That you, Jack?" A man walked through a far doorway, holding a chattering toddler. Two dressed up little girls rushed past him straight to Jack, who scooped them up with a laugh. So much joy on his face! It rushed through their link. He truly loved these children and these people. Wolves. Whatever.

She envied him this family, but was grateful he had it to draw strength and comfort from.

Grace had moved to Jack, her hand on his forearm as they spoke to the children. She'd been thoroughly dismissed apparently. The way she stood effectively shut Renee out of their little moment. She realized how very little patience for this sort of crap she had left. Couldn't she be a normal ex-girlfriend who'd make pointed and backhanded comments about Renee's shoes or how cute her face was? No, she had to be an uber werewolf doctor who looked like she could wear opera gloves and pearls and not look as if she was on her way to a Halloween party.

The man who had to be Cade Warden, and holy hotness, that man was something else, put the toddler down and within seconds, the little one headed to Renee on cautious feet.

"I'm Cade Warden. I'm very pleased to meet you. Welcome to National Pack." He bowed over her hand and kissed it. He straightened and put a hand at the small of her back. "Would you like a tour while Jack remembers his manners?"

Manners, pfft. He was being a dick and she wanted to kick him. Instead she took a chance. "Can I be honest with you?"

The stiffness in Cade's spine lessened and his formal demeanor wisped away, replaced by a genuine grin, complete with dimple. This one must have been a handful before he met Grace.

216

"I would be honored if you would be honest with me. We're family after all and I value truth over fake manners any day."

"I don't much want to walk around and pretend like I'm not annoyed my mate is having an intimate moment with another woman and her kids. I know it sounds stupid as I have another man already. And probably insulting since the woman with her hands all over my mate is your wife and all, but I've had pretty much the most trying week of my life and I find myself incapable of pretense just at this time."

Cade's head tipped back and he laughed. A rich, sexy sound that brought a shiver and *finally* Jack's attention. Grace turned and Renee sent a pointed look at her hands and back to her face.

A smile touched the other woman's mouth as she moved her hands. She spoke to Jack, who handed the girls in his arms back to Grace. When he straightened, he sought Renee out, his face relaxing into a smile made just for her.

"Sweetheart, let's go on through to the family room and the dining room. Grace tells me there are several wolves who can't wait to meet you." She felt his joy through their bond. Happiness at being with her, happiness at sharing that with his family. Her desire to snatch him baldheaded eased a tiny bit.

A tug on her sweater caught her attention. She turned and knelt to get eye to eye with the little boy trying to get her attention. Immediately she saw it in his eyes and on his skin. He was ill.

"Hello, you. I bet you don't feel well." Renee brushed the hair back from a clammy forehead.

Jack knelt with her. "Henri, this is Renee. She's my mate. Renee, this is Henri, the youngest Warden."

"It's very nice to meet you, Henri. Your pictures, and more of your sisters too, are hanging on my wall at home. We live near a park, you know. Just right across the street. There are swings. One day when you're feeling better, you and your sisters should come play. You're very special to Jack, and that's important to me. Would you like something to drink?"

"Everything okay?" Grace's tone was edged in worry and threaded with condescension. God, did everything have to be so complicated?

Jack's body language changed slightly. Whatthefuckever, this was dumb.

Henri snuggled up close to Renee, so she picked him up when she stood. "I don't think Henri is feeling well, Grace. I've got some tea that will help his tummy. It's at home, but it shouldn't take too long for me to run back and grab it. Or you probably have—"

Grace interrupted. "I'm a doctor." Grace reached and took Henri from Renee, putting him down.

She kept trying. Perhaps Grace was just one of those people who seemed bitchy at first but it was more that she didn't have social skills. "Yes, I've heard. Jack was telling me about a clinic you'd started here in the area. That's a heady achievement."

Cade and Jack had been in conversation about something or other. It was just Grace and Renee and the elephant in the room.

"I'm sure *actual* medicine would help if there were anything wrong with my children. We don't do that herbal stuff." Grace's look was smug and Renee wasn't having any of it.

"Really? I know some stuff that might help with that obstruction blocking your colon right now."

Grace looked puzzled for about half a minute until she got that Renee just told her she had a stick up her ass.

They locked horns, and Renee realized, as she spooled power from the air around where they stood, that she had something just as good as shifting into something with teeth and claws. Her mother-in-law had said pretty much the same thing on the phone to her the day before and of course, she'd been right. Renee was done taking shit and this bitch in front of her was going to learn the first lesson.

Henri head-butted Renee's leg and smiling, she stooped to pick him up again.

Grace put her hand in between them. "I think he's just tired and overwhelmed."

"Overwhelmed by what? Has he had a busy day? I'm not worried he's contagious or anything. It's no hardship to hold him." Renee saw illness around him, but nothing she could see any more serious than a stomach ache.

"No. He's just fine where he's at."

Oh no she did not.

"What is your problem?" She asked it in a light enough tone to keep Henri or her idiot of a mate from being alarmed.

"Problem? You're trying to work some magic on my kid without my permission. That's my problem."

"Magic? I picked him up and felt his forehead. I didn't—"

Grace interrupted again. "We don't need you and your tea leaves. We were doing just fine before you came along and turned Jack's life upside down."

"Tea leaves? What are you talking about? He's pasty and has a fever. I can tell just by looking at him. I offered *you* some tea for him. You said no and insulted me, but I let that pass because I have manners even if you don't. I haven't done anything to you or anyone else. I don't even read tea leaves, by the way. I'm not a fortune teller, I run a juice and coffee bar for goodness sake."

"Yes, I heard. Congratulations, it's a heady achievement."

Renee blinked a few times, her inner bitch now fully engaged. "Oh no you did *not* just say that. Listen here, I don't know who you think you are, but to me, you're a nasty, selfish bit...*person.* You want to come at me, you do it like a big girl, why don't you? I get that you don't know me and so you're not sure how I'll be for Jack. But you don't insult my work, my education and my life without even knowing me, you stuck up, elitist C.O.W. I sincerely hope your bedside manner is better than this haughty little tantrum you're throwing because you can't have Jack anymore."

Henri, who'd been patting a sticky palm against the window a few feet from them, turned and wailed as he projectile vomited. Renee only wished Grace had been closer to receive the full brunt of it. Being right was awesome, but she felt terrible for the sweet little guy.

Both men, who'd been standing by clearly not knowing what to do as they'd watched the increasingly hostile interaction between the women, managed to spring into action. Henri was not her child and his mother clearly didn't want her to be near him, so Renee moved to gather her things. She needed to be done with this situation and as soon as possible. She'd made a promise to herself on the way over. No more taking shit from anyone. This was the first step.

"Thank you for inviting us to dinner. I'm going to head out now," Renee said to Cade, who shook his head and reached for her. Reacting without thinking, Renee threw an energy wall around herself, and Cade staggered back. Wow, that was pretty cool and all, but whoa, she just assaulted the Supreme Alpha.

The room filled with growling werewolves wondering what the hell had happened. Jack yelled in the background, shoving people off him, giving orders and trying to get to her.

Great.

"I'm sorry. I didn't mean to." She halted, not sure what else to say.

"No, I'm the one who's sorry. I shouldn't have grabbed for you. You did the same any of us would do if someone rushed at us in the midst of an argument." Cade took a step back, his hands open. "Please don't leave."

"I said, stand down!" Jack ordered in a terse bark. The wolves all around obeyed. "You mind telling me what you said to Renee?" he asked Grace, who'd returned with a far calmer and cleaned up Henri. Now he wanted to deal with it? With a dozen pissed off, wary wolves in the room too?

"I was unconscionably rude." She turned to Renee, who nodded, agreeing. "I apologize. I was totally out of line. He *was* sick. He apparently ate seven pieces of sausage just a few minutes ago. Why no one thought to stop him I don't know." She sent a glare at Cade. "You were right and I didn't see it because I wanted you to be wrong."

"For Jack."

Grace nodded. "You're so lovely. Full of light and life. Calm and kind. I wanted you to be horrible. Which is stupid because I *am* happy for Jack and God knows I had difficulties with my sister-in-law at first too. I remember telling myself I'd never treat my anchor's mate the way Nina had treated me. I was worse. Nina was just a grumpy, pregnant werewolf. I was a jealous, hateful cow."

"Yeah."

Grace's eyes widened with surprise and then she laughed. "You'll fit in just fine around here."

That remained to be seen, but she wanted it to be true. "For what it's worth, I would never do magic on a person without their permission. I don't even know enough of it to do any harm. I meant peppermint tea. Nothing more. It soothes belly aches. The warm liquid tends to relax too."

Jack moved to touch Renee and she allowed it only to keep from making a scene. He stood there the whole time and did nothing. This after freaking all over Galen about what his cats had done. She needed to handle things on her own, but the way he'd just stood there while Grace had inferred she was low class and stupid had hurt her more than Grace being a bitch.

"Please stay. We have so much food and I really would like to get to know you." Grace smiled around her to Jack, reminding Renee it was time to lay out all the ground rules so there'd be no further incidents like this.

"Here's how things are going to work. First, you won't go around me to Jack. Ever. I realize he's close with you and up until I met you just now, I thought that was a good thing. It's good to have family. But you are not his wife. I am. *You* are not his mate. He is your anchor. I respect his connection to you and Cade. However, there's a difference in who we each are to him. Remember that."

Grace said nothing for a few seconds and nodded. "That's fair. For the record, I've never—"

It was Renee's turn to interrupt. "I don't care about anything between Jack and someone else before I came into his life. I care about from now forward. We got off on the wrong foot. I'm willing to accept your apology and offer of friendship at face value. But, since you alluded to all the drama in my life—" she sent the appropriate disapproving look to Jack, who responded with the corresponding hang dog look, "—and I do appreciate you sharing that without my permission, Jack. That's a habit you need to break, by the way."

"It's not like I gossiped about you. It's my job to protect you and this pack. I had to keep them apprised." Jack was caught in a difficult place and she knew he hadn't done it as a complaint. But he needed to remember other people and their wishes too. She'd talk to him about it later, and about what her real issue with that evening had been.

"No, but you shared things it took me years to share with anyone else and you did it without asking me first. I don't like that at all, Jack, and it's not the first time. You might notice these things if you hadn't simply stood there and watched as someone cut me to shreds." She returned to Grace. "Anyway, since you brought it up, yes, as a matter of fact, I've got all the drama I can handle and more in my life right now. I've made a zero tolerance rule. By that I mean, I've been walked all over for some time and that's not going to happen again."

Jack tried to move closer but she stepped away.

"I can respect that." Grace smiled. At Renee. "How about a drink? I can't have one, but I bet you could use one."

Henri put his arms out to Renee. She looked to Grace. "Is that okay with your mom?"

"My back is killing me. I'm pregnant, which is probably why I'm extra touchy. At least that's my story." She handed Henri over to Renee and he snuggled into her. "He's a picky kid. I should have taken that as a sign."

Galen strolled in, his normally handsome features hard. "Every time I go away, I come back to an enraged woman, Jack."

Renee, happy to see him, sent him a tired, but genuine smile. "I'm okay. Really."

He looked her over closely, smiling at Henri who stared at him with big, wide eyes.

"Indulge me, please. Let's talk for a moment." He held out his hand.

"The garden is quiet if you'd like to step outside for a bit." Cade took Henri, who narrowed his eyes at his father. "She'll be back, kid."

"Excuse us a moment," she called over her shoulder as they stepped outside.

It felt better out there. The quiet murmurs of the city, of the waterway, traffic, trains, all combined into a particularly comforting sound. "Nice out here."

Jack stepped outside too and Renee felt the tension between the two men spike. Galen nodded in his direction and turned his attention to Renee again. "For the last several minutes I've been headed here I've felt your emotions and there was nothing I could do to help you. Do you have any idea what it felt like to experience your shame from a distance? I don't like feeling shame come from you. I never want to feel that ever again. What happened and who made you feel that?"

"Shame?" Renee realized Jack finally got the depth of what happened between her and Grace.

"Jack, you were a few feet away." Renee didn't want to push them into a fight but really it had to be said.

"I know you were arguing but you seemed calm enough. Cade said to let it be, to let you two work it out. He's gone through this before, I figured he knew what he was talking about. I didn't feel shame from you and I don't know why. I'm sorry. What did she say?"

She just wanted to go to sleep. Even jog. Anything but have this conversation again. Or ever. "I really don't want to go into it right now. There's a house full of people waiting to meet me and I've just had a bitchfight with their female alpha within range of their hearing. I appreciate your apology, Jack, and I'm sorry you're upset." She took Galen's hands, needing him to know she appreciated his concern. "I'm sorry you felt helpless to fix it. It's okay now. I'll tell you the whole story tomorrow, I promise. After a lot of coffee."

"I don't like this, Renee. I just had a conversation with my mother about this mess and I'm already annoyed by having my wife treated like crap. I'm not really up to sitting down at a table and eating with people who found delight in tormenting you."

"And no, no, I'm not willing to wait until tomorrow to be told just what the hell happened!" Jack said, clearly annoyed. Like he or his little buddy had the right? Pfft.

"Yeah, well you know what? My warm feelings for you two are at an all time low just now, so really, you need to back the fuck off." She looked to Jack. "Both of you."

224

"What the fuck did *I* do?" Galen tried to look innocent. Which was the wrong thing to do.

"Did I not just tell you both to leave it be? Must you both push until you get your way? Even when it involves me and what I want? Fine, if you want to play it, if you want to do this right now, let's do it. You ran off to your parents to tattle after I begged you not to."

Galen exhaled sharply. "I had to. Renee, you don't understand how it felt to know you'd suffered and I hadn't seen it. I had to protect you. I had to confront my parents."

"Well, thank God all that was about you. You see, my mistake was in thinking it happened to me and I handled it myself like all the others who marry into your jamboree did. Since all this is about you then, did you get your answers, Galen? Do you feel better now that you've just undone four years of my constant fighting to fit in with your family?"

"I didn't undo anything. My mother got mad at me for going around you. But she said some stuff to set me straight. No one knows but her." Galen reached for her, sliding his thumb over her bottom lip. "I love you so much, Renee. Knowing you were harmed by my people, when I should have protected you, it made me feel like a loser."

Jack sighed, reaching out to touch her and she allowed it. "I told you I didn't mean to gossip. It's not that way. I just wanted to fill them in on our life. On you so they understood why I'd be with you more often, why I would be using more Pack resources to guard you." Jack wanted her to understand, she got that part.

"That's just part of it, Jack. You blabbed to Galen without my permission and then used guilt to get me here. I got here and your bitch of an anchor insulted me and you stood by and watched. Doing nothing. After you'd gotten up in Galen's shit for not stopping the hazing I went through."

"I didn't hear that part. Honestly. I knew you were arguing, but you seemed to be handling it and I didn't want to interfere after you'd just told us both how important it was for you to stand on your own." Jack's expression was forlorn and even with all her mad, she couldn't bear to see either of them so sad.

"I concede that larger point about doing things myself. It is important to me. Like you know, telling people stuff on my own schedule. In the future though, if your anchor is ripping me to shreds, calling me a low-rent, problem-ridden bitch, you could stop making googly eyes at her and, you know, take my side."

"I did not make googly eyes. And I'm sorry, okay? I'm sorry because if I had felt shame I would have intervened. I would have because I love you and also because it's beyond out of line."

She sighed out, hard. Part of this mess was hers to own. Most of it was them though, damn it. So sweet and overbearing, her men. Good Lord she was going to spend the next however many decades managing them and having to push back when they stepped over the line.

"If you two were bad in bed or not so pretty to look at, all this He-Man stuff would get old." She tiptoed up to deliver a quick kiss to Galen's chin, right where her favorite dent resided. "Lucky for you—" she looked around him to Jack, "—for both of you, you have lots of good qualities."

Galen wrestled a smile but lost. "You're supposed to be serious right now, Renee."

"Galen, dude, we're here. This is Jack's family and I want them to like me. More than that, I want them to understand that despite his infuriating tendency to share information he was given in confidence, I love Jack. *We* love Jack and *we're* good for him." Of course that was sort of hard to prove when there was truth to the accusation that Renee had dragged all sorts of drama into his life.

"I know you're angry with me. I can take that. But I hurt you and..." Jack reached to touch her and she leaned into the
226

palm against her cheek.

Renee shook her head, tears pricking her lashes despite her best intentions. She had brought this all on them, even though Grace had no right to say it like Renee had done it on purpose.

"Stop. It's over and I can't see the point in beating yourself up over it when I will kick your ass later." She winked and he rolled his eyes. "Please can we just go in to dinner? Seriously, I'm done with all this emotional overdose. We can talk later. I'm all right. I handled it and made it clear I wouldn't tolerate any more of the same."

"You act like we don't have a freeway into your emotions. I can feel you right now." Jack put his palm over her belly. "You hurt."

She nodded. "Sure. But I'm resilient."

"I don't want to leave it." Galen looked so sad and upset.

"If we don't leave it I'm going to punch you in the junk for ignoring me earlier and running to tattle. I'm going to resent it and I don't want to right now. If I don't leave it I'm going to start obsessing about Jack and Grace and I don't want to. I can only do so much. I'm human, okay? I'm upside down and sideways. I'm just not the same as the people in there, or in your jamboree. Even if you were human I'd be different. I'm not giving up. I'm not weak. I'm just…exhausted. I understand you're upset and you want to fix it, but there are things you can't fix, Galen. Doctors and lawyers looking down on people who own smoothie carts is not new. I'm telling you I have no room to process anything else right now. I can't."

"She said that?" Jack's shock was plain on his face.

"Shocked? Really? That your precious Grace could be a classist, condescending bitch? Come on. It's over. I believe her apology was genuine and we'll see how it goes from now on. I'm willing to give her that chance and even though I'm pissed, I don't blame you for her comments. Jack, I know you want to make things right and I know you feel bad, but I'm asking you to set it aside and let it go for now."

He sighed. "If she said that, how can we go and eat at their table?"

"You're both just determined to make me cry and get puffy and to have Jack's family hate me too. Is that it? Come the fuck on! Leave it alone for now and I'll share it with you later. If you both keep pushing, I will lose my shit." She turned and went back inside.

Chapter Thirteen

"Here." Grace put a glass of wine in Renee's hand when she walked through the doors into the family room. She heard Jack and Galen arguing quietly in the background, but decided to ignore it for the moment. She did appreciate that they cared about her and wanted her to feel better, but it was way beyond time they listened and let it go for a few hours so she could get through the rest of the evening.

"Thanks." It was gone in four gulps.

"I *am* really sorry. You don't know me so you can't be expected to understand just how out of character my behavior was out there. Honestly, I'm so ashamed of myself."

Henri saw Renee and pushed at his dad until Cade turned, noted her presence and put him down so Henri could toddle over.

"Hey there. You feeling better?" She knelt and he climbed up her legs and into her arms. "I guess so." She stood, feeling just how heavy he was as he wrapped his legs around her waist like a monkey.

"He's been saying, Neh? Neh?" I think he means you." Grace put her hand on Renee's arm. "I don't quite know how to make this all better. Are they arguing?"

"You can't. Not really. Let's just move forward." Her stomach growled and Henri put his hands on her cheeks and laughed.

"Food!" he shouted gaily.

"No more for you, little dude. But plenty for us. Come on through. They'll come in when they're ready and you look pale. How long has it been since you've eaten?" Grace led her through and she nearly balked when she noted about eight dozen people milling around.

She was introduced to so many people she couldn't remember their names. But she knew exactly who the older man using the cane was. Jack's foster father, Templeton Mancini, the male who had run this pack before a poisoning several years prior had left him severely disabled and he handed leadership over to Cade. Jack respected and loved this man and because of that, Renee really hoped he liked her too.

"I'd have known you anywhere." Templeton approached with a smile. "He talks about you all the time. *The hair, Templeton, gorgeous curls, so soft. She glows with magic.*" He mimicked Jack's voice so well she laughed. "It's an honor to meet you. I'm Templeton Mancini."

He took her hand and, in a courtly bow, kissed her knuckles before straightening again. Henri clapped but didn't seem to want down.

"I'm the one who's honored. Jack has told me about you and your wife. He talks about you with such respect and affection. You did a good job raising him. He's a good man."

The man in question entered the room behind her. She felt the pull of their connection immediately. Galen was with him and both locked their attention on her and moved as if nothing and no one else mattered. A girl had to be insane not to be flattered by that.

"I think we've been dumped for a younger man," Galen said, grinning at her and then back to Henri.

Pride on his face, Jack clapped his hands to get attention. "Everyone, this is Galen de La Vega. And the gorgeous witch holding Henri is Renee. My mates."

Templeton nodded and then hugged Jack. Renee heard the quiet inquiry about Templeton's health and the snort of amused annoyance he got in response.

"A cat and a witch? Jack, I'm pretty sure you're not even that nice. And, I happen to be way more handsome. Why is it you get two mates?"

"That huge lout is Dave. Another Warden. They breed like roaches so you'll find them everywhere." Jack indicated the giant male holding Becca. "He's Grace's personal guard. Who is nowhere near as handsome as me."

She sat, Galen on one side and Jack on the other. But Henri was having none of it. He sent a glare that she had to admit was pure Cade Warden to Jack as he pushed at his shoulder. "I sit!"

Grace held her hands out and Henri hugged Renee's neck tight. "Honey, why don't you let Renee eat? Come over here and sit with Mommy."

"It's fine unless I'm breaking a table rule. Really, he's not bothering me."

"She's this way when she's with my nieces and nephews too. They all flock to her and hog her time and attention. Can't blame them really." Galen was so charming and handsome, even as he pissed her off, she wanted to jump on him. She also found herself startled to learn he was so much more observant than she'd given him credit for. Those kids were her favorite part of being with his family.

"Yeah, yeah. But he wants my place." Jack took one of Henri's hands and kissed the fist. "Sorry, roly, you're going to have to find your own lady. This one's taken."

"Roly?" She dodged questing little fingers, moving her silverware and glass out of his reach.

"Roly-poly. When he was a baby he never bothered with

crawling. He just rolled like a little bowling ball." Cade winked at his son. "He'd barrel through the room. Becca started calling him that, saying he was like one of those little bugs that rolls itself into a ball. It stuck."

As it turned out, Jack didn't have to move over enough for Henri's high chair because Henri decided to sit on Renee's lap. He seemed quite content to play with her hair and rub his face on the softness of the scarf she wore. Jack couldn't hide how happy it made him, which in turn made Renee happy. It also helped keep things in perspective when she thought about Galen's family. Two of eight wasn't too much different than other people's families. She did like many of them. What she needed to do was make more of an effort.

It was late when they finally got out the door. Grace apologized again, thanked her for being so good to Henri and invited her to lunch the following week. When she stepped outside, she felt a million times better than she had several hours before.

They walked the quiet streets back home, her hand in Jack's and, on the other side, in Galen's. No one spoke. No one argued. It was a good kind of quiet, comfortable, easy, and Renee rejoiced in its utter normalcy.

"God what a gorgeous night it is." She breathed in deep, feeling the cold edge into her lungs. "I wish it was clearer. We have a rooftop deck. Galen got me a telescope for my last birthday. It's fabulous for looking at the stars and spying on other people through their windows."

Galen squeezed her hand, smiling.

Jack snorted a laugh. "You surprise me all the time. Just when I think I know you, or what you're like, you break out something I never could have imagined you saying but once I know, I can believe you doing it." He kissed her quickly. "I like that. It pleases me."

She shrugged, flattered and a bit flustered. "Thank you. I'm just weird. It's not special to be weird. But I like who I am. I realized that earlier tonight. I remembered that I do like Galen's family for the most part. I need to be better about remembering what my blessings are, I think. I certainly want to get along with other people, but I don't need to quest for approval. I can't be anyone but who I am. I don't have the sophistication to fake it."

"Thank God for that," Galen muttered. "Look, it's not about sophistication. But you *are* special. Not just to me or Jack, but in general. You're something rare and powerful and things are drawing toward it. I can feel it. The closer we get to home, the more I feel wrong. The air is...my cat is uneasy."

"It's not balanced." Renee realized balance was the perfect word. "It's uneven and uncomfortable. It's like the reverse nap of fabric or something. Rosemary said some of these mages prey on witches, hunt them down and take their magic."

"Like a magic jacking? This guy is so going to die." The menace seeping from Jack made her feel safer.

"More than theft. The spell to steal the prime magical force within a person is intertwined with their life essence. The witch will die a horrible, painful death as their magic is drained along with their life. Um, or so I'm told."

"So glad you decided to share that right away." Jack's jaw was clenched again.

"Pffft. I only learned it all today. Then we got dressed, had a fight, came over to Cade and Grace's, had another fight and now I'm telling you."

Jack's mouth tightened and she felt better. "Seems to fall under the really good things for Jack and Galen to know category. It's those things I like to know immediately. Helps me protect your pretty little ass."

"Hey, thanks for that clue! I'd have never known that cause I'm all girly and stuff." She rolled her eyes at him and he raised a brow back at her.

Renee knew what a freak she was, that even this silly back and forth delighted her because it was normal.

Galen, ever the pragmatist, brought the conversation back to the original topic. "How do we fight this? Should we stay elsewhere until this is cleared up? My mom told me to offer the guest house, by the way."

"That's very nice of her. I don't know, to be honest with you. I don't. Rosemary seems to believe that the warding around the house will be enough and that teaching me to use my power more effectively will be the best weapon. We can't hide forever. If this is my normal level of power, this one guy won't be the last we see."

"Which is so very comforting," Jack mumbled.

"All the more reason to find this dipshit and tear him apart." Galen kept his gaze darting around the area as they approached the front doors. "No one here but the neighbors as far as I can scent."

"If I tell you it makes me hot that you and Jack are all alpha male right now will that change the subject too obviously?"

"Hmpf." Jack tried to look gruff but failed.

"Look, they're helping me. Really. Teaching me stuff. Right now it's worse because it's all new and I don't quite know how to protect myself or even what the fuck I am. But eventually it'll be better. Eventually we will have a normal life. Or as normal as the three of us can have given the circumstances."

Jack went ahead of them and put her in the middle with Galen at her back. It felt very commando and silly, but she appreciated it nonetheless. He made them wait outside while he made sure everything inside was all right. Galen pulled her back against his chest and she listened to his heart, breathed in his scent, let him comfort her.

"What did you think of Jack's people?" she murmured.

"I don't like how you were treated. But they were friendly to me. Then again, my family hasn't been that good to you either."

"Galen, you know I love you more than breathing, but we have to let this go. I really think it's been holding me back, keeping me from really enjoying my time with your family who do like me. It sets me up for failure. I'm not the only wife in the world whose in-laws don't like her and it's not everyone. Most of them are very nice to me. Beth is Beth, I just have to avoid her as much as I can in the future."

Jack called them inside and they found themselves ensconced in their big bed, naked, just enjoying each other. She knew the thing with the Pack would come up, it had to. But she also knew they could work past it.

Jack let out a long breath after settling in, his nose in the crook of her neck as he caressed her skin and reached over to touch Galen from time to time as well. Trying to process the insanity of the last week certainly seemed nicer to do in bed with Renee against him and Galen's scent rising from his skin.

The night before they'd loved for hours. His muscles ached pleasantly as he stretched. He didn't bother opening his eyes, he knew they were there where they all belonged.

Renee made a seriously sexy snuffle of annoyance when he slid a thumb across her nipple. As if he could resist, it was her nipple in his palm after all. He was weak, what could he say?

Galen interrupted his thoughts. "How about I go and grab breakfast? I need to drop something by the office, so I'll rush back."

"Take my car. It's around the corner." Jack looked over her shoulder to Galen. At lips he'd kissed, the hollow of his throat where Jack knew Galen's taste was strong and warm. Their gazes locked as the heat rose enough to bring a soft sigh from Renee and a raised brow from Galen.

Enough to bring Galen across Renee, those lips brushing against his own and then against his throat, teeth there just enough to remind Jack of what they were. Galen's growl made Jack's system speed up with want, even as it luxuriated in their connection.

A look passed between them again. Jack knew Galen also had procured a lease on the space in his building for her cart and they planned to bring it up that day. They'd briefly spoken about it the night before when she'd been in the bathtub. Jack and Galen would present a united front. This was about safety, plain and simple. In that building she'd be guarded and away from her fucked up father and stepmother. He and Galen could afford it and they weren't going to argue.

Ha. Well, it would help if she were nice and relaxed from being waited on a bit, maybe sex drunk too. Not that either of those things would be a hardship for them. Both men not only wanted to take care of her, it was something they both found comfort in. They needed to know she was safe and happy. Not that he didn't expect a fight from her because she was independent and while he found that incredibly attractive, it wasn't going to fly this time.

"Don't think I can't feel you two scheming through the bond. And all that hot gay stuff too. That part I like."

Jack laughed and Galen grinned, rolling his eyes as he pushed from bed. "I like that part too. I'm going to rush off and be back as soon as possible."

She poked her head from where she'd buried herself in the blankets. Corkscrew curls in disarray, she rubbed her eyes and looked toward Galen. "Make it fast. I don't like you not being right here."

Galen turned from his path to the bathroom and came

back to her side. "I don't know what it is, but you live inside me. Don't ever not do that," he murmured, bending to kiss her temple. She blinked up at him and Jack watched, looking at the two parts of himself that rendered him whole, let that warmth wash through him.

"Okay. I promise." She allowed herself one caress of Galen's thigh and settled back against Jack's chest, both taking in that graceful, powerful gait before Galen disappeared into the bathroom to clean up and get ready to go to work.

He held her until she'd relaxed, breathing deeply as she'd fallen asleep again. They'd kept her awake after a rather intense discussion about what had happened during the dinner at Cade and Grace's and Jack hadn't ever seen her as angry as she'd been when she found Galen's sister had been punished when she had unsheathed her claws. But they'd worked it through, had yelled, sulked, laughed and fucked.

He got up, careful not to jostle her, and headed into the office space he shared with Galen. He wanted to check his mail to be sure there wasn't anything pressing and then grab a shower himself.

Renee woke, this time to an empty bed. She sat up and grabbed her robe before padding out into the living room. Jack wasn't around. She figured he'd gone to get the mail or perhaps had taken a run. She knew wherever he was, it wouldn't be far. Galen had gone to work and she was sure he'd get caught up in something. The man loved his job and it was a busy one. She understood that sort of dedication and passion, respected it, so it rarely irked.

Smiling, she moved toward the entry when she heard the door downstairs open up. Most likely Galen was home and he'd have breakfast and coffee. He'd have a hug that would make everything inside her stop and surge forward to soak him in.

When she opened the door though, it wasn't Galen at all. It

wasn't Jack. Yeah, make a mental note to actually use the link every once in a while.

A man she'd never seen before strode into the room, his arm shot out and with it, energy hit her body, knocking her back into the coffee table so hard she saw stars and lost her breath.

Fear rushed into her body, tensing muscles, sweat beaded on the back of her neck as she scrabbled backward, her eyes never leaving the man moving to her. He spoke under his breath and the fire of her flesh tearing open wrenched a scream from her lips. Pain twisted inside her as it began to feel as if her entire body was being pulled from her eye sockets.

She tried to get hold of herself enough to remember any of the stuff her aunt and sister had taught her. Renee even managed to send some energy back at him before agony brought a curve to her spine as she arched to try anything to make it stop. She couldn't stop screaming, sobbing, writhing as the fire of pain engulfed her nerve endings.

Stretching out as much as she could, she grabbed for the phone on the nearby chair. Bolt after bolt hit her as he never stopped speaking. The words hit her like fists, slicing into her soul and taking something important along with it.

Her feet slid in the blood and she realized he'd broken something inside as well as having rent her flesh apart in several places. She bled so much the room filled with the stench of her fear and the copper of her blood.

She was dying. She'd leave this world without ever seeing Galen or Jack again. She'd never have children, never get to meet the rest of her family. This man was stealing everything from her!

Her fingertips met the cool metal of the phone, knocked it to the floor as she crawled to reach the keypad. All the while she screamed because there was nothing else she could do. She punched buttons at random, hoped they made a call.

Her magic ebbed, passed from her, and she grabbed it back, pulling with all the strength she had left and whipped it back at him enough to stop the chanting for half a moment. His bellow of pain stoked her energy, given her a bit more, enough to keep fighting and throwing out the only magic she knew and whatever else she could muster.

"Hello? Hello? Jack? Is that you?" Cade's voice. She'd dialed Cade Warden.

She screamed again. "Help me, please. He's killing me." At least she thought that's what she'd said. This time the man picked her up and slammed her against the bar. The arm she'd put out to protect herself cracked, splintered, and she had nothing left, no feeling other than the gaping maw of unconsciousness encroaching as he blocked the bottle of wine she'd grabbed to hit him with. Each of her fingers was snapped, broken as he continued to kill her.

A roar, splintered wood. She slid to the floor, the warm pool of her blood cooling, thickening as she lay in it. The last thing she saw was a flash of fur, the scythe like claws, pale blue eyes lit with fury.

Jack had come for her and she wouldn't die alone.

Jack was torn between running after the man who'd attacked his woman and getting an ambulance. The ambulance won out.

With shaking hands, he called 911 and looked up, ready to fight again, when Cade burst through the door, followed by Galen and several other wolves and cats.

The sound Galen made echoed what he felt. Loss, rage, tenderness and a lot of fear. Her life force, normally so strong and beautiful, had receded to little more than a trickle.

He'd taken a shower and decided to run to the nearby newspaper stand, his attention snagged on a necklace he'd spotted in a shop window, the necklace he'd dropped as a wave of her fear had hit him so hard he'd gone to his knees, his vision swimming. Two blocks away. He'd been so close and yet it hadn't been enough to help her.

"Renee, honey, wake up." He cradled her body, rocking back and forth. Sirens sounded as the ambulance arrived. Galen skidded to them, barking out questions as enraged shifter males tried to rein it in to deal with the paramedics and the police.

"What happened? Jack! I need you to tell me what happened." Galen kept touching her and wincing, pulling a hand back because he worried he'd harm her. He shook nearly as much as Jack had been before the cold numbness had settled in.

"I don't know. He, there was a man here. He looked fucked up. Our girl hurt him. He got away. I let him get away. I let this happen, Galen. She was asleep, I just ran to get a paper and then stopped to buy a necklace I thought she'd…it doesn't matter. It's my fault. He got away and it's my fault he hurt her."

The paramedics rushed in, sparing a glance at the pacing, angry males, but not stopping until they'd reached Renee. It felt as if time had slowed to a trickle, as if each second took a year. Each labored breath she took cheered him and brought him dread because he heard the pain there, felt the strength inside her wane a bit more.

The police also arrived, but Jack didn't care, he only wanted her to be all right.

"Sir, move back please."

Galen bared his teeth, but held his growl back. Jack felt the desolation, the helplessness within his mate as they hesitated to let her go.

Grace crouched just to Jack's left. With one hand, she brushed the hair from Renee's forehead and murmured something Jack thought sounded like, *don't let go.* She turned to the men. "Jack, Galen, please let them help her. They're going to take care of her. She's bleeding a lot, they have to stop it."

"She's right."

Jack looked toward the male who'd spoken. It must have been Max, Galen's older brother. The resemblance was clear, though Max had more Caribbean in his features than Galen did. The other man took Galen by the shoulders and physically pulled him back, despite the snarl he received in response. Cade took advantage of that and, with Dave, pulled Jack away and the paramedics got to work. The police questioned people and looked around the house. Kindly, they interviewed Jack within sight of the paramedics, Galen getting the same treatment several feet away.

He answered, giving a timeline and a description of the man who'd broken in, all the while snared in a nightmare as they worked feverishly to save her life.

There was a bit of drama because both men were shifters, but the Boston PD were pretty open-minded and Jack had worked with them on other shifter issues in the past. They'd verify his and Galen's story, which was simply good police work, but they wouldn't let that stop them from trying to find her attacker.

If her attacker was lucky, the cops would find him before the beasts did.

At some point her aunt and sister showed up, rushing to the curb as Renee was loaded into the ambulance.

"We will begin to hunt now." A man pushed his way forward, touching Galen.

Galen nodded, his eyes never leaving Renee's very still body. "He has to be dealt with."

"Let's get to the hospital. I can start working on getting a hunt together once I know she's okay." Jack moved to get in the ambulance but they stopped him.

"Family only."

"She's my family." Jack dared them to try to stop him.

"I'm her husband," Galen said, taking Jack's hand as he got into the back of the ambulance. "He's our husband too."

The paramedic looked dubious but no one stopped him this time when he got in the back and settled in.

"We'll meet you at the hospital," Cade called out.

"She's going to be all right." Jack locked gazes with Galen as they rushed to the hospital. "There's no other way."

At the hospital, once she'd settled in and they'd rushed her into an operating room, Galen turned to Jack and put his arms around him. Jack let out the breath he felt like he'd been holding for hours and let himself fall into their link because he wasn't sure if he could survive without it just then. The fear of losing her, the pain of not protecting her battered him.

"It's not your fault, Jack." Galen kissed his cheeks, kissed away the tears.

"Whose is it then? She was mine to protect and I got distracted by a fucking shiny thing in a window. She could be dead because I didn't do my fucking job."

Galen's smile was rueful. "You might have noticed, but our woman is not one to be watched over every moment. Baby, she's ours, but she's an independent person, she would wither away if we had to sit on her every moment. We can't be there every minute. We can't. She has to be able to come and go, and if we can't have her safe in that house, we'll buy one where she can be. If I have to hire fourteen bodyguards and pay for a million-dollar security system, I will. The blame here is not yours, it belongs to the fuck who hurt her. We will end him."

"I love you." He looked to Galen as they leaned foreheads

together.

"I love you too. She's going to make it. I'd know it if she was too far gone. It was close—" Galen's voice choked with emotion, "—earlier when I first got to the house. There wasn't much left of her. But now she's getting stronger."

Jack felt it too. He nodded and they went back to the end of the hall.

Hospital personnel looked askance at the amount of people who'd gathered to wait, but no one said anything.

The man who'd spoken to Galen outside the ambulance turned out to be Galen's father. "Jack, this is my father, Cesar de La Vega. Papi, this is Jack Meyer."

The other man was an alpha, even if his eyes held sympathy and understanding as well as the rage of a male who's had one of his own hurt.

"Welcome to our family, Jack. You have our resources at your disposal. My girl is in there, broken, and I don't like it one bit." He motioned to another man who came forward. Jack recognized one of his own instantly. The male was an enforcer of some type.

"This is my brother Gibson. He's our version of an enforcer." Galen motioned at the wary eyed man covered in tats and wearing dreadlocks. His brother nodded once at Jack and looked back to Galen.

Gibson nodded in greeting before rubbing his face along Galen's jaw. "You know I'm here to help. I've got some of my people out on it already. Your woman may be little but she worked this dude over pretty well along with what Jack did. The blood spilled at your place is plenty to get a scent."

Jack pushed himself out of mate mode and into Enforcer mode. This was his job and she was his responsibility on so many levels it was written into his DNA. He grabbed Dave and Akio and began to organize a search along with Galen's jamboree. He was quite content to let Gibson take point on this one. Jaguars of all shifters were merciless hunters, far more connected to their beast than most. They would find this mage and erase him from existence.

"Thank you," Galen told his brother.

"Renee means a lot to me, too." Gibson looked to Jack. "You should be sure to keep track of your arm. You don't want the bone to heal wrong and need to be re-set."

Grace gave him a raised brow as she'd said the exact same thing just moments before.

"Go on. There's a room empty over here and we can look at it." Grace tried not to look smug as she hustled him aside. "If there's news we're only right here. I work here three days a week, Jack, they know me."

Galen walled it all off. Pushed his fear back as far as he could, letting the rage fuel him as he dealt with the insurance papers and the other stuff he needed to. He was out enough that he was able to produce the papers showing that he and Renee were married according to jamboree law. It reminded him just how much they needed to deal with the very human reality of insurance and contracts and legal status.

His mother showed up and stood at his side as he did it. Rosemary and Kendra did coffee runs and tried to contact Renee's father.

Max ordered people around, set up a watch in the hospital and then flowers started showing up by the dozen.

"Your eyes are bloodshot. Lean your head on me and take a nap. You're no good to her if you're strung out." His mother squeezed his hand. "I know you're worried, but she's going to come through this. She's strong."

"I can't sleep. Every time I close my eyes I see her, so small and pale, blood pooling around her. I feel that helplessness over and over."

Galen scrubbed hands over his face.

"I think she's also drawing from you and Jack, through the bond that unites the three of you." Rosemary handed him a cup. "Hot chocolate. Drink it." She handed a bag to his mother. "Sandwich and some soup. You look tired too."

Rosemary sat and gave him the stink eye until he finally relented and drank the chocolate. He had to admit he did feel a bit better afterward and agreed to eat the half of the sandwich his mother held out.

Jack and Grace joined them and the calls continued from friends and family. Renee's father was noticeably absent from that and Galen ached for her nearly as much as he wanted to punch the man in the nose.

"Fine way to meet your new mate," his mother grumbled and Jack laughed though the sound was threaded with fatigue and worry.

Everyone stood and tried to hold their questions when the doctor came out to speak to Galen.

"She's got a few broken bones, some major lacerations, a concussion and a lot of bruising, but there's no internal bleeding. We're going to keep her overnight and see how she's faring tomorrow. You can go in and see her if you like. She asked for you and Jack."

Galen flexed and fisted his hands. He had to relax or she'd see how agitated he was. She needed the peace right then and he'd kill everyone in that fucking place to give it to her.

"She's not very pretty right now. I just wanted to prepare you." The doctor led the way back and paused at the door before opening it up.

The scent hit him first. Pain. Blood. Fear. She'd been drugged up so her half lidded eyes widened only a bit when they entered. The hand she'd tried to raise toward them had been splinted, tubes running up her arm only added to the overall picture.

"Shh, don't try to smile, babe. I know. I know." He wanted to hug her, to press himself against her body to know she was there, living and breathing. An ache so beautiful it nearly felled him slammed into his soul. What on earth would he do if he lost her?

She shook her head, blinking back tears.

"I'm sorry," he assured her, moving closer, close enough to press his lips against an un-bruised part of her forehead. "You look like shit and it makes me want to hurt someone. I love you, God, I love you so much."

She sniffled and he dabbed gently with a tissue. "I love you too," she said, her voice slurred and rusty.

Jack groaned from somewhere behind them and he turned to see the guilt all over Jack's face.

Renee must have seen it too, felt it through the bond. "No." She swallowed hard and Galen was battered by the shards of pain she felt.

"I failed you." Jack's normally golden skin had paled, the lines around his eyes and mouth had deepened.

"Did not." Even covered in bruises, hooked up to tubes and facing some heavy recovery time, she wasn't taking any guff. "Here, please."

Jack took the two steps to her and fell to his knees, burying his face in the blankets. "I left you alone and he hurt you. He nearly killed you."

"Jack—" she paused as she swallowed, "—it was a fluke. You *saved* me. I knew you would. Don't you understand? I knew I would not die alone, I knew you would come. You said you would and I believed you and you did."

"I just found you. What would I do without you?"

Her exhaled breath was shaky and she wasn't good enough

to hide her state of exhaustion and pain. "I love you both too much to go anywhere."

"Don't talk anymore. It's okay. It isn't Jack's fault, I told him that already and now you have too. Your job is to get better so stop talking and go to sleep. We'll be here when you wake up."

"Did you get him?"

Jack growled and her bottom lip trembled a bit. Galen hated to see her scared. Hated to know this sick fuck was still alive.

"He got away. I'm sorry. I should have..."

Galen interrupted. "He chose to save you instead. I endorse that plan. Not to mention his own broken arm and wounds."

She tried to sit, her eyes widening. Both men urged her back to the pillows as gently as they could.

"I'm all right. We heal fast. The bone is knitting back together right now. Once I shift fully and then back, I'll be good as new." Jack kissed her shoulder. "He broke your fingers. He stole into your soul, hurt you. He's on borrowed time."

"Don't. Let the police handle it. I gave them a good description when they interviewed me before you came in. I don't want this sort of thing on your hands. On your conscience. Don't harm someone on my behalf. Love me, that's all I ask."

She was so earnest, Galen might have listened to her more if she hadn't been covered in bruises and had each one of her fucking fingers broken one by one by a sadistic bastard who wanted to steal her power and leave her for dead.

"He's a dead man. It's not just about me, Renee. He's disrespected my jamboree by attacking one of us. He's come into my home, touched my things, nearly killed my fucking wife. This cannot stand."

"Can you live with this on your conscience?"

"We can." Jack shrugged.

"I don't want to be the reason you murder someone. Don't you see? I should be bringing you up, not dragging you down."

Her breath strained with each word and aside from the rainbow sherbet bruise on her face, she'd grown whiter than the hospital sheet from the strain.

"First things first." Jack leaned over and pointed at a button. "This is pain medication. You need it. Push the button or I will."

Galen wanted to cheer and simultaneously cry at the way she did it without argument. That she had simply obeyed meant she had to be in pretty awful pain.

Jack's gaze met his for long moments before moving back to her face. "Better. Now, you do bring me up. I didn't realize how empty I'd been until I met you. You fill me up. You make me a better person and I do love you. So damned much that seeing you like this makes me crazy. So damned much that when I came into that room and saw you covered in blood, a madman trying to kill you, my entire world went inside out. I've been that way for hours. You are the reason, Renee."

"The reason you're inside out?"

Jack snorted. "The reason for everything. You are everything."

She sighed and her eyelids slid down a bit. "Let the cops deal with it."

"He's not human, you're not human and we're not human. This is not for them. It's for us." Jack crossed his arms over his chest.

"I'm not?" She tried to glare at him but gave up when all she could manage was a blink of sorts.

"You're more than that. You're magic. This asshole who attacked you is more than that only in a twisted way. The point is, he didn't steal your car at gunpoint, he tried to kill you by stealing your magic, your life force. This isn't a crime the cops are prepared to deal with. He's dangerous, Renee, he has to be removed."

Chapter Fourteen

Renee woke up, relaxing when she realized it was her own bed and she was home. The hospital overnight when they wake you up once an hour wasn't her idea of comfort. Still, the sight of a dozen wolves and cats, all there to protect her, did make her feel a heck of a lot better. She'd also had a lot of nurses and other female staff just stopping in to check on her because few men were as smoking hot as shifter men. It almost made up for the fact that her father had never called to see how she was even though he knew she'd been assaulted.

Jack and Galen had treated her as if she'd been made of glass since they'd returned. Waited on her hand and foot and not let her out of their sight. They'd hovered and coddled and made her feel utterly loved. The bedroom door currently stood open and she could see Galen walk by, shirtless and in low-slung jeans.

Well then, thank goodness the attack hadn't killed her sex drive because hellllllo there, sailor!

He turned, interrupting her perusal of the strong line of his back and the utterly stellar ass so lovingly hugged by the pale blue denim.

"You're awake."

"You're handsome."

He grinned, moving to her.

"What are you doing?" she asked when he began to sit in a nearby chair.

"Sitting. Are you still tired? I can go back out."

"Here, in bed with me. I need to rub up on you unless I smell horrible or something." She remembered some hours before she'd laid down for the nap, that Jack had washed her hair and cleaned her up. Sponge baths were a lot more appealing when administered by Jack Meyer.

"I don't want to hurt you."

"I'm just sore, but you know how to deal with that." She waggled her brows at him.

Carefully, he slid between the sheets and she attached herself to him like a limpet. Immediately his warmth, the scent of his skin, the way he felt against her, it all combined to calm her, to comfort.

"Mmmm. I've missed this." And she had. She'd taken for granted just how much she gained from touch too. She knew shifters did, but humans, or more than humans or whatever, did as well.

"Babe, if the next year of my life looked like me in bed with you holding me like I was the best thing on earth, I'd be the happiest man alive."

"You are the best thing on earth. You and Jack."

He smoothed a hand up and down her spine. "Not good enough to get here on time. I'm sorry. You don't know how much."

"I was scared. Terrified. He—" she shuddered, remembering the darkness he tasted of, the desolation, "—he was wrong inside and it got all over me. I was dying, but I knew one of you would get here, I knew I wouldn't die alone. And Jack, when he came in, everything was all right because I wouldn't die without one of you with me. My only regret was not having you here too."

"I saw it." Emotion choked his voice. "You wrote my initials." In her blood. But it wasn't like she had a pen and pad nearby.

She had wanted him to know her mind had been with him too. "I wanted you to know. You know, um, after I was dead."

His muscles tensed and he shivered. "I can't." He pressed his face into her neck. "I can't think about it, it's too much."

Need bloomed from low in her belly, her nipples beaded. "It's been days since you've been in me."

He took a shuddering breath. "It's too soon."

"I need you."

"You need to heal seven broken fingers."

"But you have ten working fingers and that mouth. I could just, you know, lie back and enjoy it."

He shook with laughter, bringing her own.

"Goddamn, what the fuck would I have done without you?" he asked, pulling back to look down into her face.

"You don't need to know now." She'd faced it, believed she was gone, but at the same time, she could let go knowing Jack and Galen had each other. The fear that her men would be alone if she passed was gone. It took a weight from her.

"I think about it all the time. Leaves a cold sweat in its wake."

"I have something else for you to think about."

He laughed. "I love it that you're trying to flutter your lashes with a black eye."

"Am I hideous now?"

He gave her the lawyer face. One raised brow, no expression otherwise. And still, holy crapdoodle, he was hotter than the sun. She'd blame her concussion but she already found him irresistible long before the attack.

"Hideous my ass. You're beautiful, even with a black eye.

But you just got out of the hospital two days ago. You need the rest. Jack and I are here to service you when you're ready."

"If you're not going to fuck me or make me come, how about some food?" She tried to pout but it pulled at the stitches on her jaw.

"Are you leaving our lady high and dry?" Jack strolled in, tossing his shirt to the side and leaving her breathless in the process.

"I was trying to explain she was still too hurt to get involved in any sexytimes." Galen's voice cracked when she leaned up enough to brush her nipples over his chest.

"Stuff and nonsense! I didn't volunteer for anything acrobatic, but I sure as hell can lay back and enjoy myself."

"You do have a point." Galen sat up and peeled the blankets back. He traced around her nipples and then down her belly, over her mound through her panties. "You do know how much I love this particular pair of panties."

"Wasn't my idea, though I do approve of the results. Jack chose them."

Jack got in bed on the other side, leaning over to look. "Yes, I thought so too. Opening her panty drawer was a treat."

He bent, leaving an openmouthed kiss on her hip. She couldn't really care less about fancy underpants but Galen loved her in them and she left the purchase of said frilly panties to him. If it had been up to her, she'd wear plain white cotton granny panties and do so quite happily.

"Close your eyes, babe. Let us take care of you."

"Finally!" Laughing, she closed her eyes and laid back. But she sure as hell wasn't thinking of England.

Hands caressed over the non-stitched, non-casted parts of her. Thank goodness those were the best parts. She couldn't keep her eyes closed though, what was better to imagine than her reality?

Galen situated himself between her thighs and slid her panties down her legs. "You're so beautiful. Even bruised and battered, you're so gorgeous it steals my breath."

"You say the most awesome things." She gave her best imitation of a grin, trying not to wince when the movement tugged at her stitches.

Jack's teeth caught her nipple through the thin material of her sleep shirt. A satisfied moan slid from her lips.

With his head bent over her body, Galen looked nearly reverent. How she ended up so loved, so taken care of and worshipped, she didn't know. But she loved it.

She wanted to grab the sheets or a handful of hair, but her splints wouldn't allow for it so she settled for writhing instead.

"Oh God, yes, right like that," she panted out when Galen's tongue fluttered over her clit.

"God, I want to be in you," Jack murmured as he kissed up her chest to her neck.

"Be in me then. I won't break."

"You're already broken," he said, agitation clear in his tone.

"Don't." She turned and then arched on a gasp as Galen's tongue slid through her pussy and pressed up, into her gate. Magic, warm and familiar, rushed through her, pushing aside aches. Wow, that was awesome. Her aunt had told her it was within her power to heal, but it was one of those lessons they hadn't gotten to yet. Perhaps she knew without really knowing, perhaps she could just let her body do it. Of course thinking about it would probably jinx it and, gah! She turned her mind away from that, back to this moment with her mates.

When she let go, the energy pulsed through her again like a warm caress.

Galen pulled back, kissing the inside of her thigh. "You taste like power," he said, his eyes lit with the yellow-green of his cat.

She was in a place beyond words. Instead she pushed to sit. Galen's hands tightened on her thighs, like a boy who wasn't giving up his sweets any time soon.

"Lay down, gorgeous." Jack licked the hollow of her throat and she sighed happily. This was good and right. What they had was what was supposed to be.

"No. I feel better. I'd feel even better with a cock inside me. Any takers?"

"I was in the middle of something." Galen's mouth found its way up her thigh and to her cunt. Jack knelt behind her, bringing her body to a lean against him. His clever fingers tugged and rolled her nipples as Galen pushed her thighs wide and set back to licking her pussy like a starving man.

Long, wet strokes of his tongue as his fingers teased her gate, slid back to tickle her rear passage. All she could think of was his cock. His cock in her mouth, deep in her body, the way he tasted and felt against her. Even as he continued to drive her up, she couldn't stop thinking about it.

"Christ, what are you thinking about?" Jack pressed into her back, his cock behind the zipper of his jeans hot against her skin. "I fell into a movie in your head, felt Galen's cock in my cunt."

Galen's surprised laugh was the last bit of sensation she needed to tip into orgasm. Still, he pressed his face into her flesh, never stopping, pushing her into an aftershock climax that brought a rush of pleasure through her and a flush to her skin.

His kiss on her belly and around Jack's fingers brought her attention again.

"I was thinking about Galen's cock. About the taste, how it feels inside, how it makes me feel when his control slips and he pulls my hair just a tad too hard. So hard it hurts really good."

Galen groaned. "Your mouth on me is like nothing in the

world."

"Just like being inside her is like nothing in the world." Jack bit her earlobe.

"One of you should prove it before I die." She stopped as the words hit them like a slap. "It's laugh or cry. I'd rather laugh. I'm not dead. I'm here with you two and I'm not going anywhere."

"It's not funny." Galen's voice was very nearly a snarl. Something he rarely unleashed in her presence. For some reason, this made her feel better, like he trusted her enough to show that part of himself to her.

"It happened. We can pretend it didn't, but that won't make it true."

"Damn it," Jack cursed low, just in her ear, and suddenly she was picked up and plopped onto his lap, his cock sliding deep in one thrust up as she moved down.

Yes. That was what she needed.

"Hold her up, Galen," Jack said, his voice strained. "Sweet heaven, your pussy feels so good I can't stand it."

"Thank you, God you feel right. I think I may be a Jack junkie. I'm afraid there's no treatment but more of you so I don't go into withdrawals."

He laughed against her neck, his breath stirring the tendrils of her hair.

Galen moved to her, his front brushing against hers. With exquisite care, he cradled her body, careful to avoid her various injuries. He tasted her lips, her taste on his tongue, melting into her senses. She expected an urgency from him, instead he touched her with gentle hands, kissed with a mouth that tasted rather than demanded.

"I need you so much. I don't know that I'll ever get enough," he said against her lips.

"Good," she managed to gasp out as Jack continued to

thrust into her body slow and deep. It felt so good, *he* felt so good, for the first time since the attack she felt okay. Normal. "I still want your, *ohfuckyes,* cock, Galen. Be patient and you'll be next. Or if you can't, I'm sure Jack has some energy left. Though—" she paused to grind herself down on Jack, "—he's working awfully hard here so perhaps he'll need a break when we're finished."

"I've already had Jack's cock," Galen said, kissing her lips, her cheeks, her eyelids. "I want your pussy."

"You really need to be sure I'm awake and watching the next time." Nothing was more beautiful than the two of them, writhing together, touching each other the way they did.

"Are you objectifying me, gorgeous?" Jack nipped the back of her neck and a full body shiver worked through her.

"Hell yes, I'm sure you understand each time you look in the mirror."

"You don't care that Galen and I are fucking too?" Jack thrust deep, holding her in place for long moments, a groan rumbling through his chest.

"Why should I? Aside from being ridiculously sexy, what would I be jealous of? Afraid of? You're mine, I know that. I believe that to my bones. You two are each other's as well, that's how it's supposed to be so why fight it when I find it beautiful?"

Galen's gaze locked with hers. What they had as a threesome wasn't just titillation, it was deeper. She accepted it was supposed to be the way it was. No, it wasn't what most people had and she wasn't entirely sure it would have worked if there hadn't been this bond between the two men and her. But none of that mattered. She had it and she had it good. There were no doubts in that department.

"I want to be here forever," Jack whispered.

"You are." She turned her head, met his mouth with her

own, even as the muscles in her neck and shoulders screamed in protest while she brushed her lips against his.

His teeth dug into her shoulder, marking her as he came. Flashes of light and pleasure buffeted her behind closed eyes.

"Each time I'm with you I think it can't get any better. And then there's the next time." Jack laid her on the mattress so gently tears welled up again.

"You're a gift, Jack. I've brought all this drama to you and yours, but you're a gift."

He shook his head and kissed each broken fingertip. "Stop. None of this is your fault except the being irresistible part, which I'm quite happy about."

"Mmm," was all she could manage until Galen touched her again. His cat slid against her and her magic caressed him in return. Jack's wolf curled around her, his scent comforting and familiar.

When she opened her eyes, Galen's face was just inches from hers. "Hiya, handsome. Wanna get lucky?"

"I already am."

"Smooth fucker."

Jack laughed and Galen nuzzled her neck. "I want in. Can you take me so soon after Jack?"

She hooked her calf around his hip, pulling him down toward her.

His entry was slow, dreamy, like the pace he set. Her arms lay to her sides, helpless. She wanted to grasp and hold. Instead she had to rely on her body in other ways, on her eyes to let him see how much she needed him.

So much gentleness, this man who could just as easily rip her apart. He chose kindness, he chose to cherish and that made it even more important.

"I love you. Both of you," she said drowsily after he'd come and made her come once again. The spot he'd bitten tingled just right, the occasional throb in time with the mark Jack had left on her other side. "I'm glad you both marked me again." Normally she'd touch the edges, this time she couldn't. Instead she let them be, let her body experience them in a totally different sense.

"Hungry? Kendra brought over some food. She said she'd come back by later today for tea." Jack kissed her chin. "I like your aunt and sister. They're good people."

"They are. I'm, well this is going to sound stupid in the wake of this last week, but I'm lucky. I'm blessed with unexpected gifts. I'm not that woo woo, not really, but this is all for a reason. That's what I hold onto and that's what's important. You, me and Galen."

Her men smiled and helped her from bed. This time the sponge bath came from Galen and she had no complaints either way.

Galen ran long and hard, working the kill from his system. Somewhere behind him, lay their house, on their street, their garden and his woman. His woman watched over by his man.

The threat to her had been removed. This pleased man and cat immensely. No one would miss the piece of shit who'd erected a fucking shrine to Renee in his boarding house. Pictures of her on the walls, spells Galen had packed away and would pass on to Rosemary. This man had Galen's wife's name on his lips, wanted to steal her life to make himself stronger, and Galen would not allow it.

When he reached his parents' house, he went inside and cleaned up. No one spoke of what had happened and no one ever would again. Their business with this mage was finished, any further actions by men like the one they'd just dealt with, would end up exactly the same. It would now be up to them to impress the point the only way the mages would listen. By repeating it until they learned.

On his way to the front door via the kitchen, he bumped into his brother. Max nodded, satisfied with their work and now on his way to find a woman. Max would work out his energy in bed as would Galen now that he'd run off the excess, sloughed off the parts of his energy that were too dark to ever bare in Renee's presence.

"Do you want me to drop you back home?" his father asked from his place at the breakfast nook.

"Yes, please." Galen took the thick sandwich his mother handed his way and devoured it in four bites.

"I expect to see you three this Sunday. Your mother worries about Renee." His father navigated the streets with the ease of a man who'd lived in Boston his entire life.

"Ah, *Mami* worries about Renee." Galen didn't bother hiding his grin.

"Your little witch has stolen my heart, what can I say? She's small and fragile. You protect her well. My worry isn't about that. Her father, bah!" Galen's father went off on a string of half-English, half-Spanish insults for a full three minutes before he returned his attention to Galen. "I'm her Papi now. I want her to know that."

Poet yes, a warrior poet. Galen couldn't imagine a finer man, a finer example than the one he had. Of everyone in his family, it had been his father who'd seen Renee truly, right from the start.

"I'll tell her, but she knows already anyway."

They pulled to the curb. "Can't hear you're loved enough. That girl deserves it. I imagine we'll be making a trip to meet with whoever it was that sent this bastard."

"Yes. Renee will balk. Give me some time to work with Rosemary and Jack on it."

"She's got a good heart. But she's not stupid, Galen. Your

little witch would kill to protect those she loves, she'll understand."

He looked at his father and nodded.

The wolf guard stationed at the end of the block sent a tip of his chin to Galen as he unlocked the front door and re-locked behind himself. He knew that just because the threat this one particular mage had been erased, that didn't mean there wouldn't be more. There would.

He turned the security back on as he headed up the stairs.

Rosemary and Kendra sat with Renee on the couch, laughing, looking so much like one another it still caught him by surprise. They'd simply been there, every day, and Renee had come alive in a completely new way as she'd learned more about her power and how to use it.

She looked up and grinned at the sight of him. "Hi there. We're about ten minutes from dinner. Jack is in the office."

He bent to kiss her. Between her magic and time, she looked far better than she had just two days before. One hand was free of the splint, which made her very happy because she could manage her own baths, though he and Jack were quite content to do that work themselves.

She got up and followed him down the hall to the office he shared with Jack. He'd decided on the way over to have the unfinished bottom floor renovated. It would give them more space. Eventually there'd be babies and they'd need the room.

"It's done. We found some evidence of who sent him and we'll be needing to pay him a visit," he said to Jack, who nodded gravely. He turned to Renee. "You're safe for now. He's no longer a threat."

She swallowed hard and he figured she was working up an argument. Instead she simply nodded. "Thank you."

While she was being so agreeable, he may as well get it all out on the table. "Jack and I have taken a two-year lease on the empty space in my building. It's ready to go when you are. We had it painted two days ago and the lettering has been put on the door."

Her eyebrows flew up and her jaw clicked as she locked it.

He did his best to harden his features. "Don't think of arguing. You can't have your old space, and I'm sorry for that. You couldn't afford to do two years all at once and we could. So we did. I used the money Susan had to pay you so don't start. It's safe, guarded by my people. This is the best option and you know it."

"What I know is that you two can't just do things without consulting me! I won't be managed, Galen."

"I'm not managing you, dumbass, I'm making you safer. It's your business and now you can do it in the safest place possible. And now I can invite you up to my office and fuck you on my desk. You know how much I love that."

She threw her hands up with a snort.

"We're your men. It's our job to be sure you're safe and to make you happy. We're not forcing you to quit and stay home where you'd be way safer." Jack probably got loads of ass with that smile, hell, it made Galen hard just looking at him. But Renee wasn't so easy.

"You're paying my way! This just makes what they say about me true. You know how much it means to me to make my own way."

"I really fucking hate your sister, Galen."

At the moment, Galen couldn't agree with Jack more. Beth had been avoiding him, but he'd confront her eventually.

"You! Get that look off your face, Galen. *I* will deal with Beth." She growled and stormed from the room, heading into her work room and coming back shortly, holding a checkbook.

"I'll be paying you rent then. You'll need to let me know the monthly amount. I'm sorry I can't give it all to you at once but I just don't have it."

"For fuck's sake, Renee. I make a ridiculous amount of money, why can't I just help you? I'm not a bank. I don't expect you to pay me back. This is *our* money. What's mine is yours. By human law and the law of the jamboree."

Jack coughed and then gave over to a full laugh. "Laugh while you can, dog boy," he grumbled.

"He's right." She spun, turning her attention to Jack, and Galen sent a triumphant smile over her shoulder. "How long have you two been up to this? And don't even *think* about lying to me."

"Since the afternoon you got thrown out of your own place of business by your crazy and possibly criminal stepmother. We needed to know you'd be safe. You can't possibly complain about having a bigger place, a safer one. You're like magical catnip, Renee! These fucked up asshole mages are going to keep sniffing around. You're in the best possible place."

"Oh you, shut up. I'm not complaining about being safe or even having a lovely space for my shop. These are good things and things I'd have loved to *discuss* with you, had I been consulted in something regarding my own life for a change. Are you both deliberately ignoring the real reason I'm annoyed?"

"The check from Susan covered the last five months of your lease payment and a penalty for breaking the lease. That'll cover the first four months of the lease. Save your money right now so you can be sure you're stocked."

Jack rumbled his disagreement. "No. Damn it, Renee, let us do this for you. It's nothing to us."

Galen shook his head. On so many things, Jack was the most reasonable and intelligent man Galen knew, but sometimes he said the most stupendously ridiculous stuff.

Still, he took a breath, risked his life and waded in between them. "What Jack means is the money is not a problem for us.

Lauren Dane

Of course we both understand this is important to you, your independence and your business. We respect that."

"Oh, uh, yeah, that." Jack sent a grateful look to Galen. He'd collect on that later, with Renee in between them.

"Hmpf." She turned and began to walk from the room only to stop at the doorway and turn. "Thank you."

As if he wouldn't walk through the fires of hell for her.

"I love you, babe."

Chapter Fifteen

Renee looked up in time to catch sight of Galen stalking through the lobby, toward her. Everything in her body sped at the sight, and then she had to grab the counter when Jack caught up and the two, side by side, moved to her.

They'd been gone three days while she stayed with Grace and Cade. It had been stupid, she'd have preferred to stay in her own house with her own things, but of course, no one really cared what she wanted, not when it came to her safety. Secretly, not that she'd admit it out loud, she found it achingly tender and sexy that they went out of their way to protect her.

She raised a hand, her senses caught up in them, their scents rolling through her, the sight of those eyes, the flex of masculine muscle sending her into her very happy place.

"Close to closing time?" Jack asked, his gaze on her intent. She managed to look up and down his body. It made her breathless to look at him.

"Ten minutes. I was just cleaning up."

Galen walked around her counter and swept her into a hug. She breathed in deep, letting him slide into her system again, settling her jangled nerves.

"I missed you so much."

"We missed you too. Clean up. Jack's going to wait here and I'm going to run upstairs a moment. We'll all go home and take the phone off the hook." The smile Galen sent her promised all the best sort of sweaty, sticky loving.

"Now it's my turn." Jack's hug was different than Galen's, though no less affecting. The raw energy he gave off filled her as much as his scent. Her need for them both staggered her. "I have this need inside only you can fill up. Galen and I can touch each other, love each other, but you're essential in a way I'd be scared of if I didn't trust you to take care of it."

"I'll always take care of it." She held his face in her hands, his heart in hers.

"I know. Soon I hope, because it's painful to walk at this point." His wink made her laugh.

"You're the one who came in here all sexy and hot and stuff. Stand back and let me finish cleaning up." She laughed, wiping down her counters, shutting things down, putting the juices away. By the time she finished, Galen had come back and the three of them nearly ran back home.

"The mage knows that if he sets foot in Cascadia or de La Vega territory he will die begging for mercy and getting none." Galen hustled her toward their bedroom.

"I'm safe?"

"For now. They'll find you, others will. You're metaphysical candy to them, they will find you." Jack pulled his shirt off one handed.

"Rosemary is helping a lot. Kendra is moving here to Boston." This made her happy, the happiest she'd been her whole life. Her men, their life, her aunt and her sister, Jack's pack had accepted her and things within the jamboree had eased once she simply remembered it was better to celebrate all the people who did love her instead of mourning those who didn't.

She would be a powerful witch. She had it within her heart, within her capabilities. She trained every single day and would continue to do so. Kendra already had a job offer at a local private school. She'd set up in Jack's old apartment and found the neighborhood suited her well. Rosemary would spend time in Boston every month as she traveled back and forth between coasts.

Four hands and two mouths roamed over her body as her clothes disappeared. Their connection glittered between them, no sharp edges, just curves and paths they all could follow. It wasn't easy sometimes, these two, overbearing men who wanted to protect her from every hurt. They struggled, tussled over things nearly every day. If she didn't keep her guard up and not let them get away with too much, they'd steamroll her, not to harm, but to protect. It was infuriatingly comforting.

For years she'd been empty and apart from others and then Galen had landed in her life like the gift he was. He'd healed her broken parts, had brought her out of her shell and made her believe in herself. And just when she thought her life was as perfect as it could be, Jack stumbled in.

Magic was real. She felt it rushing through her veins as it was her birthright. But she felt it each time she touched Galen or kissed Jack. Experienced it when she turned the corner and watched them kiss or touch. Knew it when they flipped the stereo on and didn't complain when KC and the Sunshine Band began to play.

There were paths yet unforged, territory she knew she had to explore and conquer. She'd find the truth of her past. She'd do it and succeed because she was blessed in matters of the heart, blessed with two warriors at her side and their extended family who'd taken her in too.

Magic worked in ways she knew she'd never understand all of. But it was made flesh and bone right here in her bed, in her heart and that's what meant the most.

As she dropped into sleep, she remembered to tell Jack and

Galen that Rosemary had worked a spell on her earlier that may help with her memory. They'd tried a few others but this one had come from an old friend of her aunt's.

If it worked while she slept, it would most likely mean the memory loss was worked through dark magicks, much like the stuff she'd dealt with during the attack. A great deal of her hoped it didn't work.

She played out in the backyard with Peaches, their mutt of a terrier mix. The tire swing her mother had put up for her just a few weeks before was perfect. Renee loved the way her hair flew all around as she toed herself up higher and higher.

A woman came outside with her father. Immediately Renee didn't like her. This woman looked at her dad wrong. Not like her mom did, her mom tried not to look at him very much and it made Renee sad.

Her mother had drawn little curlicues into her skin with pretty smelling oil. She'd told Renee it would protect her, even as she'd urged her not to show her gifts in front of her father, ever.

She didn't say anything because she shouldn't speak unless she was told to. Her father liked children when they were seen and not heard. She was glad her mom didn't think that.

"Just do it already. The cops will be here shortly." Her father barked it at the other woman, who frowned.

She turned, the woman, and while speaking, she flicked a hand in Renee's direction. She was knocked off the tire swing. She stood, dusting herself off and wondered what she'd done to lose her seat that way.

"What the hell?" The woman glared and looked at Renee closer before turning back to her father. "Change of plans. Your stupid witch wrote spells into her skin, into her muscle and bone. There's years worth of magick here. She's probably got more stored from that than her natural gifts. This one would taste a lot sweeter than her mother."

"*Just put a pillow over her face then, if you can't do it with your power. Let's be done.*"

"*This little rug rat will give me enough power for years and years to come. When she's older it might be possible to unravel the protections to take all that stored magick. Like sucking marrow from bones.*" *The woman stood.* "*If you kill her in your way, the cops will find her and wonder how it is that a child dies the same day as her mother.*"

Renee's heart beat fast. She tried not to cry but she was scared. "*Mommy's dead?*"

"*Yes, kid.*" *The woman looked back to Renee's father.* "*We'll have to adjust her head a little bit. Memories can be fixed.*"

Renee sat up on a strangled gasp of emotional pain. Her father? Susan? That fucking bitch had been around that long? Why?

A Quick Note For Readers

Trinity is the first in a two book story arc. While the HEA between Renee and her men is standalone, there's an overarching story arc that will carry into the second book, REVELATION.

About the Author

To learn more about Lauren Dane, please visit www.laurendane.com. Send an email to Lauren at laurendane@laurendane.com or stop by her messageboard to join in the fun with other readers as well. www.laurendane.com/messageboard

LaVergne, TN USA
30 August 2010
195143LV00009B/2/P